I0673192

Revenge

REVENGE

A LADY BETHANY ADVENTURE

CHRISTOPHER C. TUBBS

LUME BOOKS
A JOFFE BOOKS COMPANY

Lume Books, London

A Joffe Books Company

www.lumebooks.co.uk

First published in Great Britain in 2025

ISBN: 978-1-83901-618-9

Assignment

The Right Honourable Sebastian Ashley-Cooper and his wife, the Right Honourable Bethany Ashley-Cooper, walked into the Foreign Office, having made their way to London from their house in Surrey that morning. The weather was cold but sunny: a light mist had covered the ground but burnt off as they travelled. They were accompanied on the journey by Beth's bodyguards/special operations team, known as the Wolves, and Sebastian's batman/valet, Titherton. The Wolves comprised four girls and Mike, their leader, who went almost everywhere with the couple and would certainly not have allowed them to take a three-hour coach journey without protection. Not that the couple were helpless — between them they carried enough weapons to deal with any eventuality and the coach had a hidden cache below one of the seats. However, Beth knew she could not deny the girls the chance to spend some time in London if she wanted a peaceful life.

Mike rode up front with the driver and carried a short-barrelled ten-gauge shotgun loaded with deer shot. That fearsome weapon would kill at close range, and he carried it on his lap in full view as

1

a deterrent. Perhaps due to that, or the cold, they saw no one on the trip and arrived in good order.

When Sebastian and Beth reached the Foreign Office, the clerk in the entrance politely checked their names off his list. A messenger showed them to the waiting room outside the secretary of state's office, where an assistant brought them tea. After half an hour the door to the office opened and John Ward, 1st Earl of Dudley, showed a pair of men out. The departing men's accents suggested they were French. Once they had left, Ward turned to the couple.

"Sebastian, Bethany, please come in."

They exchanged greetings then took seats at an impressive mahogany table.

"Have you had tea? Would you like some more?"

"We are fine, thank you," Sebastian answered.

Very soon after, there was a knock on the door, which opened to admit the Ashley-Coopers' boss, Admiral James Turner. As he entered the room they both stood up, and James shook Sebastian's hand and kissed Beth on the cheeks, French style. When they were all seated, Ward started to tell them why they had been called to London.

"South America is a mess; Simón Bolívar has achieved independence for most of it, but internal factions are tearing it apart. The former Spanish region is the worst. It is beginning to split into separate states and there is a danger that the Spanish could use this as an excuse to go back in and re-establish control. We need intelligence from the region, and operatives there who can do whatever is necessary to maintain British interests and keep the Spanish out. We have a mission there with an ambassador. What we would like, Sebastian, is for you to join his team as an envoy."

Turner stepped in. "The two of you will be working together, of course; it is a three-year posting. Beth will be kept busy gathering information. Together with the ambassador, you can make decisions on how to act. You will have your team with you — all the girls speak Spanish and Portuguese, I believe?"

Beth replied, "The sisters do. It is harder for Netta. Mike has learned a lot working with the girls and he can now speak Portuguese."

Turner smiled at that; her team was building nicely and all of its current members had achieved excellent scores at the Intelligence Service Academy. However, more was needed, and he told Beth, "You need one more agent to complete your team. None of them are specialist housebreakers. If you check the crews of your ships, you will find there are several with skills and experience that would be suitable." He passed over a piece of paper that had the relevant names and skills written on it.

Beth took it and raised her eyebrows at some of the names listed. She recognised them all but had — until now — no idea of their criminal pasts. Two were topmen — one had also been a housebreaker specialising in entry through the roof, and the other a cat burglar. Another on the list was a former locksmith; she wondered what *he* had done wrong to end up in the navy. She began to consider the fourth name but another thought intruded.

"My ships? Do I get the *Fox* and *Cub*, then?"

"You do indeed — you will need to move around, and sailing is the fastest way," Turner replied with conviction.

Ward said, "Your main task is to help Bolívar stabilise the region — if that is even possible. You can decide on how you do that locally; you have complete discretion. Just try not to leave too many bodies lying around."

At this Turner barked a laugh, and Beth fluttered her eyelashes at Ward.

"Why sir, as if I would!"

The ships were brought up from Chatham, where they had undergone a scheduled refit, to the Pool of London. Beth got them a mooring at her family's berth in the India Docks and she and Sebastian visited them to check all was well. The *Fox* was moored with the *Cub* against her seaward side. The couple stopped at the gangplank and Sebastian called up, "Permission to come aboard, Captain."

Richard Brazier came to the side and smiled down at them. "Permission granted."

The couple walked up the gentle slope of the gangplank to the deck, where Richard shook Sebastian's hand and kissed Beth's hand as he bowed over it.

"Where are those hellcats of yours?" Richard asked Beth.

"Shopping. Mike is looking after them."

Richard laughed. "It's more likely that he's protecting the poor shopkeepers from them! Those girls haggle like camel dealers."

Beth looked around at the deck, then up at the rigging. "So, what's new?"

Richard became serious. "We have new rigging and canvas, the knees have been strengthened, and we have replaced the forward two carronades with twelve-pound longs as fore chasers. To compensate for the extra weight at the bow, we have added a thirty-two-pound carronade at the stern."

Beth looked aft and pursed her lips. "I don't see it on the main deck."

Richard looked slightly uncomfortable as he explained, "It's in the day cabin."

"*My* day cabin?"

"Um … yes."

Beth strode aft and down the steps to her cabin. There, tied tight up against the bulkhead, was the carronade — swung around to the limit of its truck and tied tight against the side. At two yards long and a yard wide it took up some space, but not too much.

Having given Beth time to look at it, Sebastian came into the cabin.

"I suppose it doesn't take up *so* much room," she said.

"You left before Richard had time to finish explaining the refit," her husband said.

Beth was unrepentant and simply walked past him and out of the door with a swing of her hips. Sebastian shook his head with a wry smile and followed her. Titherton, who had been unpacking in the sleeping cabin, which lay beside the day cabin, grinned.

"Anything else?" Beth asked Richard as she approached him.

"New copper and several new planks, a slightly taller mast and a new galley, but most important is the fact that the rudder and its pinions have been replaced. The new one is bigger, which gives us a better turn rate."

Beth, who was pleased to learn of these changes, then walked the main deck and said hello to the crew members, who were mainly above deck waiting to go ashore. Then she crossed to the *Cub*. Stephen Donaldson, the skipper, met her as she boarded.

"Hello, Stephen, are you well?"

"Very well, thank you, boss."

She liked being called that and smiled as she looked over the rigging.

"New rigging and spars?"

Stephen grinned; he had heard Richard's report.

"Copper an' all. Same guns though."

Beth laughed, then asked, "Is Harry Bean onboard?"

"Yes, he is. Why?"

"I've heard he has a colourful past."

"Oh, that. He ran away to sea to escape the clutches of the constables. He was an all-round bad lad: robbery, burglary, housebreaking, ran a gang of kids. Then he robbed the wrong man and the constables went after him. Now he is settled in the foremast watch, and not a bad topman."

"Can I see him?"

"Are you going to steal him?"

Beth smiled sweetly. "I don't need to; the admiral is gifting him to me."

Stephen rolled his eyes then roared, "Harry Bean, get your arse up on deck!"

A minute later Harry appeared, looking confused. "Skipper?"

"The boss wants a word."

Stephen walked away, clearly having nothing to do with this. Beth chuckled and led Harry off the *Cub*, across the *Fox* and down the gangplank to her carriage.

"There, now we can talk privately," Beth said as Harry closed the door, still looking puzzled and more than a little awkward. "Can you pick a lock?"

Now he looked embarrassed. "Yes ma'am, I can."

"Do you know what this is for?" She produced a slim jim.

"Opening windows and doors with catches; useful on skylights as well."

"Open the seat you're sitting on."

Harry stood and felt along the edge of the seat until he located the catch, then pressed it and lifted the lid.

"Cor blimey!"

Beth waved a hand at the contents. "Pick a weapon for use during the night when you are on a job."

Harry went through the pistols and paid particular attention to the revolvers. Then he put them down and looked over the selection of knives and coshes. He picked up a stiletto with a five-inch blade, then a smaller dagger with no cross-guard and finally a leather blackjack.

"These two and this."

"How would you wear the knives?"

"The stiletto on me right forearm. The dagger on a cord around me neck hanging down between me shoulders."

That confirmed what she had observed: he was left-handed. "What are these?" she said, and tossed him a wallet she took from her own bag.

He opened it and grinned. "That, boss, is the finest set of lockpicks I has ever seen." He went to hand them back.

"You can keep them, if you agree to join the Wolves."

"What? Mike and the girls?"

"Yes, I need a good breaking-and-entering man."

The young seaman looked overjoyed. "Not 'alf … I mean, yes please, boss."

And that was that.

Now a team of six, the Wolves sorted out the sleeping arrangements on board the ship. The girls had a cabin that had been fabricated in the forward hold of the *Fox*, which had room for four hammocks and — when those hammocks were rolled up — ample room for dressing and washing. Most importantly, it was private. The men slung their hammocks in the cockpit with the two midshipmen. Fede, Beth's dog, had his bed in Beth and Sebastian's cabin.

Leaving England in late winter guaranteed that the crossing would be somewhat entertaining, and the fun started almost as soon as they entered the Atlantic. Storms rolled in from across the sea. The waves were large even along the coast of England, and they had to fight their way west to gain enough sea room to clear the Bay of Biscay. When they turned south, they had the wind and waves on their port quarter, which made the ships roll and pitch in a corkscrew fashion. Paola was sick, and while Netta nursed her, the other two sisters went up on deck.

Sebastian was a landlubber, and like Paola he didn't have his sea legs. He was so very sick that Beth worried that he was losing fluids too fast. Youngs, the surgeon, came and suggested sugared water with lime, a small pinch of salt and a dash of rum. Sebastian drank it and almost immediately threw it up. He was saved when, after a week's sailing, they passed Spain and Portugal and the winds turned south. Even so, Beth ordered them to stop at Gibraltar to give him a couple of days to recover.

That also gave her time to do a bit of shopping. Her ships had fifteen marines, whose regiment had issued them with Baker rifles. That, she decided, was not good enough. Her father had told her of a weapons dealer in the town who had a full warehouse and stocked the latest in small arms. She and Sebastian, who was still weak from *mal de mer*, took a walk.

"Is that it?" Sebastian asked incredulously as they walked towards a shabby shopfront. There were cutlasses and knives in the window along with a couple of nice, but old, pistols.

"Looks, apparently, can be deceiving," she replied with a frown.

They approached the door, which was half-glassed and filthy. "Well, we won't know until we go inside," Beth murmured as she pushed it open.

Inside was not much better than outside. Dust motes drifted in the shafts of light coming through the grubby window as a cracked bell announced their entry. Racks full of second-hand swords lined the walls and muskets were stacked in a corner. A scruffy old man came out from the back. He had a kippah on his head.

"Good morning," he said cheerfully. "Ebenezer Fineman at your service."

Beth treated him to a smile. "I am told that you stock the latest in rifles."

Fineman looked at her, then took out a pair of round glasses and put them on. "Who are you?"

"Bethany Ashley-Cooper. You know my father, Martin Stockley."

The old man chuckled. "I knew your mother as well. You look just like her. Are they both well?"

"They are in excellent health. He sends his regards."

"A fine man. Has he made admiral yet?"

"Yes, he has."

Fineman smiled. "Now, what can I do for you?"

"We are looking for twenty breech-loading rifles," Sebastian said, tired of playing second fiddle.

Fineman looked him up and down. "You have been sick; do you need a chair?"

"No, thank you," Sebastian said, finding himself unable to stay annoyed for long.

"Then come with me."

Mr Fineman led them through a door at the back of the shop, which, surprisingly, led to a set of stairs that descended into the rock the house was built on. He explained. "The whole island is a honeycomb of caves and tunnels. The army dug a lot during the war but this was a natural cave before I built the house. In fact, it's why the house is built where it is, as you will see."

Lamps placed at regular intervals lit the stairs, and at the bottom was an iron-clad door. A large key opened the lock, and it swung inwards on well-oiled hinges.

Beth gasped at what she saw inside. Holes in the ceiling let in shafts of sunlight to illuminate the interior, albeit dimly. The ceiling holes were too small for a person to get through and in any case had bars over them on the inside. The cave was huge — at least forty feet high and probably a hundred feet long by thirty feet wide. It was dry, so Beth knew it must be above sea level. Crates were stacked in rows, which she soon realised marked off various separate areas.

Fineman walked unerringly to a particular stack. He lit a pair of lanterns to fully illuminate the area and in particular a box, which lay with the lid at a slight angle. He lifted it off. Inside were new rifles, all still wrapped in oiled paper except one, which he lifted out and passed to Beth.

"That is an M1819 Hall rifle with percussion cap ignition. Made at the Harpers Ferry Arsenal in Virginia. Fires a half-inch ball over one hundred grains of powder. Good out to at least eight hundred to fifteen hundred yards."

Beth didn't mention that she already had one.

The gun was loaded front to back with the ball inserted first, then the powder, which was tamped down with a hand tool rather than a ram rod. It could be loaded faster than a muzzle loader and was more accurate because the rifleman didn't have to ram the ball down a rifled barrel. Also, it didn't need a patch around the ball, since that could be made large enough to fully engage with the rifling.

Sebastian took it from Beth and checked it over. "Can we fire it?"

"Certainly, come with me."

They were led to a tunnel at one side of the cave which, after lamps were lit, turned out to be a firing range. Fineman walked him through the loading procedure. Sebastian wrapped a handkerchief around his head to cover his ears to protect them from the noise in the confined space, brought the gun to his shoulder and aimed at the target, some fifty yards away at the end of the range. Beth put her hands over her ears, as did Fineman. Sebastian squeezed the trigger and when the smoke cleared, he saw he had edged the bull. He reloaded and fired again. He got closer to the centre this time — it would count as a bullseye.

"Let me try," Beth said. She hit the ring of the bull, getting slightly closer than Sebastian's first shot.

She looked thoughtful after she had given the gun back to Fineman. As they walked back to the stack of crates, she murmured, "These would make excellent gifts for any allies we may want to encourage."

"That's my thinking as well … we may want to stock up," Sebastian murmured back.

"How many do you have in stock?" Beth asked Fineman when they reached the stack.

"There are ten to a case and I have—" he counted them — "seventeen cases."

"A hundred and seventy," Beth said. "We will take fifteen cases with tools. What is your best price?"

They haggled and Beth paid him when they had agreed. "Please deliver them to the *Fox*," she said, and smiled sweetly.

Fineman smiled back. "You haggle like your father. He should be proud of you."

The crates were delivered later that day and went down into the *Fox*'s hold. The marines were issued with the guns and their first job was to clean the grease off and make them fireable. Beth watched as they studiously scrubbed them clean. All still had their Baker rifles beside them. The *Fox* and *Cub* marines did not wear uniform and mixed in with the rest of the crew when it came to manning the guns. However, they were under the command of Sergeant Harris on the *Fox* and Corporal Fines on the *Cub*. The two NCOs reported to their respective skippers, and all deferred to Beth as "the boss".

Once the guns were clean, they were inspected by the NCOs, from whom the slightest hint of grease would earn the culprit an ear bashing of the first order.

"There is grease on this action! Do you want to misfire in the face of the enemy? You have embarrassed yourself in front of her ladyship. Do it again!"

The first gun passed inspection as they were setting sail. Sebastian had by now recovered and was eating well, and the wind was on their sterns. As they moved south it became warmer and they changed their clothes to suit the climate. Lighter fabrics — especially linen, silk and cotton — and looser-fitting clothes were the order of the day.

Sergeant Harris organised rifle practice. First Sebastian demonstrated how to load one, then the men practised loading their new weapons. That went well, and after Sebastian had checked they all had their guns' breeches closed properly, they fired.

"Bloody hell!" Marine Tibs exclaimed as burning gases escaped from the gap between the breech and the bore.

Sebastian chuckled; he had deliberately not mentioned that the guns did this. He told them, "When you line up, allow a little more than the usual gap between you and the men to your sides. You don't want to singe their eyebrows."

The men practised and were soon able to get off six rounds a minute. Sebastian felt they could do better and should aim for eight or nine, so the practice continued. Meanwhile, Beth and the Wolves joined in with their personal rifles, which were of the same type but polished with use. Practice kept her team sharp, and Mike set the bar they all had to reach. The man was a crack shot and could knock the eye out of a goat at three hundred yards.

The Wolves practised fighting constantly: the use of knife, sword pistol and unarmed combat predominated and any member of the crew could join in. The new Wolf, Harry, suffered to start with. He had no particular weapons training other than what the crew got, so Mike showed him the basic moves, then Paola took over and he learned a lot more.

"Do I detect a certain *friendship* growing between those two?" Sebastian asked Beth one day.

"It would seem so."

"It doesn't worry you?"

Beth shook her head. "As long as the other girls do not mind, it is all right."

Sebastian frowned. "All the same, I will have a chat with the young man."

Beth grinned; she knew *exactly* what that chat would be about.

Jamaica

February 1828

The ships entered the Wag Water River, Jamaica, after a reasonably drama-free crossing of the Atlantic. They made landfall in Barbados on 4 February and took another five days to get to Wag Water River. In theory they should have continued directly to Cartagena, but Beth wanted to look in on the plantations and stock up with coffee beans.

"Do you think they will be expecting us?" Sebastian said, as Beth was looking up at the hills towards the Den, the plantation closest to the river.

"I think so," she replied, and pointed at a group of dots on the hillside.

Sebastian grabbed a telescope from the rack on the quarterdeck and focused it. He chuckled. "I see two men on horseback leading two Friesians and a half-dozen other saddle horses."

Thirty minutes later the dots arrived. Beth greeted Emperor and Gregory, the Friesian stallion and gelding, with apples taken from a nearby wild apple tree. The two field hands that had brought them looked at their princess in awe. Within the past half-hour she had changed into a riding habit and packed a smallish bag. Sebastian had followed her lead and now admired the horses, noting the Spanish-style saddles.

"They are a pair of beauties," he declared.

"You can ride Emperor," Beth said as she swung up into Gregory's saddle. Mike handed up her rifle, which she slid into the saddle holster. One of the hands took her bag and tied it to his horse's cantle. When the Wolves were all mounted, with Titherton sitting behind Harry, they set off for the Den. Fede loped along beside the horses, keeping an eye out for anything he could catch to eat.

This was Sebastian's first visit to the Stockleys' Jamaican plantations, since the last time they were in Jamaica they had been too busy. The journey was not without challenges; Emperor didn't know him and decided to test this new rider by doing a sneaky sidestep and then a buck. Sebastian was far too experienced to fall for that and maintained his seat without effort. He was not used to a Spanish saddle, but the longer stirrup actually helped, and he brought the stallion under control with a laugh. Emperor snorted and rolled his eyes.

Beth laughed with him and then kicked Gregory into a canter, which prompted Emperor to try to keep up, and soon they were galloping side by side. The horses' manes flew back in the wind and Beth's hair streamed out behind her head like fire in the sun. The Wolves kicked their horses to keep up but they were soon left behind — as was Fede, who was built for fighting and not for chasing down horses. The couple laughed as they enjoyed the speed and power of their mounts, but all too soon the gates of the Den appeared, and Beth dropped Gregory back to a walk.

"Why slow down?" Sebastian asked.

"Children and animals."

"Oh."

She was right: as soon as they were ten yards inside the plantation, children and dogs ran up and surrounded them. Sebastian caught the word *princess* more than once and thought they were talking in some kind of patois. Fede caught up and pointedly walked at Beth's left stirrup.

They arrived at the plantation house and were met by Bertram Berkley, the plantation manager, and his wife.

"Welcome, Miss Bethany!"

Beth swung down and Gregory was taken by a groom. "Hello, Bert. This is my husband, Sebastian. I am Mrs Ashley-Cooper now."

"Congratulations, and nice to meet you, sir," Bert said, and smiled.

Beth was chatting away to Sandra, Bert's wife, as the two men shook hands and got to know each other.

"Will you be staying long?" Bert asked.

Sebastian shrugged. "A day or two here, then on to the Blue Mountain. Beth wants some beans but I think it's all an excuse so she can see the people again."

"She has told you about them?"

"And about her great-whatever-it-is-times grandmother."

At this, Bert looked thoughtful. "She does seem to have a spiritual connection with this place."

Later that evening, before the sun set, Beth took him down to the crypt below the house that ran off the cellar. She unlocked the door and stepped inside; he followed a little tentatively. Inside were two coffins; one had some exquisite emerald jewellery laid out upon it. Beth stood at the foot of the coffins and closed her eyes. Then she said, "Grandma Scarlett, this is my husband and soulmate, Sebastian. He is a good man, and worthy."

Sebastian was surprised and then shocked as he felt a warm glow of something … was it *approval*?

Meanwhile, Beth opened her eyes and turned to him with a beaming smile on her face and her eyes wet with happy tears. "She likes you."

This was the strangest thing he had ever experienced and well outside his understanding of the world. He stuttered, "Tha-that … that's good."

Beth turned back to the coffins and closed her eyes again. Did he imagine it, or did the air *move*? He was very relieved when she opened her eyes and turned to leave, taking his hand.

"Aah, does that happen every time you visit?"

"What?"

"The *feelings* … and air moving and that stuff."

"Oh yes, and she comes to me in my dreams."

She had told him that before, and he had put her experiences down to stress — but now he was decidedly unsure.

Dinner that night was an outdoor feast attended by everyone on the plantation. Sebastian found out that their ships had been spotted — by one of the boys who herded goats — as it passed through the sandbar and into the river. Knowing that Beth was always followed by a team and expecting Garai to be with her, Bert had despatched the horses.

Having eaten, Sebastian was again surprised — this time by an old lady, who approached him and started some kind of ritual. This involved sprinkling something that smelled like rum on him and then blowing some powder in his face.

"That's Mama Felice, she's the medicine woman and priestess of the people. She just blessed you."

"What *was* that stuff?"

"The dust was probably a mix of herbs and ground bone; the liquid was rum and chicken blood."

"Delightful," Sebastian said, and grimaced.

"She will tattoo you later," Beth said, absolutely straight-faced.

"She'll *what*?"

Beth held out her hand and pulled her bracelet away so he could see her iguana tattoo. "You need to have one of these to be part of the tribe."

Sebastian swallowed; a tattoo was the last thing he ever thought he would get. He knew Beth had one, as he had explored every inch of her body during their lovemaking, but to have one himself ...

"Do I have a choice? No, silly question. I mean, do I have a choice about where it goes?"

"Oh yes, she will put it anywhere you choose ... even on your bum."

Sebastian snorted a laugh. "I had my shoulder in mind, so it will not show when I am in uniform."

In the end, not only was Sebastian tattooed that evening, but also Mike and Harry. The girls had already been tattooed and wouldn't let the boys off. And so the boys endured the procedure without a flinch, mainly because the girls claimed that they hadn't flinched at all for theirs. After that, the night was long and the rum punch flowed. They danced and made merry.

In the morning, the horses were brought around and they set out for the Blue Mountain plantation. The ride was pleasant and not too hot, since they travelled and arrived before the sun got too high.

As soon as they entered the plantation boundary, children and dogs gathered to escort them to the house. Fede was immediately approached by a frisky bitch who, after sniffing him, invited him to play. Beth laughed at the sight of the pretty little dog making eyes and playing catch with the big Alpine. Then they were greeted by Phineas Calthorpe and his wife Jasmine. Beth and Jasmine were old friends and were soon deep into a girls' catch-up. Sebastian scratched his head and looked at Phineas who said, "Fancy a coffee? You can call me Finn, by the way."

Seb replied, "I would love one."

So the two men sat in the shade of the porch around the main house and drank coffee. The Wolves had dispersed and were looking around the grounds.

"How big is this plantation?" Sebastian asked.

"We have around one hundred and seventy-three acres of planted land. We are one of the biggest plantations in Jamaica."

Sebastian was impressed. "That's a good size. How much do you produce?"

"About three and a half tons per acre and we sort the crop into normal and peaberry beans."

Sebastian looked at him quizzically. "Peaberry?"

Finn smiled. "Normal coffee beans come in pairs. Every now and then a cherry will produce a single bean, which we call a peaberry. We separate those from the regular beans, as they produce a superior coffee, and sell them for a premium price."

At that moment Beth walked up with Jasmine who asked, "Do you want to try some peaberry coffee?"

"Jasmin is an expert coffee maker," Beth said.

The coffee, when it arrived, was unlike any Sebastian had tasted before. A deep pocket of sweetness followed by a brighter acidity gave it a very balanced structure.

"That is delicious," Sebastian said after tasting it for the first time.

"Lady Caroline always takes some with her when she comes here," Finn said. "Seb, do you want to have some?"

Beth noted the use of 'Seb'; clearly her husband was making friends here.

"Oh, yes please. Can you show Titherton how to brew it?"

Quite by chance, Malakai — the Stockleys' company agent — visited the plantation when they were still there. He lived in Kingston and used a dog cart to get around. The large wheels were helpful when travelling over unpaved roads.

"Any news?" Beth asked.

"Nothing much, everything is pretty quiet really," Malakai replied, and frowned. "There is one thing, though. Some former slaves have gone missing from a number of plantations — quite a few, by all accounts."

Sebastian looked up at this. "How many is 'quite a few'?"

Malakai frowned even harder. "Well, now I think about it, they have gone missing from lots of places, and when you add up the incidents, it must be between eighty and ninety."

"That's a schooner full!" Sebastian said.

"It is, isn't it?" Beth said thoughtfully. "Are they still using slaves in South America?"

Malakai considered for a moment. "Brazil does, and I think Mexico, Uruguay and Bolivia still import slaves."

"So, there is a ready market. Has the navy done anything?" Sebastian said.

"No, not a thing."

Sebastian looked at Beth. "The posting won't go away; we could look into this."

"First, let's think it through. Where would you collect together one hundred not very happy people, to get them onto a ship?"

Sebastian shrugged and Finn went to the door and called for someone. An older worker eventually arrived.

"This is Bo. He used to be a fisherman and knows the north coast really well. Bo, if you were gathering stolen slaves to be loaded onto a schooner, where would you take them?"

"Where no one would see, boss?"

"Exactly," Finn said.

"Where they stolen from?"

Malakai reeled off a list of plantations.

"All them be in the west," the old man said with his thick local accent, then thought for a moment or two. "I think that I would use Explorer beach or Dunn's River beach. No one live there and the water is deep enough. Everywhere east of that has too many people and fisherfolk."

Sebastian thanked him and gave him a silver coin for his time. Bo took it and went to leave, then he stopped.

"There is an old salt pan east of Dunn's River. That might be a good place to look."

They went back to the ships and Beth, on board the *Fox*, had Richard dig out a small-scale chart of the island. They soon located the places that old Bo had mentioned and saw he was probably right.

"Get us out of the river and have the *Cub* scout ahead, but not engage," Beth said to Richard.

"Do you think they have holding pens on land?" Sebastian said.

"They might; they will lose fewer slaves if they keep them on land rather than in the holds," Beth replied.

"Then can I suggest a pincer movement?"

The sound of shouting from outside interrupted Beth's thinking: the *Cub* was casting off.

"How do you mean?" she replied as the cutter headed downstream.

"We lead a shore party of the Wolves and marines that will cut off any escape of the perpetrators on the landward side while the *Fox* and *Cub* engage their ship."

The *Fox* moved and the bow started to swing around to face downstream to follow the *Cub*. Shouts and thuds came from above. Meanwhile, the couple pored over the chart with a magnifier, noting the depth of water at likely landing places.

"If we disembark here, it's a one-and-a-half-mile trek to get into position. I have sailed up that bit of coast and it's predominantly wooded or covered with brush."

"That shouldn't be a problem," Sebastian said, and smiled.

Beth gave him a look. "Have you ever tried to march through the brush on a Caribbean island? The scrub has thorns that are two inches long and sharper than needles. If you want to go through it, you have to hack a path with a machete. A mile would take hours."

"Ahh ... do you have any other suggestions, then?"

"There is a coast road that runs a half-mile inland. We take that and make our way to behind the cove. There must be a track leading down to the landing."

Sebastian agreed, and so the choice was made.

The *Fox* took a lot longer than the *Cub* to exit the river and the cutter was well away by the time they got under sail. The wind was from the south-east and the *Fox* set minimum sail to give the *Cub* a chance to complete its reconnaissance. They pootled along and just before sunset the *Cub* came into view, tacking to get back to them. They pulled alongside and both ships hove to, and Stephen shouted across, "We spotted a pair of masts here, inside the reef at Explorer beach. The coastline there is heavily wooded, and you cannot see it from the road. There is a cove with a beach to the east and just past that is another cove, which is Explorer beach. The reef carries on west, with a passage to get into the cove. Behind it there must be sufficient water for a schooner to get in, as that is where they are anchored. Behind the bay is a beach with trees coming up as far as the waterline in places."

Beth, Sebastian, Fede, the Wolves and ten marines boated ashore from the *Cub* at the first cove. The coastline was forested, and they used machetes to cut a path inland. Birds flew in the canopy and lizards scuttled away from under their feet. Beth spotted a large snake in a tree and took care to avoid it. The terrain was fairly level, and they found the coast road five hundred yards inland.

Beth and the girls were in fighting leathers and armed with rifles, revolving pistols and each woman's preferred choice of blade. Fede wore his fighting collar, which was covered in spikes and reinforced with metal plates.

"You might not even know the coast was there along this stretch," Sebastian said, and swatted a mosquito that was biting his neck.

"It's like that here, where no one has built anything," Beth replied.

They spread out in single file, ready to hide in the forest if anyone came down the road. Mike led the group and a marine was rearguard. They moved quickly and quietly with rifles ready. Mike held up a clenched fist and Fede moved up beside him, sniffing the air.

They stopped, and all took a knee. Mike disappeared into the forest with Fede; the rest waited. He soon reappeared, took a knee and signalled with a clenched fist and four fingers. Beth understood: *fourteen bad guys.* Then he made a roof shape with his hands followed by seven fingers. *Seven in a hut.* Three fingers followed by a mime of walking using two fingers. *Three on patrol.* Four fingers and hands in a boat shape. *Four by the boat.*

Beth nodded and looked down the road to her husband. Sebastian nodded and signalled to the marines that they were to go with him, to take the hut. The Wolves would be with Beth, naturally, and would take out the sentries and the men by the boat. Beth signalled to Mike to proceed.

There was a trail that was concealed well enough to fool a casual or passing glance. It was well used and easy going. They moved down it at a trot until Mike stopped them at a point where Fede sat watching. Beth had the Wolves spread out into the trees, ready to come at the camp from multiple directions. The marines would charge in. When they were ready, Sebastian fired a signal rocket.

Beth moved and the Wolves followed. She had pinpointed one of the sentries, who was moving around a stockade that was packed with people. She exited the forest rim, knelt and shot him. Other shots rang out and, with a roar, the marines charged. Beth ran to the stockade and opened the gate. A bullet slapped into the ground next to her and she spun, pulling a pistol from its holster on her leather bodice and scanning for the shooter.

A shot rang out and a man fell from a watchtower built into the palisade. Beth looked around and Netta waved, smoke coming from the barrel of her rifle. The captives surged out of the gate, almost trampling Beth in their rush to escape.

* * *

Sebastian led the charge. The ten marines instinctively formed a line behind him once they had room, and they descended like demons from hell on what was a shelter rather than a hut. Bayonets were used on the slavers, and they took no prisoners. Some slavers fought bravely but the result was the same — they were outnumbered and surprised, and didn't stand a chance. Fede chased down one man who started to run and hauled him to the ground for a marine to finish off.

Sebastian ran one slaver through the chest and then kicked him off his blade. A glance told him the boat was well on its way to the schooner, which was now on full alert and running out its guns. But behind it, on the other side of the reef, the *Fox* appeared around the headland with the *Cub* racing to get through the gap in the reef and into the cove.

As soon as the *Fox*'s guns bore on the target, they roared and the schooner's upperworks were shredded. The *Cub* made the passage through the reef and came alongside the stricken schooner to board her. The fight was brief and vicious. The slavers surrendered.

Beth spoke to the captives that hadn't run into the forest. Those who had would make their own way home. One of the remaining men stepped forward and introduced himself.

"I am Laurence Stone, and I thank you for freeing us."

Beth noted his educated manner of speech and the intelligent look in his eyes. "What is your profession, Laurence?"

"I am a teacher, ma'am." He looked at her hand and saw the iguana tattoo. "You are the princess of the Children of Scarlett."

"Is that what they call my people?"

He laughed. "It is an old name that translates from Twi, the language of the original slaves she freed, *Nnipa a wɔwɔ Scarlett*."

"My ancestor is well known, it seems."

"Like you, she did much for her people."

"Can you all make it home from here?"

"We have some sick that will need to be carried," Laurence said.

"We will take them, and any that need to go to Kingston, on our ships," Beth assured him.

Over the course of that day, more people came out of the forest as they realised it was safe to do so, and they ran boats out to the ships to get them aboard. The skipper and crew of the slaver were confined on their own ship. Beth and Sebastian went over to see them.

The crew knelt in a line, hands tied in front of them down the centre line of the deck, watched over by the *Cub*'s marines. Beth came aboard and looked at them, counting thirteen survivors. Most were European but there were a few dark skins amongst them.

Stephen came up from below and handed her a sheaf of papers. They were the ship's registration documents. She walked down the row of sailors until she got to the skipper.

"Sylas Morgan, owner and skipper of the *Celeste*. British, out of Bristol. Says here you are shipping agricultural tools. Well, you certainly pushed *that* definition to the limit."

"Fuck you, bitch."

"Oh, a man of few words." She smiled at Mike, who stood behind him. "Would you be a dear?"

Mike grinned and kicked the man in the kidneys, sending him flat to the deck.

"Thank you," Beth said, then smiled and set a knee on the writhing man's chest. A stiletto had appeared in her hand and now pricked the skin beneath his eye.

"The hangman won't care what shape you are in when he drops you. So do not think that just because you are going to die anyway, you can get away with not answering my questions."

His eyes were wide and defiant.

"Your choice." The stiletto jabbed forward and pierced his eyeball right through the pupil. Morgan screamed and when that scream died down to a sob, Beth hissed, "If you want to keep the other one you *will* talk. Now, who is your customer?"

"Bruno Rocha, he is in São Luis. There is a slave market there."

Beth stood and walked away. Her colleagues in England would track down his associates once they received her report.

Sebastian left her alone; he could see that she was fired up and her blood was running hot. She needed time alone to cool down. However, one of the slavers made a grab for her as she walked past, probably hoping to use her as a hostage. She turned on one foot and caught his arm while rotating into him for a hip throw. It was purely instinctive, and the man ended up on his back on the deck. What followed was driven by the cumulation of her enduring anger at having once been raped, and her visceral hatred of slavery. Her main gauche was in her hand and it flashed as she swept it down. The man screamed, then died with a gurgle as blood fountained from his mouth.

"Get this offal off the deck," she said as she walked away.

Sebastian looked down at the corpse. His trouser crotch was soaked in blood and his left lung had been pierced where the main arterial blood supply joined it, between the second and third ribs. She hadn't got near his heart, but opened his lung to fill it up with blood. He knew his wife had studied anatomy and could only conclude the stab had been deliberately aimed. He gingerly pulled the man's trousers away where she had sliced them open.

"She did a good job of that," Mike said, and winced as he looked over Sebastian's shoulder.

"Yes, she has the precision of a surgeon," Sebastian said, as he covered the mutilation up.

On their return to Port Royal, Beth looked into the history of the case. She found and talked to the governor, Sir John Kean.

"Sir, when did you have the first report of former slaves going missing?"

He brushed some lint from the sleeve of this jacket. "Oh, I don't know, probably two months ago."

His disinterested manner annoyed her. "Can you remember how many reports you saw?"

He missed the edge in her voice.

"About half a dozen, then I passed it over to Staincliffe to look into. Thought it was a bit rum."

At least he noticed it was unusual, thought Beth. "What did he report?"

"That blacks were going missing from plantations all over the western end of the island. His conclusion was that someone was taking them, to put back into slavery. We couldn't have that — government policy and all that — so I told Charles Ogle."

Vice Admiral Sir Charles Ogle was the Commander-in-Chief North America and West Indies Station.

"What did he do?"

"He said, 'The damn blacks shouldn't have been freed in the first place and have probably run off,' but that he would send the cutter *Calypso* along the coast to see if there was anything unusual."

"Is the cutter still in Jamaica?"

"It is, it's moored near your ships."

Her interview with Sir John Kean having concluded, Beth, escorted by Mike and Harry, went to the prison where the slavers were being held. She asked to see the skipper. She was shown to his cell, where she found him with dressings around his head and over his eye. He looked at her with a mixture of fear and hatred. She returned the look dispassionately.

"Were you visited by a navy cutter while you were in the cove?"

"What if I was?"

"If you were and you paid its skipper off, I want to know."

He sneered. "What's it worth?"

"Your other eye, if you don't talk. If you *do* talk, and willingly, I can make sure you get a quick death rather than a slow one off a short drop."

He snorted a laugh. "That's worth somethin', I suppose. Yes, I did, and I paid him twenty guineas to turn a blind eye."

Beth didn't laugh at the dark humour of his idiom. "How will I recognise your coins, if I find them?"

"I put a nick on the rim between the G and the E of George. Stops my men from stealing them."

"Thank you."

Her next task was to talk to the former captives and ask if any of them had seen the *Calypso* in the cove. It didn't take long to find several who had, including one who had served drinks to the slaver and captain.

A carriage took Sebastian, Beth, Mike and Harry across the causeway to the peninsula on which Port Royal lay. There, the Royal Navy had a replenishment station and a hospital. The *Fox* was anchored a hundred yards offshore, and as they rode along Beth tried to imagine how the area would have looked before the great earthquake sank two-thirds of the peninsula.

They signalled, with a shot, for the *Fox* to send over a boat, which Beth asked to take them to the *Calypso*. She climbed up the battens, hitching her dress up with concealed ribbons, and was met by a midshipman.

"Can I help you, miss?" the seventeen-year-old said, trying desperately to keep his eyes off her legs.

"Is your captain aboard?" Beth released the ribbons and decency was restored.

"No, miss, he is in town."

She smiled sweetly at him, and he blushed. "When will he return?"

"Soon, miss, we are due to sail in an hour or so."

"Then I will wait." She walked to the stern and down the steps to his cabin. The boy started to object but Mike placed a hand on his shoulder and shook his head.

Mike, Harry and Sebastian waited on deck. Harry and Mike looked like regular sailors so could hide in plain sight; Sebastian hid. By the time Lieutenant Robertson returned, Beth was below, searching his desk. Robertson was slightly tipsy and still had rouge on his cheek from a recent encounter with a high-class whore.

The mid, on the instruction of Mike, said nothing about Beth, and the lieutenant suspected nothing as he went down to his cabin. So he was surprised when he opened the door and saw a woman sitting at his desk with his pile of gold sovereigns and his papers.

"What the … ? Who the hell are you?"

Beth produced a pistol and pointedly cocked it. Robertson's eyes widened, and he sobered up almost instantaneously.

"Stand there," Beth said and waved the revolver at a spot in front of the desk.

"You can't order me around on my own ship! Who the hell are you? Answer me, woman!"

"I am an agent of the British security service, and *this* gives me all the authority I need." She waved the pistol at him then pointed it at his groin. He stepped forward onto the spot she indicated, and waited.

"You took a bribe from a slaver operating on this island to ignore what he was doing; you are under arrest for that and for dereliction of duty."

"I did not!"

"Then kindly explain where you got the eighteen guineas I found locked in your drawer."

"I … aaah …" He was obviously trying to think of something, and suddenly he smiled. "I won them in a card game."

"Really? Must have been high stakes. Where and who were you playing?"

"I can't remember."

"That's convenient. No matter, I have a confession that states the slaver paid you. Unless you can provide witnesses to the contrary, that is all that will count."

"I want to see your authority!"

Beth pulled her letter of authority from her bodice. It had been signed not only by John Ward, but by the Duke of Wellington as well. It basically said she had authority over all British assets in the Caribbean and South America. She smiled as Robertson read it, then took it back from his shaking hand.

"I see you are not wearing a sword. You will leave it off and come with me."

31

She led him out onto the main deck, where Mike and Harry closed in on either side of him. The mid came over, his face bearing a look of concern. Beth asked, "Is the admiral in port?"

"No, miss. He is in Bermuda."

"Is that where you are sailing to?"

"Aye, miss."

"You are now in command of this ship; your skipper is under arrest and will be held on board my ship, the *Fox*. You will proceed to Bermuda as planned, escorted by my ship."

Beth gave Sebastian the *Cub* and told him she would meet him in Cartagena. She wanted to confront the admiral, with her prisoner, personally.

"Tread lightly around admirals, my sweet," Sebastian cautioned.

"Don't worry, I will. I want to verify his views on slavery and make sure that a court martial takes place. I do not want this swept under the carpet."

Soon after, the *Cub* sailed for Colombia and the *Fox* set off with the *Calypso* in her shadow. The lieutenant was held in their brig in chains and turned out to be not only dishonest but a misogynist as well. He was rude to Delfina when she served him food and made disparaging remarks to the guard about Beth. That got him a professional beating from the guard — professional in the sense that it left little evidence but caused a great deal of pain.

Beth wrote her report, which would go to Turner as well as Vice Admiral Sir Charles Ogle. As she wrote it, she contemplated her actions against the slaver as he grabbed her. These had been purely instinctive and driven by a deep psychological need for release of the tension and anger she had inside her. She had not realised, until now, that she carried with her so much from the rape. In the version of her report intended for Turner, she chided Ogle, as Commander-in-Chief North America and West Indies Station, for failing to act when it became known that black people were being taken. She stated that, after some investigation, his view was that they were only blacks so not worth the trouble. She would change that part, if her interview with him proved otherwise.

In any case, an unedited version of Beth's report was taken to England by a Stockley ship and was in Turner's hands twenty days later. Beth wanted his response before the admiral hurried the trial through, with his own officers.

Court Martial

March 1828

It took over a week to reach Bermuda and as soon as they made harbour, Beth went to the flagship. The watchman at the side of the ship hailed her as she approached and her cox answered, "Government official," which caused a certain amount of confusion as the officers did not know how to form an appropriate side party. In the end, the captain settled for the party suitable for a captain.

Beth tied up her skirts and climbed aboard the flagship, causing the side boys to blush. Then she let her skirts down upon gaining the gun deck and introduced herself.

"I am Senior Agent Chaton of the British Secret Service, and I wish to see the admiral immediately."

The captain, caught completely by surprise by a woman arriving on his ship, took a moment to gather himself.

"Madam, one cannot simply arrive and demand to see the admiral."

Beth smiled vacantly and cocked her head to one side.

"Oh, silly me." Then her face went hard as she gave him her authority. She gave him a moment to read it then said, "The admiral?"

The captain re-folded the paper and handed it to a midshipman with a whispered message for the admiral. The boy walked away as fast as he could without running. Beth waited. The boy returned and said, "The admiral's compliments — and would you show miss to his cabin, sir?"

The captain bowed to her and said, "If you would care to follow me."

The admiral stood as Beth entered, after a barked introduction from the marine guard. His expression changed from one of annoyance to one of interest as she walked towards him. He gave her a long look up and down, which she noted.

"Admiral."

"My dear ... ahh ... Chaton? What can I do for you?"

"That is my designation in the Intelligence Service. In fact I am the Honourable Bethany Ashley-Cooper, wife of Major Ashley-Cooper, who is the military envoy to the ambassador in Colombia."

The admiral knew the aristocracy and recognised that her husband was a son of the Earl of Shaftesbury and, having read about their marriage in the newspapers, that she was the daughter of Rear Admiral Viscount Stockley. She was also well connected in government, according to the signatures on her papers. So, he smiled and behaved in as gentlemanly a fashion as he could.

Beth continued, "I have, unfortunately, had to arrest Lieutenant Robertson, who was in charge of the *Calypso*, for taking bribes and dereliction of duty. I have brought him to you, to stand before a court martial."

Robertson had been given the *Calypso* because he was the third son of the admiral's cousin. So this was not welcome news and the admiral was immediately defensive.

"I am sure there must be some mistake. He is an exemplary officer, and his report says he did not see any ships acting suspiciously on his patrol."

"Not according to my evidence."

"And what is that?"

Beth had seen this coming and was prepared. "The confession of the slaver he took the bribe from — in clear opposition to the law and government policy — and the pile of gold sovereigns I found in his desk."

"The confession of a slaver will not count for anything, and he could have accumulated the coins over time."

Beth kept her cool. "I can prove the coins were from the slaver."

The admiral wasn't beaten yet. "Where is this slaver now?"

"In jail in Jamaica, awaiting trial for kidnap and slave-trading."

"*Kidnap?*"

"Yes, all the people he was going to sell into slavery in Brazil are freed slaves who were innocently going about their lives on the plantations."

"Free men?"

"Yes, otherwise he would also be charged with theft. Several of the men have given evidence, stating that they saw the *Calypso* arrive and her captain come ashore and parlay with the slaver. Two even saw the coins change hands."

"Blacks? They will say anything."

Beth had heard enough. "Obviously my report will go to the Admiralty and the secretary of state as well as Admiral Turner and Arthur Wellesley. I will send the lieutenant home on the next ship with it."

That was too much, and the admiral lost his temper. "Damn you, woman, how dare you! He is under my command!"

Beth looked at him calmly. "The lord high admiral, King William, is totally against slavery. I can ensure he sees my report."

"*What?*"

Beth unashamedly used her family connections. "My father is a confidant of his." She paused, then offered him a lifeline. "All I ask is that he gets a court martial that is fair and impartial."

The admiral was enough of a politician — and chess player — to know when he was about to be checkmated. He huffed. "Where?"

"Jamaica. He will be charged under Articles Three and Thirty-Two of the Articles of War."

These articles were:

III. Holding intelligence with an enemy, or rebel. If any officer, mariner, soldier, or other person of the fleet, shall give, hold, or entertain intelligence to or with any enemy or rebel, without leave from the king's majesty, or the lord high admiral, or the commissioners for executing the office of lord high admiral, commander-in-chief, or his commanding officer, every such person so offending, and being thereof convicted by the sentence of a court martial, shall be punished with death.

XXXII. Apprehending and keeping criminals. Bringing offenders to punishment. No provost martial belonging to the fleet shall refuse to apprehend any criminal, whom he shall be authorised by legal warrant to apprehend, or to receive or keep any prisoner committed to his charge, or wilfully suffer him to escape, being once in his custody, or dismiss him without lawful order, upon pain of such punishment as a court martial shall deem him fit to deserve; and all captains, officers, and

others in the fleet, shall do their endeavour to detect, apprehend, and bring to punishment all offenders, and shall assist
the officers appointed for that purpose therein, upon pain of
being proceeded against, and punished by a court martial,
according to the nature and degree of the offence.

Breach of Article III could mean the death penalty. The admiral made
a final play. "Will you release him into my custody?"

Beth looked at him, her head on one side, weighing him up.

"No, but I will let a defence officer of your choice come aboard
the *Fox* for the trip back to Jamaica."

The *Fox* returned to Jamaica with the flagship and two frigates as
escorts, the *Calypso* tagging along behind. Having to go against the
current and the prevailing wind with the big second-rate, whose bottom
was filthy, meant that it took them three weeks to make it back to
the island. The slaver had not been tried yet and Beth asked for that
process to be delayed so that he could testify. This request was granted.

Beth used the time wisely. She appointed Richard Brazier, captain
of the *Fox*, as the prosecuting officer and spent every spare moment
working with him on their case. The defence would be carried out
by the admiral's flag lieutenant, who was aboard the *Fox* so he could
spend time with the accused.

The admiral would appoint four frigate captains to preside at the
court martial and intended to chair it himself, but Beth stepped in
and asked that an independent officer be appointed and that, as the
accused was only a lieutenant, it should be a captain. She also asked
for Sir William Anglin Scarlett, the chief justice of Jamaica, to be
present. The admiral objected strongly … so she waited.

Ten days after they arrived in Jamaica, the admiral was pushing for the court to be convened when a fast packet came into harbour under full sail. On it was Turner's reply to Beth's report and, more importantly, Captain Francis Boyle of the Judge Advocate's Office, who was designated to preside over the trial accompanied by a judge advocate, Graham Niccols. The reply told her that the admiral was not to be touched, but that the lieutenant was to be made an example of. That had the support of everyone from the lord high admiral (the king) and the Navy Board to the prime minister and secretary of state. He also said that the admiral had received orders accordingly. Turner had also turned up the fact that the admiral and lieutenant in this case were related; he warned Beth that she had probably made an enemy, as the admiral was also linked to Admiral Gambier, her father's old adversary.

Now the admiral insisted that Sir William Scarlett should attend, saying he wanted proof this was a fair trial. When Beth agreed, he got in his ship and went back to Bermuda, leaving his flag lieutenant to manage the defence on his own.

Francis Boyle was a trained lawyer from Edinburgh Law School and had been practising in naval law since being called to the bar in 1819. Beth found he had a dry sense of humour and pleasant character, although before the trial he very much kept himself to himself. He had brought along his own writer and a clerk.

The trial of Lieutenant Robertson was held on the *Jupiter*, and the board was made up of four captains plus Captain Boyle. The captains were Captain Benjamin Clement of HMS *Shannon*, Captain John Tower of HMS *Curacoa* (in port from duty in South America to suppress the slave trade), Captain Travis Smythe of HMS *Brilliant* (in port for repairs while returning from the Galapagos) and Captain William Redford-Pipkins of HMS *Horatio*.

Beth knew that two of these were Ogle's men, but with Boyle, Tower and Smythe she had a great chance of getting the result she wanted.

The captains were sworn in by the judge advocate with the oath:

> *I, [name], do swear that I will duly administer justice according to law, without partiality, favour, or affection; and I do further swear, that I will not on any account, at any time whatsoever, disclose or discover the vote or opinion of any particular member of this court martial, unless thereunto required in due course of law. So help me God.*

Then the judge advocate was sworn in by the president:

> *I, Graham Niccols, do swear that I will not on any account, at any time whatsoever, disclose or discover the vote or opinion of any particular member of this court martial, unless thereunto required in due course of law. So help me God.*

Lieutenant Robertson was brought in, and sat before the court and Richard as the prosecution opened his case.

"Captains of the court, I present to you Lieutenant Amos Stanford Robertson, who is charged under Articles Three and Thirty-Two of the Articles of War with the taking and receiving of a bribe from a known felon and for failing in his duty to arrest said felon for kidnap and the trading of slaves."

The advocate general asked the accused, "How do you plead?"

Robertson replied, "Not guilty."

Once that was recorded, the president asked Richard to present his case and witnesses. Sylas Morgan was called. He was brought forward in chains and took the seat in front of the captains.

He was sworn in and asked to recount his meeting with Robertson, which he did clearly and without hesitation. Richard then asked him if he could identify the coins, and he told how he marked them. Then it was the defence's turn to cross-examine.

"Your eye is injured; would you care to tell us how that happened?"

"She stuck a blade in it to make me talk."

"Can you identify the woman you are referring to?"

He turned and pointed at Beth, who was dressed prettily and looked as if butter would not melt in her mouth. "Her."

"Did she threaten you at any other time?"

"She did, when I was in me cell."

"So, is it safe to say that the confession you made was tortured from you?"

"I object!" Richard cried. "He is putting words into the witness's mouth."

"Agreed," the president stated. "Please confine yourself to direct questions."

The flag lieutenant changed tack. "You are a convicted slaver and kidnapper?"

"I am."

"Sentenced to death by hanging?"

"Yes."

"No more questions."

Richard was surprised at the sudden stop and called Beth. She was sworn in and he asked the first question.

"Can you introduce yourself, please?"

"I am the Honourable Bethany Ashley-Cooper, née Stockley, and I am a senior agent in British Intelligence. I am codenamed Chaton. I am married to Sebastian Ashley-Cooper, who is the military envoy in Colombia."

Captain Boyle leaned forward. "Your father is Admiral Stockley, Earl Purbeck?"

"Yes." She smiled proudly.

She was asked to describe how she got involved in the case, which she did before describing the raid and her interrogation of Morgan. Then the coins were produced as evidence.

"All twenty are there," Beth said.

Boyle counted them and handed them around to the captains.

"You said you only found eighteen in his cabin, where did the other two come from?"

Beth replied, "From the whorehouse Robertson visited prior to his arrest. He spent two guineas on two whores."

After Beth, the two people who witnessed the meeting at the slave camp were brought forward and gave their evidence. After his cross-examination the flag lieutenant made a statement, for he thought the prosecution's case was closed. "All the evidence against Lieutenant Robertson is from dubious sources, a convicted slaver and former slaves. I propose that it cannot be trusted and should be dismissed," he said.

But before Boyle could reply, Richard stepped forward.

"Mr President, I have three more witnesses."

The flag lieutenant looked surprised and opened his mouth to say something, but Boyle interrupted him.

"Please bring them forward."

Two pretty women came in, one with brown hair, the other blonde. One of the captains broke out in a fit of coughing. The blonde smiled and waved at him. The other captains grinned at his discomfort.

"Please introduce yourselves, ladies," Richard said after they had been sworn in.

"I am Annabelle Smith, a courtesan at the Bird of Paradise," the blonde said.

"And I am Jenny Jones, also a courtesan at the Bird of Paradise," the other stated.

Richard asked, "Do you recognise the defendant?"

"Him and others," said the blonde, and then laughed.

"Just answer yes or no," the advocate snapped.

She pouted at him, obviously enjoying the occasion. "Yes."

"When was the last time you saw him?"

Now Jenny spoke up. "Why, about a month ago. He came in flashing golden guineas at everyone and asked for me and Anny."

"How long was he with you?"

Jenny grinned wickedly. "He paid for a day and a night, but he spent most of the time drinking and boasting. Could only manage one time with each of us."

Richard suppressed a grin. "What did he boast about?"

"How he made twenty guineas — more than a year's pay — from a slaver who was shipping some blacks off the island."

"You both heard that?"

"We did as the Lord is our witness!" Anny said, and fluttered her eyelashes at the unfortunate captain.

Richard asked one last question. "And he paid you with golden guineas — what happened to them?"

"Her ladyship over there turned up with a bunch of girls who were all armed to the teeth and asked if he had been with us and how he paid. We showed her the guineas, which she exchanged for two of her own."

"Did you notice anything odd about the guineas he gave you?"

"Only that they carried the mark of Sylas Morgan. We have seen them before."

Richard handed them over to the defence, who had no questions other than to verify they were whores.

The final witness was the midshipman from the *Calypso*.

"State your name, rank and ship."

"Archibald Nugent, midshipman on the *Calypso*."

Nugent testified that the ship had called in at Explorer beach and that Robertson had gone ashore. He had returned rather the worse for wear, and jubilant.

Richard asked him, "Mr Nugent, why did you come forward to testify against your captain?"

"Because what the slavers were doing was wrong, under law and God — and my conscience wouldn't allow me to stay silent."

Richard continued, "Even though you know that the lieutenant has interest that could damage or even end your career?"

"Yes, sir."

The court took several hours to review the evidence and come to a decision. The verdict was a four to one majority vote that Robertson was guilty on both counts. The dissenting captain was never named but Beth guessed it was Redford-Pipkins, a follower of the admiral.

Sentencing was carried out after a further hour of discussion. The court was reconvened the next morning, and Robertson stood in front of the captain's table. Robertson's sword was lying on the table with the point towards him.

Boyle addressed the court.

"The accused has been found guilty on both counts. To have an officer of the Royal Navy fall so low is a disgrace and must be dealt with severely."

The judge advocate took over.

"The court has decided by majority that under Article Three the condemned should be stripped of rank and face the maximum penalty of death, commuted to life in military prison. The court has further decided that under Article Thirty-Two the condemned should be stripped of rank, dishonourably discharged from the Royal Navy and forfeit all pay and pensions. The court has so ruled."

Robertson collapsed, but was lifted up by the master-at-arms and a bosun's mate and taken from the court. The admiral would not be happy.

Beth talked to Boyle after the trial. "Should we give him the opportunity to do the decent thing?"

"It would mollify the admiral somewhat," Boyle replied. "Will you … ?"

Beth nodded. Enough had been said.

Beth visited Robertson in the brig on Port Royal, taking Mike. Robertson was scheduled for transport to a prison in England at the end of the week. They stood outside his cell and addressed him.

"What do you want?" Roberson said from where he lay on his cot.

"I am here to offer you the chance to recover some of your honour."

He knew what she meant. "Fuck off, I have none, hadn't you noticed?"

"It would make things so much tidier if you did."

Beth turned to the guard and said, "Open his cell." The guard, being no fool, opened the cell and walked away. Beth took out one of her older single-barrelled muff pistols.

"It is loaded."

"I would rather spend my life in prison."

Beth sighed. "Have it your way."

Mike stepped into the cell and punched Robertson in the gut as he lay there. He doubled up and Beth put the gun to his temple, then pulled the trigger. A quick rearrangement of the corpse meant observers would be in no doubt that he had shot himself, and Beth abandoned the gun for the guard to keep as evidence. In due course, the navy's hierarchy was happy because an embarrassment had been removed. There was no investigation, and Robertson was buried in an unmarked grave in the naval cemetery.

Beth kept her word to Sylas Morgan. She persuaded the courts to change his sentence from death by hanging to death by firing squad. She made sure it was done properly and selected men who had killed before so they would not deliberately miss. No coup de grâce was needed.

Midshipman Archibald Nugent was taken back to Britain and reassigned to a command that had no connection with either Ogle or any of his friends.

The Road to Bogotá

May 1828

The *Fox* pulled into Cartagena two months after the *Cub*, and pulled up beside the dock. It was now early May. The city walls were stark, high and formidable with the barrels of cannon poking out between the crenelations. Beth remembered that her five-times-great-grandmother Scarlett had lost her first love on these walls and felt a shiver run through her. That event had led to Scarlett's feud with the priests of the Inquisition.

The *Cub* was anchored nearby, and Stephen came across with a message from Sebastian telling her he had been summoned directly to Bogotá and to meet him there. He warned that the roads were often dangerous and to be prepared.

Beyond the walls, Cartagena's buildings were multi-coloured, with balconies that dripped with flowering plants. There were arch-lined walkways and bustling markets. The place smelt of humanity and the scent of flowers. It was bustling and busy. As they walked, the girls spread out ahead of Beth, and Mike and Harry bracketed her. A pair of sailors with handcarts followed with her baggage.

Just before they parted ways, Sebastian had left her a note that told her of a boarding house-cum-cantina called the Casa Mara on the western side of the town, where she could hire a coach. Beth enjoyed the walk and having the opportunity to stretch her legs after being at sea. The directions given led them to a plaza where street food was sold from carts and booths. She bought a dozen aborrajados: these were deep-fried ripe plantain, stuffed with cheese and coated in batter. The whole team munched on the snacks as they looked for the hotel.

They almost walked past it, but a large gate which gave access to a busy courtyard gave it away. Horses stood patiently waiting to be harnessed or brushed; a large coach was being prepared. Beth entered the cantina, went to the bar and asked — in Spanish — when the next coach would leave for Bogotá.

"I am sorry, señora. The one that leaves today is full. The next one is in a week."

Beth was not to be put off. "Do you have a coach, or even two, that I can hire?"

He cast an eye over the Wolves and her luggage. "Yes, and you will need a wagon for the luggage. I have some that you can rent, but I will want a large guarantee held against their arrival at my place in Bogotá."

Beth was intrigued. "How does that work?"

"You deposit the guarantee here, and when you arrive in Bogotá at my establishment you get it back — when you present the receipt and the carriages in good condition. There are places every thirty miles where you can change horses or stay for the night. They are also owned by me."

He has this all worked out! Bright boy! thought Beth.

As it was now early afternoon, she decided to stay at the boarding house and leave early the next day. The journey was five hundred and fifty miles, and if all went well it should take six or so days. That afternoon, appropriate clothes were chosen for the morrow. The girls would wear their fighting leathers, while Mike and Harry would sport tough, serge-de-Nîmes trousers that had been made in France. The material, a twill made of wool and silk, had become known as denim in recent years. Cotton shirts, bandanas, broad hats and Wellington-style leather boots would complete their dress.

However, for that afternoon the girls could stay in their colourful frocks and blouses, while the boys remained in their ship outfits, to explore that part of the old city. They were all armed, of course, and escorted by Fede — so anyone who thought they could take advantage would be in a heap of trouble. They ate in a cantina overlooking the water, and as the sun went down it outlined the fort of San Felipe de Barajas on its hill.

They returned to their boarding house without incident.

They rose early and breakfasted on fried arepa de huevo — corn cakes stuffed with egg and ham. They were tasty and filling. Outside, a pair of horses was harnessed to what looked like a post chaise, cut off at the top of the doors with a canvas canopy mounted above it. Luggage was being loaded onto the wagon. Beth and the girls climbed aboard and sat under the canopy. Harry took a seat next to the driver of the wagon and Mike next to the driver of the carriage. The carriage was sprung with leaf springs, which was just as well as the roads left much to be desired. The wagon was of a buckboard design and both the wagon and the carriage had larger wheels at the back than the front.

As they travelled, the sun got higher and the air got hotter. The horses, having started out at a trot, were soon plodding, and by the time they got to the first post stop they were going at no more than walking pace. Food for the people and a change of horses got them moving again — more slowly during the heat, but faster as the day cooled. Regular water stops kept the horses in reasonable condition.

On day one, they covered sixty miles according to the driver. They stayed overnight at a town called Santiago de Tolu. The second day took them to the village of Colomboy. The third up into the hills to Caucasia. The fourth day took them to Medellín, where they took a break.

The first priority for the girls was to have baths. The dust from the trail had gotten in everywhere and their fighting leathers had become hot and smelly. Beth decided that she would wear loose trousers tucked into high boots, a blouse and jerkin from then on. She took the girls shopping, as they still had at least another four days' travel to get to Bogotá and she wanted them all to be comfortable. A maid at the boarding house had a brother who was a leather worker, and she recommended that they give their leathers to him for cleaning. Beth took her advice and was fascinated by the array of belts and chaps he made for the Llaneros, the local cowboys.

"What are these for?" he asked when he saw the holsters for her pistols on her bodice.

"Carrying guns," Beth replied.

He looked at the simple tubes that Beth had made. "Can I see the gun?"

She opened her bag, took out one of her revolvers and handed it to him. He turned it over in his hands and tested the balance point. Then he took a piece of charcoal and traced the outline onto a stiff piece of hide. He stood back and looked at it thoughtfully.

"How do you carry them when you are not wearing this?"

Beth was surprised. "Why, in my bag — or if I am travelling, in a sash."

"Do you ride?"

"I do."

He nodded in thought, then turned the gun over so it was back to back with the first outline. Then he drew a line around the outside of the two profiles and cut out the shape using a razor-sharp knife. He took the piece to a clamp and, using a bradawl and needles, stitched the edge around to make a holster. He trimmed the upper edge so it cleared the butt and trigger.

"Does this work for you, if I mount it on the bodice or a belt?"

Beth tried it by holding it against her side and pulling the gun. "Yes, it does."

"And here?" He took it and held it against her left hip, where it would hang from a belt so the butt would be forward. She reached across with her right hand and drew it.

"Yes."

"You carry two?"

"Most times."

He nodded. "Come back tomorrow morning. I will have these done for you."

The next morning, she arrived at the shop with the girls in tow. She wore what were now her riding and travelling clothes. Rodrigues, the leather worker, brought out a tooled leather belt with a fancy brass buckle which had two tooled leather holsters and a pouch for cartridges fitted to it. Beth gasped at the workmanship. It was beautiful.

She buckled the belt around her waist then took her pistols from her bag and slotted them home. Simple loops of leather slipped over the hammers to hold them in place. The girls were fascinated and all talking at once. Beth grinned and said, "They will all need belts as well — and two for my men and one for my husband."

She paid Rodrigues in advance and left him to it. He promised that all would be ready that evening.

Medellín was a green and pleasant town. Its altitude gave it temperate weather and it was spring, so the flowers were out. Beth changed into a dress and wandered around the town with the girls in tow. Everyone was benefitting from the break in the journey; moods had improved and kinks caused by the jarring ride in the carriage eased out. But then it was time to move on. Fitted out with their new belts and holsters, they started the second leg of the journey, the two hundred and fifty miles to Bogotá.

They set out with fresh drivers as well as horses, with the former ones taking goods wagons back to Cartagena. Their route would take them up into the mountains.

As they got more deeply into the hills, Mike noticed that their driver was nervously looking around at the land beside the road.

"What is the matter?"

"This is a bad place, bandits live here."

Mike picked up his sawn-off shotgun and checked the primers, then swapped it for his rifle. The girls and Beth took his cue and pistols were checked.

Beth watched the ridge line that ran parallel to this stretch of road. It was covered in low scrub with occasional trees. She saw nothing unusual for about a mile, when the road started down into a valley. Then a glint on the ridge line ahead of them caught her eye.

"Mike!"

"I saw it, boss."

The driver was now shaking in fear. Beth climbed forward and took the reins, sending him back to sit with the girls. Mike grinned at her, then resumed scanning the surroundings.

"Here we go," he said, and raised his rifle to his shoulder.

Several horsemen blocked the road ahead, rifles couched on their hips. Beth spotted more moving through the scrub on the left and signalled to the girls. The terrain sloped down and away to their right, so she didn't expect an attack from there. She slowed the wagon. Harry brought the luggage wagon up as close behind them as he could so they would cover him with their fire. His driver had hidden himself in the luggage as soon as they saw the bandits.

"Move aside," Mike called out.

The horsemen grinned and brought their rifles to their shoulders.

Mike didn't hesitate. He fired and took the central horseman out of his saddle. Beth grabbed the shotgun, stood up — to clear their horses' heads — and let fly with both barrels. The recoil sat her back down with a thump.

"Bloody hell, what did you load that with?" she gasped. Mike just laughed; he had double-charged the gun, figuring that the shorter barrels would need the extra thrutch that would give. He grabbed the reins and slapped the horse into a run. The two remaining men were wounded by buckshot from the ten-gauge and their horses skipped out of the way as Fede charged at them, barking furiously.

The girls were keeping up a steady fire to cover the luggage and prevent the flanking men from getting near. Harry had his hands full with driving the horses as the coach and wagon careered down the road. Alie shot one of the horsemen as they passed and shouted imprecations in Spanish.

Their next stop was in the valley — which was just as well, as the horses were blown by the time they reached the bottom and the village. Men were waiting at the edge of the village with guns in hand, having heard the shooting in the hills. At first Beth thought they were on the side of the bandits, but smiles greeted them rather than bullets.

The village was called Narino and had a small garrison of soldiers. The commandant asked them what had happened. When Mike told him he had shot the middle of the three riders, the commandant slapped him on the shoulder.

"You have killed El Puma, the bandit. He always sits between his two lieutenants."

"Well, they are wounded as well — milady shot them with a ten-gauge and one of the girls shot one of them again with her pistol."

The commandant was so happy, he bought them all wine at the cantina — although he remained puzzled as to why all the women of Mike's party wore guns.

The next day took them forty-five miles further on, to Norcasia, during which time they were left alone. The following day was another forty miles to Guaduas. Two more days saw them in Mosquera, and with Bogotá being the next stop, the ladies changed into dresses. The final leg was a short one of just ten miles and took them onto the plateau Bogotá Savanna in the Andes mountains.

Bogotá itself was relatively peaceful and was becoming a thriving city that grew year by year. They entered the Plaza de San Victorino with its ornate stone-built wellhead, which had spigots dispensing water where women filled pots. The Andes mountains dominated the skyline.

They arrived at the residence of the ambassador and were met by the soldiers guarding the gates. Mike told them who Beth was and they were admitted under escort. Curiously, it felt like entering an armed camp.

. Word of their arrival soon reached Sebastian, and he appeared in the doorway. Beth was swept up into Sebastian's arms and kissed roundly. Then Fede demanded attention from Sebastian — after all, he hadn't seen him in forever! He knelt and ruffled the big dog's neck while looking up at Beth. "We have our own house, two doors down. This whole block contains the embassy and residences."

Beth was given time to settle in and that gave her time to ask Sebastian the obvious question. "Why here? It's ten days from the coast and in the middle of the mountains."

"Bolívar has chosen Bogotá as his capital. It is roughly in the middle of Colombia and the climate is perfect. We have Venezuela to the east, Brazil to the south, Ecuador and Peru to the west and Panama to the north. He has dominion over Venezuela, New Grenada, Ecuador and Panama as the Republic of Colombia and presidency of Peru. He founded Bolivia and it is part of Gran Colombia as well."

"You would think that peace would reign."

Sebastian sighed. "Unfortunately not. There are juntas with varying political stances and objectives and there is always someone stirring the pot."

Their house was pleasant and cool, as the climate was sub-tropical and the temperature a perpetual five degrees on either side of sixty. It was by now the wetter season: it rained more in March through May and in October and November than it did the rest of the year. The women, having endured a long journey, wanted to bathe. With the house being part of the embassy, a bathhouse was included and this had three baths, which the Wolves soon took over. Beth had her own bathroom, which was attached to her and Sebastian's bedroom.

Within an hour of their arrival, she lay up to her neck in hot water scented with aromatic oils and salts. "God, that feels good," she sighed.

Sebastian sat on a rattan chair beside the tub. "It is a long journey," he smiled.

She snorted a laugh. "I have a feeling we will be doing a lot of travelling in the next three years."

"Gran Colombia is made up of a lot of countries; luckily we have agents in all of them."

Beth suddenly recalled the agent she had worked with in Mexico. "Does Troupial report here?"

Sabastian nodded. "She does."

Beth ducked under the water and washed her hair. Sebastian knew it would glow after she had dried and brushed it. He stood and walked to the head end of the bath, rolling his sleeves up as he did. "I'll wash your back."

She looked over her shoulder at him with a smouldering look. "It would be easier if you were in here with me."

Sebastian grinned and started unbuttoning his shirt.

With Beth suitably refreshed and in a summer dress, her hair styled in an ancient Grecian fashion so that it flowed over one shoulder, the couple went to the embassy for Beth to be formally introduced to the ambassador's wife and the rest of the embassy staffers. Great Britain honoured Bolívar with a full embassy and staff— after all, he controlled or at least influenced the whole of Spanish-speaking South America.

Beth rested her hand on Sebastian's arm as they walked up the steps and entered the hallway. He led her through the embassy building to a grand pair of doors. "The ambassador is throwing an afternoon tea party so you can meet everyone; it's being held indoors because of the rain," he said.

"That's nice of him," Beth replied.

Sebastian pushed the doors open and inside was a sight one would expect to see in an upper-class London house. Tables with tea stands laden with dainty sandwiches, scones and cakes and tea sets were dotted around the room, and the people were sitting in comfortably cushioned rattan chairs or otherwise standing, nibbling on the food or drinking tea.

The couple walked through the room to where Alexander Cockburn — the envoy extraordinary and minister plenipotentiary, to give him his proper title — sat with his wife. As they passed, men nodded to Sebastian and the women either smiled or looked envious of Beth. The ambassador rose as he saw the couple approach. His wife gave Beth a slightly haughty look, which was noted.

"Bethany," he said, greeting her expansively, "I am so pleased to meet you at last."

He bowed over her proffered hand, his lips not quite touching it. His wife's look hardened a fraction. Beth treated him to her best smile and then turned to his wife. "Mrs Cockburn, so pleased to meet you," she said pre-empting the ambassador's introduction. "Your tea party is wonderful."

Mrs Cockburn's face softened as Beth turned the full force of her charm upon her. "Please call me Agnes."

"And I am Beth."

"How are your parents?" Cockburn said.

"Oh, you know Daddy, he is off with his ships looking after the Greeks and Mummy is tutoring Princess Alexandria Victoria," Beth said as if it were nothing.

Agnes noted the connections carefully, knowing they had potential to benefit her husband.

They sat and chatted while taking a cup of tea and a scone or two. Beth was hungry but ate sparingly. She found Agnes to be sophisticated and entertaining; she couldn't be described as pretty, rather she was handsome, which might have contributed to the hard look Beth had noticed at the beginning. But when Beth made her laugh with tales of the goings-on in London and shared an insightful view of current politics, they started to get along famously.

Sebastian interrupted them after twenty minutes as he wanted Beth to meet the rest of the staff. Most were married, and she soon learned that the wives had an active social life both as a group and with the wives of men posted to other embassies. The staff varied in age: the youngest, the ambassador's clerk, was twenty-five, and Sir Walter Cunningham, the deputy head of the mission, was in his fifties. There were eight full-time officers, two of whom were Colombian, and a number of secretaries and clerks. Beth impressed the Colombians by speaking Spanish.

Later on, Beth told Sebastian about the bandits, and he reported this to the ambassador in case there were any repercussions. So, it was no surprise when he was summoned to Cockburn's office a few days later because the Colombians had raised a concern. He was surprised when Cockburn told him what it was.

"It appears that your good lady and that Wolf pack of hers did the administration in that area a favour by eliminating El Puma, and there is a reward. Who actually shot him?"

"Michael Holder. He had a rifle; the others all had handguns except Beth, who had a sawn-off ten-gauge shotgun."

Cockburn raised his eyebrows at that and tried to imagine the woman he had met holding as brutal a weapon as a shotgun. He shrugged and read from a hand-written report.

"Well, according to the report from the mayor, they found El Puma dead on the side of the road with a bullet through his heart. One of his men lay not far from him with multiple wounds and another in the brush on the hillside. Blood trails showed at least two more were wounded."

He handed the report, which was in Spanish and written in a fancy script, to Sebastian. He deciphered the handwriting enough to read it.

"They are assuming the wounded will not survive."

"Yes, that adds up to five bandits killed, and a total reward of two hundred and ten onzas. El Puma had a reward of one hundred and fifty onzas on his head, and the other three, twenty each."

As an onza was a coin containing an ounce of gold which had a value of four pounds and five shillings sterling, this was a substantial sum. Sebastian whistled. "The Wolves will get it all and I am pretty sure they will divide it equally."

"Bethany will not keep any for herself?"

"No, we have enough," was the simple answer.

The Wolves did split the reward, but only took a portion of it. The rest they gave to Beth for safekeeping and to invest in bonds against their retirement. The national bank of Colombia had an arrangement with Coutts in London, who would manage the money for them in an investment account in Beth's name. The account invested in bonds that gave a net return of 4.7 per cent.

Cartagena

It was just a few days after they arrived that Simón Bolívar requested the presence of Beth and Sebastian at his home.

Cockburn came with them, and they met the great man in the central courtyard. Bolívar was accompanied by Manuela Sáenz, his Ecuadorian lover, who was actually married to a British merchant. She was a heroine of the revolution in South America and despite not being married to Bolívar was acknowledged as the first lady of Colombia. She was small, at barely five feet tall, and curvy with jet black hair and smooth skin. She wore a sash with the Order of the Sun medal on it. Beth liked her immediately and sat next to her during the meeting. She sensed that the diminutive woman had a core of steel.

Bolívar was pensive. "I have received word that there is a Spanish-backed rebellion in Venezuela which I intend to help crush. However, there is a second problem that needs attention. José Prudencio Padillo has occupied Cartagena and that is where I would like your help. I need someone to evaluate his strength and deployment so I can turn to him after I crush the rebellion."

Sebastian looked confused; Beth felt he was overdoing it.

"Why ask the British for help?"

"It is simple; I do not know who to trust there. The British can be trusted when their interests are at stake."

"Our interests?"

"Yes, as long as Padillo holds Cartagena, your ships will not be allowed to dock there. He is an ally of Santander."

Francisco de Paula Santander was the leader of the opposition in Colombia. He had once sat beside Bolívar as his deputy, but now their political differences meant he opposed Bolívar's centralist policies and especially the retention of Venezuela in Gran Colombia.

"If we help with this, can the British expect something in return?" Cockburn said, and smiled. Beth thought he looked like a snake when he did that.

"I will grant you the right to have the first pick of the coffee crop," Bolívar conceded.

"Excellent! That is more than generous," Cockburn crowed, knowing that gave the British traders a huge advantage in the marketplace.

Sebastian gave him a sideways look which he hoped Bolívar did not notice. "We will leave in the morning; can we count on you to supply horses?"

Bolívar did notice, and smiled at the couple. "How many?"

"Eight saddle horses and eight pack horses," Beth answered.

Bolívar stood, indicating that the meeting was all but over. "They will be supplied this afternoon. You can get remounts at any army post. I will provide you with an authority."

Beth smiled at him. He kissed her on both cheeks then held her at arm's length. "I knew your father," he told her.

"I know, he told me. He said a lot of good things about you."

"If he had stayed, we could still be friends. Send him my best wishes when you write to him."

"I shall."

The horses were delivered by the army as promised and a letter authorising remounts arrived with them. Further to that, they received a letter of authority from Bolívar stating that they were acting on his behalf and that all aid must be given if asked for.

The next morning at dawn found Beth and the girls dressed in cowboy-style outfits including broad-brimmed hats. The men wore clothes suitable for a long ride. Everyone wore their gun belts, and rifles were slipped into saddle holsters.

Fede took up position beside Beth's horse, where he would run beside her. Cockburn was there to see them off, with Titherton beside him. The latter would stay behind as he disliked horses and was unable to make a long journey on one.

"Be careful. I do not want to tell Wellesley you got killed being reckless," Cockburn said.

Beth glanced over her shoulder, one foot in the stirrup ready to mount. "He would tell us to be bold."

Cockburn smiled. "Yes, I expect he would."

With that, they all mounted and exited the embassy courtyard at a canter, a pace they kept up to the edge of town and beyond in the cool morning air. They crossed the plateau and started down into the first valley. The horses were fit and kept up a quick pace overall with regular breaks where they walked. The initial leg was about thirty miles to the first garrison, where they would change horses so they could push on. Fede kept up without any problem and seemed to enjoy the exercise. Beth checked his paws periodically and found no signs of injury or harm.

* * *

The first garrison came into sight after they had travelled about thirty miles, and they rode up to the gate in the palisade that protected it. The two gate guards recognised the horses as army beasts, but stopped them entering as neither could read the paper. They called for an officer, and a man who closely resembled a strutting peacock arrived.

"We need a change of horses," Sebastian said, and held out the letter.

The officer, his rank indecipherable as it was hidden under all the gold braid he wore, snatched the letter from Sebastian's hand. He read it and his attitude rapidly changed. "Yes, sir," he said and clacked his heels together, Prussian style. He shouted at the guards and then at some soldiers who were lounging around. They reluctantly got up and went to a corral built on one side of the compound containing fourteen horses. Beth dismounted and followed the men over to it. She quickly examined the animals and pointed out two that didn't come up to scratch.

"Not those two."

The officer came over and looked in horror at the horses that *were* being brought out by his men. "That one is mine!" he squawked, pointing at a nice black gelding.

"It has an army brand," Beth said. She stepped forward, took its lead rein and proceeded to switch her tack from her former horse to this one.

"But ..."

"You read the authority. The two horses left in the corral are in no condition to do thirty miles quickly, so we have to take this one. The horse I am leaving is as good as yours. Rub him down, give him some oats and water, let him rest and he will serve you well."

The soldiers were all grinning behind the man's back, amused to see him put in his place by a woman.

They changed horses three times that day and covered more than a hundred miles. Sebastian had Mike help him hoist Fede up across his saddle whenever he got tired. The big dog was quite comfortable up there. They lodged for the night in the last garrison they came to. Saddle-sore and weary, they slept well and were back on the road at first light.

They got to Mamonal, a town near Cartagena that was still in the hands of the government, in four days. Beth decided that if she ever saw another saddle, it would be too soon. They found a cantina that could take them all, and rested for a day.

While they rested, they listened to the local people chatting. It appeared that Cartagena was in rebel hands because they controlled the castle of San Felipe de Barajas. Rumour had it they had slipped in posing as government troops aided by the commander and simply evicted the government soldiers.

Whether that was true or not didn't matter, as they went to see for themselves. However, in such a situation, riding into town on army horses might get them arrested, so they found a couple of livery stables and a farm that rented them local horses and tack.

Suitably mounted, they went onto Manga island in Cartagena Bay, entering across the southern bridge. They were not challenged, and the bridge was only guarded by a couple of soldiers. The town was unusually quiet, and their horses' hooves echoed as they walked down mainly empty streets. Faces appeared at windows and disappeared when looked at. The bridges to the castle of San Felipe and the town of Cartagena were blocked with makeshift barricades and armed troops.

"This is a city under siege," Mike commented.

They made their way to the fort of San Sebastián del Pastelillo on the south-western corner of the island, which was still in the hands of the government. The fort that had been built to protect the bay from attack now had most of its guns pointing at the approaches from the castle and the town of Cartagena, whose walls were clearly visible from the ramparts.

They approached the gate, which was closed. A man looked over the rampart and shouted, "Who are you and what do you want?"

"We have come from President Bolívar in Bogotá. We have a letter of authorisation," Sebastian called back.

A hatch in the gate opened and the nervous-looking face of a soldier peeked out. "Give him the letter," the man called down.

Sebastian shrugged at Beth, who smiled encouragingly. "You can't blame them, they are not the Rifles."

Sebastian dismounted, walked to the gate and handed the letter through. The soldier slammed the hatch in his face, barely giving him time to get his hand out. "Charming," he muttered.

Several minutes went by, during which voices were heard inside, one more dominant than the others. Then the gate creaked open and an officer stood in the open doorway, holding the letter. An honour guard stood at attention at either side.

"Welcome to my fort, señores. Please come in."

His face when he realised that five of the eight people were women was an absolute picture. To make it even worse, Beth was a good six inches taller than he was. He looked up at her and blinked.

"My name is Chaton, I am the leader of this group of fighters." She pointed at Sebastian, who was grinning as he led his horse to a hitching rail. "He is my husband, Lancelot." Her arm swept over the others. "These are the Wolves." She turned back to him and gently extracted the letter from his fist. Then she folded her arms and waited.

The man's mouth opened and closed a few times before he found his voice. "I am sorry, I thought *he* was the commander."

"A common mistake. Now tell me, who are you? And how did José Prudencio Padillo gain control of Cartagena?"

The man suddenly rediscovered his manners. "Please … let me provide you with refreshment and I will tell you everything."

While Sebastian and Beth were taken inside, the Wolves checked out the fort. It consisted of a barracks, an armoury, an underground magazine and the boundary walls. The guns mounted on those walls were nine-pound field pieces, and old. Harry examined one. "I wouldn't want to fire that more than a couple of times."

Mike agreed: the barrel, when tapped, had an odd ring to it which might suggest it was honeycombed.

"There are only three walls with guns and there's hardly any wall at all at the barracks end," Paola said.

"That is because it was designed to protect the harbour against pirates and smugglers, not the town," Mike replied.

The soldiers were a mix of infantry and gunners. Without exception they ogled at the girls until at last Delfina grew tired of it. She walked up to a group and thoroughly berated them in machine-gun Spanish with a bit of Portuguese mixed in for good measure. One of the men must have said something about her wearing a gun, because she took an empty wine bottle that was laying in the dirt and marched across the courtyard to place it on a stone pillar. Then she returned to where he stood and invited him to shoot it. He raised his musket and aimed carefully. He missed by inches. Paola shook her head, turned on her heel, drew her pistol and fired all in one movement. The bottle shattered.

There was a stunned silence.

In the commandant's office, Sebastian and Beth were served a rough local wine as he told them how Cartagena had fallen.

"It was quite simple. Padillo approached the castle of San Felipe de Barajas with about fifty men at his back and demanded entrance. The commandant, who is known to be stupid and a sympathiser of Santander, opened the gates and let them in. He turned the castle over to the rebels, and the next morning Padillo ordered all loyalist troops out of Cartagena. With the commandant on his side, he had no resistance."

"Where are the loyalist troops now?" Sebastian asked.

"Some went home, if they came from nearby; the ones that come from far away are still here, scattered amongst the houses on the island and other towns."

There was a musket shot from outside, followed closely by the sound of a pistol. The commandant looked alarmed, but Beth just smiled. "Do not worry, that's just my girls showing your soldiers they can shoot. Now, how long would it take to gather the loyalists together?"

"A few days at the most. Why?"

Sebastian grinned. "My lady is thinking about taking the town back."

Beth leaned forward and kissed him. "You know me too well."

Beth found that, as well as the castle, the rebels held the city walls. The gates were guarded and ready to be slammed shut in the face of any type of counter-attack and the simple fact was, a few men on the walls could hold off an army. She tasked Paola, Delfina and Alie with scouting the city.

The girls changed into the type of clothes that local women wore, concealed their weapons and set out, crossing the north-east bridge to allow them to approach the city from the landward side. They carried baskets of fruit on their heads and walked with the typical hip swing that the local girls employed. The guards at the gates flirted with them.

"Well, look who we have here!" a guard said, openly admiring them.

"Hello, boys," Delfina said, and sauntered up to them.

The chatty guard patted her on the backside. "If you want some fun, ask for Pedro at the Cantina de Sementales."

Another of the guards stood close to Paola. "I will be there as well. My name is Vencedor."

"Such a strong name!" Paola said. "A good-looking guy like you should have the ladies running after him." The guard grew an inch taller at the praise.

Alie stood back, her hand on her concealed pistol butt in case of trouble. There was none: the guards flirted until a farmer arrived with a horse and cart and they had to get back to work.

"Idiots," Delfina muttered as they walked away.

Like the island, the city was quiet, and they moved through relatively empty streets to one of the marketplaces, where they surprised a fruit vendor by depositing their baskets on his stall. Alie blew him a kiss as they walked off. Militiamen patrolled but seemed pretty relaxed.

The steps up to the walls at the west end had sentries posted and they saw that only the walls on the landward side were manned fully, with the others being patrolled by a handful of men. They obviously feared an attack from there and not from the sea. A head count revealed that there were around a hundred troops in the city.

"What we need is a prisoner," Alie said as they walked through a market towards the end of the day.

The others agreed and Paola asked, "How do we get him out of the city?"

Alie was watching a cantina. "I think I have an idea."

The cantina was one of the type with stables for horses at the back, and she led the girls into the small courtyard. There were several carts, used by market-stall keepers to bring their wares in. Most were horse- or burro-drawn but there were two handcarts as well.

Alie checked all the carts over and chose one with a tarpaulin covering the empty bed. Then they went into the cantina, where the stall holders were having an end-of-day drink along with several militiamen. As this was her idea, Alie got the job of flirting with a militiaman. She soon had him in the palm of her hand and led him out of the back door, to the stables.

There was a solitary, well-shielded lantern in the stables that just made the shadows deeper. No one heard the thud and grunt as a blackjack was applied just behind the militiaman's ear.

The market traders started to leave and when one harnessed his burro to the cart with the tarp, he suddenly found he had company. Three pretty girls were asking if he would escort them out of the city as they were afraid to travel alone in the coming dusk.

"This place isn't safe for good girls like us," Delfina said while looking as innocent and vulnerable as she could.

"I've got daughters, and I know what you mean," he said.

The three climbed in the back and he set off, the burro trotting along happily despite the load. The guards on the gate knew the man and, as he was the last to leave, shut the gates behind them.

* * *

Back at the fort on the island, the hapless militiaman was unloaded from the surprised trader's cart. The latter complained bitterly at how his living could have been ruined and how his good nature had been taken advantage of. He shut up when Beth gave him a silver peso and told him to go home.

"How many men do you have in the city?" Sebastian asked the militiaman as he sat in a chair placed in the middle of an otherwise empty room. Harry stood off to one side, just within his field of view, toying with a vicious-looking short whip.

"A hundred and ten, s-señor," he stammered.

"Where do they come from?" Sebastian said, and walked out of his field of view.

"Some, like me, are from Zulia, but there are many from Magdalena and Venezuela."

"How many men at the castle?"

"Fifty, señor."

Other questions followed, about weapons and the training of the men. When he had finished, Sebastian sat down with Beth and the commander.

"Basically, the militia are all infantry and poorly trained. They can march in line and shoot maybe two shots a minute. As the girls reported, they are spread out on the walls facing the land with a few patrols in the city."

Beth looked thoughtful. "Who is watching the seaward side?"

Sebastian knew what she was thinking. "A few sentries."

"Twenty-five men, led by someone who knew what they were doing, could roll up the force manning the wall."

"How would you get them there?" the commandant asked, catching on to what she was planning.

Beth looked at Sebastian and grinned. "I have two ships."

"There are no English ships in the bay. The rebels told them to leave."

Beth smiled like the cat that had got the canary. "They aren't in the bay; they are behind Tierra Bomba island."

That surprised Sebastian, as he had thought they were offshore somewhere.

"I ordered Richard to move there if anything were to happen here," Beth continued, somewhat smugly. "We can put fifty men on the *Cub* and land them on the beach below the walls, take the top of the wall and sweep it clean of militia."

"The gates are closed and barred," the commander said.

"I don't think Beth is thinking of entering through the gate," Sebastian said, eyeing her suspiciously.

"Not at first. The *Cub*'s marines will scale the wall and eliminate the sentries. They have been trained to do that. Then they will open the gate so your soldiers can enter the town. Half will go with Sebastian and the marines to clear the wall, the other half under your command will go directly to the barracks and take care of the rest."

Sebastian made a gesture of approval but then looked at her suspiciously. "While we are doing all that, what will you be doing?"

"Oh, not much. Just re-taking the castle."

Sebastian swore as a soldier dropped his musket as he climbed over the side of the *Cub* and into the long boat. It landed butt first in the bottom and clattered loudly. Everybody froze, waiting for a challenge from the walls, but nothing was heard so they continued. It would take two trips with the boats they had towed behind them from Bomba island to get the men ashore. The *Cub's* five marines were already in the ship's gig and on their way.

Corporal Fines and his four men wore dark clothes and blackened their faces and hands. They could all see enough by the light of the quarter-moon to do their work. The gig landed them on a stretch of shingle in front of one of the lower parts of the wall. They watched the wall carefully for the appropriate moment, when the sentry was turned away, to advance to the base. A padded grapnel on a strong line, thrown by a well-practised hand, flew up and over to catch on the other side.

Fines was first up, his rifle slung across his back and a dagger between his teeth. He gained the parapet and, crouching, waited for his men. Hand signals sent two one way and two the other. He joined the two that headed towards the gate. They moved silently on soft-soled boots. Fines held up a clenched fist and the three of them stopped. Ahead, silhouetted against the starry sky, was a sentry leaning on the wall, apparently looking out to sea at the *Cub*.

Fines moved quietly forward; he was relaxed because as far as he was concerned, there was only one possible outcome. Confidence in these situations was everything. He came up behind the sentry and his dagger flashed forward, penetrating between the fourth and fifth ribs on his left side, piercing his heart. The sentry died without a sound.

The other two men crossed the bridge above the gate to eliminate any other sentries. Fines went down the stairs in the bastion to the gate and heaved the heavy bar out of its hooks. One of his men arrived to help him lower it gently to the ground.

Sebastian stepped ashore and hoped that the sentries had been eliminated as the soldiers made a terrible noise as they debarked. He had made them blow out the priming on their guns to avoid accidental discharges giving the game away, and they now chatted as they re-primed those guns.

"Silence!" he hissed.

He had his twenty-five, and the commandant was coming ashore with his twenty-five.

"Adelante!" he said in a hoarse whisper, and set off towards the gates.

He had just reached them when they opened, and Corporal Fines saluted as he said, "Good job we did for the sentries. Could hear you coming a mile away."

Sebastian grunted something unintelligible and led his men through the gate and up the steps behind the corporal.

The marines formed up in front, bayonets fixed. The parapet was wide enough between the bastions for two men to walk abreast and widened at the bastions to carry guns. They met no one except the dead until they had rounded the south-western end of the wall, where they caught up with two marines who had gone ahead. A whispered report told Sebastian that the next bastion was manned, and the disposition of the gunners. He and the marines advanced with the soldiers behind them and, as the parapet opened out, they spread out into a skirmish line.

Silently, they moved in on the sentries and killed them. The following soldiers swept the bastion from top to bottom to eliminate any sleeping men.

That was when a gun went off.

"Well, there goes our surprise. Form them up!" Sebastian said.

The corporal gathered the men into a column and Sebastian shouted, "Charge!"

From then on it was a matter of move and shoot. He sent the men forward in two waves. The first wave into a bastion would clear it, while the second went through to prevent any reinforcements coming from the next one. Once a bastion was cleared, the cover wave became the lead wave and so on.

By dawn, the wall was in their hands.

Beth, the Wolves and ten marines from the *Fox* went on foot to the castle and the base of its huge sloping walls. At the stroke of two in the morning, the *Fox* started firing its cannon at the castle from the other side of Manga island. Her main guns slammed balls into the walls, making a tremendous noise and attracting the attention of the occupiers.

That was Beth's cue; she and Harry twirled grapnels and threw them to the top of the first wall. Beth's stuck but Harry had to re-throw before his caught. They shinnied up, followed by the rest of their party. A second pair of grapnels was thrown over the second slope of the wall, which was almost vertical, and they shinnied up to the top onto the gun platform.

Beth saw a silhouette of a man and stabbed him in the back through the kidneys before stabbing him in the neck and wrenching the blade out through his throat. A fountain of blood shot forward. She took a breath — her knife was razor sharp, but it still required considerable effort.

The team assembled and moved along the gun platform. Men were loading and firing the big guns. Stealth was not needed now, and speed was called for. She charged forward, confident that her team would be right there with her.

Pistols were fired at point-blank range. Beth had a mantra for this type of work: *two through the body and one through the head.* That got her four bodies per pair of guns, which was more than enough as there were ten men to a gun. The second gun was harder as the gunners were now aware of being attacked, but the result was the same even though they had to get in closer and grapple with some. The girls used their daggers and pistols ruthlessly.

Before the third gun, Beth grabbed a lantern and threw it down into the central bailey of the castle. It smashed and sprayed fire around, illuminating the area. Men were coming out of what she assumed was the barracks.

"Grenades!"

The last four marines carried pouches of grenades and started raining them down on the men in the bastion. They retreated rapidly.

Beth almost forgot to pay attention to her own job as she watched the chaos below. Alie barged past her and shot a man that was creeping up on her.

"Thanks," Beth shouted.

"*Es nada,*" Alie shouted back as she stabbed a man holding a ramrod in the belly.

They cleared the three guns that were manned. Now to clear the rest out. Beth took a moment for everyone to reload. It also gave them time to catch their breath. She found the stairs down to the bailey and descended them, flanked by Mike and Harry with the sisters behind them. They were halfway down when a squad of militia met them coming up.

Beth and the boys crouched and fired to allow the girls to fire over their heads. It was a move straight from their playbook and had been rehearsed many times. A volley of twelve pistol balls slammed into the squad, followed in seconds by a second volley. What was left was kicked out of the way.

Beth was keeping count. They had killed or disabled forty men so far, so there should only be another ten. She was right, and they were holed up with their commander, Padillo, in his quarters.

Beth moved up to hailing distance with Mike beside her. At her instruction, Mike shouted out, "You are the last. We have control of the town and the castle. Give up now and you will live. Resist further and I will take no prisoners and mount Padillo's head on a spear."

There was a pause, and then a soldier came out carrying what looked like a white napkin. He stood, looking very nervous, and said, "If we have your word of honour that we will be treated fairly, we will surrender."

"You have my word of honour," Mike called back.

The rest of the soldiers came out and dropped their guns in a pile. Last out was Padillo, who looked completely surprised at the sight of a red-haired woman dressed in leather pointing a gun at him. As she was obviously in command, he offered his sword to her.

"Do I have your parole?" she asked.

"You do," he replied.

"Then you can keep your sword."

The sun came up and the gates of the city were thrown open. The people came out tentatively, having listened to the fighting during the night. The city was back in the hands of the government and the militiamen were either dead or imprisoned. It was as good an excuse as any for a fiesta as they had feared a bombardment.

The commandant and Padillo were under arrest at the castle. Sebastian questioned Padillo, in quite a civilised way, and entertained him in what had been the commandant's sitting room. Padillo knew he wasn't Colombian but did not know he was linked to the British embassy. Sebastian asked, "I am puzzled. You and Santander were allies with Bolívar during the fight for independence from the Spanish. Why do you now rebel against him?"

Padillo smiled sadly. "We are not rebelling against him; he is a great man. We are opposing his idea of Gran Colombia being a centralist state with a centralised government. The territory is too big and communications too slow for that to be effective. We prefer a federal government where each state has its own powers along with powers shared by the central government."

Sebastian understood. "So, this is primarily over a difference in political philosophy?"

"It is. We needed to make a gesture to get his attention. You know what happened at the Convention of Ocaña?"

Sebastian shook his head.

Padillo continued, "Bolívar proposed a compromise based on a new constitution he created for Bolivia. It was unpopular with both the federalists and the centralists and the pro-centralist delegates walked out rather than sign even a slightly federalist constitution."

Sebastian thought for a moment. "Where is the federalist cause most prominent?"

"Venezuela; the liberals supported Spanish liberalism in the years before independence and now align themselves with the conservatives under José Antonio Páez. You know our ideas do not differ much from those of your country's government. You have local government in the shires and a central government over that. What Bolívar wants is more akin to Napoleon's arrangements."

Sebastian laughed. "That is true for England but the United Kingdom is centrally governed. Wales, Scotland and Ireland do not have autonomous rule. The land area is much smaller, so it works, after a fashion. I do see your point about the similarities with Napoleon, but Bolívar does not have his expansionist ambitions."

Two weeks later, Bolívar arrived at the head of his army. Sebastian and Beth learned that the Venezuelan revolt had been quashed before he got to it and he found that he had marched two hundred and fifty miles to Cartagena for nothing as well.

Padillo was tried, imprisoned and then exiled.

Assassination

August 1828

Beth was concerned. They had returned to Bogotá, where Bolívar awarded them medals to recognise their actions in Cartagena. It was now approaching the end of August 1828 and Bolívar was depressed, ill and increasingly frustrated by the political manoeuvrings that both his allies and opponents seemed to relish. He was also becoming paranoid and had lost trust in his own people.

He visited the embassy, where Cockburn sat with him in one of the reception rooms.

"Congratulations on being made President-Liberator of Colombia," Cockburn said.

Bolívar sighed and looked unhappy. "I have sent Santander to Washington as a diplomat; he is no longer vice president. It is better I do that than exile him."

"Do you think his absence will weaken the opposition?"

"Frankly, no. He has too many allies."

"Is there anything we can do to help?"

Bolívar smiled for the first time that day. "I want to engage Sebastian and Bethany as my bodyguards."

Cockburn was surprised, but managed to keep a neutral expression on his face. "Aah, Sebastian is a registered diplomat—"

Bolívar interrupted him. "Then de-register him. I know that he and his wife are agents, her father was one when he was the so-called governor of Aruba. She may or may not be Sebastian's real wife, but I want them and that pack of theirs as my bodyguards."

Cockburn blew out his cheeks. This was definitely not in the playbook for ambassadors, and it would take far too long to check with London. The decision was down to him.

"If I do this, they will have to be disavowed."

Bolívar's temper flared. "I don't care if they become mercenaries, or if I have to throw the rest of the delegation out of the country!"

Cockburn held up his hands to mollify the unstable leader. "I will find a way to make it work for both of us."

Cockburn called Sebastian in to see him.

"Our host is becoming more unstable by the day," he said by way of introduction.

Sebastian waited to hear more; Cockburn was agitated, and he wanted to know why before saying anything.

"He is obviously suffering from depression, and I have my doubts over his general health. You know he has signed a decree to dissolve the congress and to impose military law?" He looked at Sebastian for a reaction.

Sebastian replied, "The long marches to Venezuela and Cartagena affected his health. The constant infighting gets him down, and he thinks the solution is to take power away from the agitators and infighters."

Cockburn nodded in agreement. "And he has lost trust in almost everyone, except you and Beth. I think he sees you as neutrals."

Sebastian felt there was more to come. Cockburn sighed and leaned towards him, hands on his desk.

"He wants you two and the Wolves as bodyguards."

"Really?"

"Yes. I will have to release you."

Sebastian thought quickly. "That's not enough, we can't have any suspicion fall on the British government in case he is overthrown and the federalists gain control. You need a good excuse to throw us out and for us to run to Bolívar."

Cockburn sighed. "Why do spies always have to complicate things?"

Sebastian smiled reassuringly. "Let me talk to Beth and we will come up with something."

Cockburn half smiled. "Good, I will send a note to the Washington embassy and ask them to be nice to Santander in the meantime."

Beth was fencing with Mike when Sebastian returned. Actually, describing their combat as fencing was like calling a brawl a pillow fight. The two had swords, which was where any similarity to fencing ended. They fought to win as if their lives depended on it. The sword strokes were fast and vicious, kicks and punches landed. Sebastian waited; interrupting this could be dangerous for the participants.

Finally, they both froze, Beth's sword at Mike's throat. They were both sweating from the exertion. Sebastian clapped. Beth looked at him and grinned, Mike grunted and stepped away.

Sebastian said, "She got you with that damn pirouette, Mike. She does that to me all the time and I never see it coming."

"She hides it well, but I think I can get her next time."

"In your dreams!" Beth laughed.

"We need to talk," Sebastian told her.

"After I have bathed. I'm all sweaty," she said, and kissed him on the nose.

A bath was waiting for her. The servants, warned by the cessation of hostilities downstairs, were filling it with hot water. She stripped off her leathers and stepped in with a sigh.

Sebastian sat on a stool and watched. She had a slim, athletic body that was toned and muscular like that of a dancer. There were scars which marred her otherwise perfect skin but told a little of her history. Her breasts were high and firm, and she had the perfect backside in his opinion, although it might be considered boyish by some. Her legs were long and shapely. He considered himself a lucky man.

Beth was aware that Sebastian was examining her and loved it; her stomach did a little flutter as she sank into the water, her long auburn hair tied up in a loose bun. Maybe she could persuade him …

"I just came from Cockburn, who has had a visit from Bolívar," Sebastian began.

There goes that idea, she thought, and sighed. Then she asked, "Oh, what was that about?"

"Simón wants us as his bodyguards."

She looked over her shoulder at him quizzically. "By 'us' you mean you, me and the Wolves?"

"Exactly."

"But you are a registered diplomat."

"And there lies the problem."

Beth's brow furrowed as she thought it through. "As you are telling me, I assume that Cockburn wants us to do it?"

"He does, and he also realises that we need to be disconnected from the embassy to do it."

Beth made a face. "Yes, and if they release us with no reason, it looks highly suspicious."

"Any ideas?"

Beth thought, then giggled. "You could seduce his wife, but then I would have to kill you."

Sebastian raised his eyebrows. "Ha-ha, not helpful."

Beth cocked her head to the side, a sure sign she had thought of something. "But a duel would do it."

Sebastian shook his head. "We can't hurt anyone."

"We don't need to. We set it up and, just in the nick of time, Cockburn intervenes. You get fired and we go over to Bolívar."

Sebastian stood, bent over her and tipped her chin up with a finger.

"I married a very smart woman," he said, and kissed her.

The duel was between Sebastian and the commercial envoy, William Dickinson. It was scheduled for dawn in the Bolívar Park. William was a renowned fencer, so naturally Sebastian chose pistols. The men and their seconds assembled — along with a sizeable audience as duels were a rare spectacle, and word had got around the embassies and consulates. The master of ceremonies got the proceedings underway. The combatants stood back to back and moved off ten paces before turning.

Right at that point, Cockburn arrived on horseback. "You will cease this nonsense now!" he bellowed, reining in his horse dramatically.

Someone booed.

"I will not have my people fighting duels! Who is the challenger?"

Sebastian looked disappointed. "It was me; he offended me."

Cockburn had dismounted and walked up to face Sebastian. "You know the law. Duelling is forbidden on British soil."

Sebastian replied a little glibly, "That is why we are in the park."

Cockburn exploded in rage. "Don't be insolent with me. You are sacked!"

"Sacked?" Sebastian said, apparently in disbelief.

"Yes, sacked! Be out of your house by tomorrow."

The news travelled around the embassies like wildfire that an envoy at the British embassy had been discharged for duelling and had been kicked out of their compound. When it reached the ears of Bolívar he smiled, and sent a messenger to invite the couple and their retinue to stay with him.

"Well, that worked out very well," Beth said as they took up their new rooms in the Palacio de San Carlos.

They had rooms near to Bolívar's, with the team in close attendance. Inquisitive as ever, Beth went about finding out why Bolívar felt threatened. She questioned his close advisors and confidants, of whom there were only a few.

"It appears that some of his ministers are getting cosy with the French. Their ambassador is almost a permanent fixture in the centralist camp. The Neogranadian liberals have grown more militant since he was declared dictator and have formed secret societies called Sociedad Socrata Parlamental, or SSPs."

Sebastian frowned and pursed his lips. "We need to get into one of those ... or find someone we can turn."

Beth shook her head. "Getting in will be impossible, they only admit known people. But we might be able to find someone we can blackmail."

Sebastian grinned at her. "You are the expert at that. Why don't you go and find someone?"

Beth got the girls together — including Netta, who could lip-read Spanish — and instructed them to circulate amongst the servants at the palace and government building, to find out if there were any rumours or gossip about any of the liberal ministers. It took a couple of weeks, but then Netta came up with a name. Soon after, Beth sat with Sebastian and the boys.

"Our target is José Luis Fernandez; he is rumoured to be having an affair with a young man from the music school."

"I thought sodomy was illegal here," Sebastian said.

"It is, according to both the state and the church; and homosexuality is socially despised," Beth said.

"How good is the gossip?" Mike asked, ever practical.

"Fernandez is known to host parties for the artistic and musical members of Bogotán society including boys from the school. He is single, good-looking but not a lady's man."

"It's worth checking out to see if he's a shirt-lifter," Harry said.

"We know where he lives. We will pay him a visit," Beth said. "Harry, be ready for an outing at midnight."

On the stroke of midnight, Beth left her rooms through a window. As she climbed out Sebastian whispered, "Good luck. I love you."

"I love you too," she replied, and faded into the dark.

Harry was waiting for her. Like her, he was dressed in black and carried only a small leather pack containing his tools. The house was on Avenida Carrera, a fair way from the palace, and they slipped through the streets avoiding contact with watchmen and anybody else who was out at that time of night.

When they found Fernandez's home, they saw it was a typical Colombian three-storey house with barred windows on the ground floor and balconies on the windows of the first and second floors. Harry used the iron frames of the bars of the ground floor to climb up and get hold of the balcony above. He pulled himself up, and once on the balcony dropped a rope for Beth to climb up. Once she was up, he wound the rope around his waist out of the way. While he did that Beth examined the window, slipping the quill of a feather between the window and the frame and sliding it around to check for traps. It was unlikely that there were any, but it was good form to check.

Satisfied, she left Harry to take a slim jim, slip it under the catch and gently wiggle it upwards. The catch gave way and the window opened.

They slipped inside and closed the curtains behind them. Harry lit his small, shuttered oil lamp that had a concave silvered mirror inside to shine the light forward in a beam. The room was a bedroom that had not been used for some time, so they ignored it and opened the door to a landing. This had four doors including the one to the room they were in, and Beth crept carefully down the landing, testing each step before placing her weight on her foot. She wore calfskin shoes with chamois soles, which allowed her to feel for any movement in the floorboards. She listened at each door, and gestured to Harry when she heard gentle snoring.

The door opened silently after an application of light oil to the hinges as a precaution. They entered and Harry shone the beam of his lamp on the bed.

"Jackpot!" Beth whispered.

There in the bed was José Luis and beside him a pretty young man of about twenty years old, with a mass of curly brown hair. Beth signed to Harry, who took a cloth and a sealed bottle from his bag and carefully dripped some fluid onto the cloth before resealing the bottle. He kept it far from his own face and gently placed it over the man's nose and mouth. After around thirty seconds he took it away and dropped the cloth on the floor well away from the bed.

Beth gently uncovered the man, who was naked, and examined him, putting her anatomy studies to good use. She snarled when she saw evidence of sodomy. It was enough, and she took out a stiletto before moving around to the other side of the bed.

"Wake up!" She pricked José Luis's throat.

"What? What are you … ?" He stopped when the point of the knife dug into his Adam's apple.

"I should cut your throat," Beth hissed, "but I will give you a chance to save yourself."

"What do you want?" He tried to avoid swallowing.

"Information, and you are going to give it to me, or your crimes will be exposed."

To give him his due he knew the game was up and didn't deny anything. "What information?"

"Tell me everything about the activities of the SSPs, and tell me what they talk about."

The information, when it came, was mostly mundane and uninteresting, but then in early September, they got a report that a man called Luis Vargas Tejeda, a politician and poet, had made an address in which he stated — in the form of a poem — that Bolívar must be killed for peace to reign.

Si de Bolívar la letra con que empiezay aquélla con la que
acaba le quitamos, «oliva» de la paz símbolo hallamos. Esto
quiere decir que la cabezaal tirano y los pies cortar debemossi es
que una paz durable apetecemos.

The last sentence translated as:

This means that we must cut off the head and feet of the tyrant
if we want a lasting peace.

"They are going to try and assassinate him," Beth said as she handed the note to Sebastian. "We had better try and find out by whom and when."

They instructed José Luis to listen out for conspirators, and subtly increased security at the palace. They did not tell Bolívar as he tended to be rather direct in his solutions, and the wholesale arrest of the liberals wouldn't solve anything and could even tip the country into civil war.

The twentieth of September came around and all they had heard were rumours that *something* was about to happen. No details were given, nor any hint of a timescale. The Wolves were on watch twenty-four hours a day. Working in pairs, they escorted Bolívar everywhere. During the day, either Sebastian or Beth was with him, albeit in the background with a pair of Wolves in attendance. At night a pair of Wolves, plus either Sebastian or Beth, would prowl the corridor outside his bedroom, and they persuaded him to change the room he slept in every week.

Five days passed and nothing happened, then at midnight on 25 September, a commotion was heard. The noises came from the main entrance to the palace.

"That sounds like fighting," Paola said to Alie.

"I'll go and check it out," Alie said and slipped away.

Beth appeared from another part of the palace. "Did you hear that?"

"Yes. Alie is checking on what's happening."

The noise continued and Beth had Paola rouse the rest of the team. When Alie returned, she reported back. "About forty soldiers and civilians have broken into the palace and killed the guards. They are searching for Bolívar."

Sebastian joined them with the rest of the team. "We can blockade the ends of this corridor. With our weapons we should be able to hold them off until the army arrives," he said.

The door to Bolívar's room opened and Manuela came out. "What is going on?" she demanded.

Sebastian left the Wolves, who were busy stacking furniture across the corridor at either end, and quietly informed Bolívar's partner what was happening. "A large group of men have invaded the palace; we believe they are looking for Simón. We will try and stop them here, but you must get him away."

Manuela slipped back into the room and shook Bolívar awake as the first shot rang out in the corridor. "What is happening?" he asked.

"Men have invaded the palace, meaning to kill you. You must dress and get away, quickly."

Bolívar threw on some clothes and grabbed his sword and pistol — a single-shot flintlock — clearly intending to fight. Manuela pleaded with him, "My love, you cannot fight. Leave that to Sebastian and Bethany. You must escape."

The only escape route was through a window, which was

undignified, but he managed. Before he left, Bolívar reached up to Manuela and kissed her hand before disappearing into the dark. He ran through the night to a low bridge that crossed a dry riverbed, and hid under it.

Back at the palace, Beth shot a soldier who tried to charge the barricade she was behind. That should have dissuaded the rest but a pair of them, probably thinking she would have to reload, followed him. They went down to a hail of fire from Beth and the three Wolves that were with her. She could hear the invaders talking from around the corner where they hid.

"Tell Sebastian to be ready; some of them are going to try and get around to the other end."

As his orders were to conceal their real strength — and that would not be helped by shouting warnings — Harry slipped down to the other end of the corridor where Sebastian, Mike, Netta and Delfina waited.

"Get ready, they are coming around this way."

Shots were fired by the attackers, the flashes briefly illuminating the corridor and filling it with smoke. Under the cover of that smoke, they charged both ends at once.

Beth snapped off shots at faces that appeared in front of her and a bullet fizzed past, cutting a slit in the sleeve of her blouse and stinging her arm. Paola fired her pistols in the direction the shot had come from.

It was chaos; the corridor was full of gun smoke and the fight came down to hand-to-hand fighting. Knives replaced pistols as those armaments emptied. It was cramped and inelegant, brutal and vicious.

Suddenly, there was shouting from beyond the attackers. The army had finally arrived and immediately there was quiet.

"Bethany, are you hurt?" Colonel Whittle, the English officer in charge of the relieving battalion, asked her while touching her arm.

Beth looked down and saw the blood on her sleeve where the bullet had cut it. "It's just a nick, I'll be fine. You need to find Bolívar, he escaped."

Bolívar was found and safely returned to the palace. He was, to say the least, angry. He commanded Generals Rafael Urdaneta and José Maria Códova to round up the conspirators in the capital and imprison them.

What followed could only be described as a purge. Anyone who was even remotely suspected was arrested and put on trial including Santander, who was tried in his absence, and Admiral Padilla, who was nowhere near Bogotá at the time. The central conspirators — Luis Vargas Tejeda, Florentino González, Captain Emigdio Briceño Guzmán and Pedro Carujo — were all summarily tried by a reconvened council of ministers and found guilty. They were sentenced to death, commuted to exile, except for Carujo, who for some reason was pardoned.

Santander was tried *in absentia* and found guilty without any evidence being presented. He was demoted, dishonourably expelled and sentenced to death by being shot in the back. After Sebastian intervened — by having a quiet word with Bolívar about the international consequences of that — Bolívar commuted the sentence to exile.

On 29 September, annoyed by the acquittal of eight people by the court, Bolívar dissolved it and appointed Rafael Urdaneta as the sole judge. Without impartiality or neutrality, he sentenced anybody who had been arrested to death whether they were young or old, whether they participated in the event or not, and whether there was any evidence to support the charge or not.

Sebastian and Beth did their best to moderate his behaviour, and it was with a sense of relief that he left Bogotá and all its complexities behind in December, taking Beth, Sebastian and her team with him to go to war with the Republic of Peru over their intervention in Bolivia and invasion of Ecuador.

Panama

Gran Colombia had always claimed the provinces of Jaén and Maynas. The borders to these provinces were quite literally unknown, as they were sparsely populated, except by Indians, and largely unexplored. According to the *uti possidetis juris* established by Bolívar, the viceroyalty of Lima should have been part of Peru and the viceroyalty of Granada should have been Colombian, given the location of borders in 1809 at the beginning of their independence from Spain. However, due to uncertainties around the precise nature of those borders and their locations, claims could be and were being made on the provinces in the zone of uncertainty by both Peru and Colombia.

Bolivia, which had been named after Bolívar, had briefly had him as president, but in 1826 he resigned and Antonio José de Sucre took over. Two years later, on 3 July 1828, Peru launched a campaign against Bolivia to remove it from Gran Colombia and force the Colombian army to leave. To make matters worse, the Peruvian navy had beaten the Gran Colombian navy in August and now blockaded the strategic port of Guayaquil in Ecuador.

93

Bolívar prepared his army to march to the aid of the provinces and to expel the Peruvians from what he considered his territory. However, he had other things in mind for Sebastian and Beth.

"You have ships, yes?" he asked Beth while he drank a morning coffee in company with her and Manuela.

"We do — a schooner and a cutter."

"I wish for you to go to Peru and attack their navy and shipping. I will grant you a letter of marque."

Beth looked at him carefully in case this was a jest. It appeared not to be, so she asked, "Um, how are we to get them across to the Pacific? It will take months to sail around Cape Horn and back up."

Bolívar looked smug. "Your ships do not draw more than ten feet of water?"

"Less, if they are unburdened; we can float them in less than eight feet."

"My engineers have been working on the Rio Chagres and you can now sail it to Cruces, where my engineers will transport your ships twenty miles overland to the estuary of the Rio Grande. From there you can sail down to Panama City and the Pacific."

"You have obviously thought this through."

"Yes, and discussed it with my engineers, one of whom will accompany you to Panama."

Beth thought for a while. "Why not send us and our crews and give us ships on the other side?"

"I could, but then you would lose the advantage of your superior guns. No, I prefer to get the ships there as well."

Beth looked at Manuela, who shrugged with a look that said, *You cannot argue with him when he's like this.*

* * *

94

Beth frankly thought the whole idea to be somewhat ridiculous, but Bolívar would have his way, and she was, to be honest, intrigued as to whether they could pull it off. Consequently, they returned to Cartagena with Rodrigo José Ahogado, the engineer who had convinced Bolívar it could be done, and boarded the *Fox* for Chagres in Panama.

Rodrigo pestered Richard with questions about the *Fox* and *Cub* as soon as they were at sea. He went below with the carpenter and measured all the frames from bow to stern, then created exquisite scale models of both ships. Then he made similar scaled models of wheeled contraptions that the hulls would be floated onto, once they had been de-masted and unloaded. These would be towed overland by huge teams of horses to Panama City and the estuary of the Rio Grande.

Beth found Rodrigo likeable, if a little odd. He was a mathematician and engineer and very focused on whatever problem faced him. He did not think in terms of what-ifs, only absolutes, which made Beth think that this adventure would not go as planned. He was often distracted, as his mind seemingly wandered off into whatever problem he was trying to solve, and prone to outbursts of joy when he found the answer. Rodrigo wore the uniform of a soldier, but it was decorated with the tools of his trade. Pencils and sheafs of paper held together with string protruded from pockets, a pouch on his belt held drawing instruments instead of cartridges and across his back he carried an extending measure. This stick, a yard long when folded, extended out to five yards long when unfolded.

One evening, Beth and Sebastian had Rodrigo dine with them.

"How are your plans coming on?" she asked.

Sebastian kicked her under the table, but it was too late.

"Well, the problem was calculating the exact displacement of the *Cub* without masts and guns. You see the ..."

Beth tuned out. He would carry on explaining even if they got up and left.

You just had to ask, Sebastian said to himself, and rolled his eyes.

Four days later they reached Chagres, where Rodrigo had them dock. A small flotilla of flat-bottomed barges was waiting for them.

"What are they for?" Richard Brazier asked, although he had a sneaking suspicion.

"They will carry your guns and anything else we can unload to reduce your draft."

"All our guns?"

"Oh yes, they all need to be offloaded. See — the sheerlegs are being raised as we speak."

He was right. A team of soldiers were erecting sheerlegs on the dock which were large enough to lift their biggest guns.

Richard went to Beth and said, "He is taking all our guns."

Beth, who was watching the engineers working, replied, "I know, he told us last night at dinner; I almost missed it. He was droning on about some mathematical problem when he suddenly changed the subject."

"That will leave us defenceless!"

A frown furrow appeared between her eyes. "Not entirely, we will keep the swivels."

Richard shook his head and went off to make sure no one dropped a gun barrel through his hull.

As it happened, the unloading of the guns went without a hitch. The engineers on shore were professional and the crew handled everything on the ship. By the time the third gun had been swung ashore and replaced on its carriage, they were working as a well-oiled machine, separating the barrels from the carriages and sending them over separately to be reunited on the dock.

Rodrigo constantly monitored the amount of water the *Fox* was drawing and when it reached the point he wanted, he called a halt to the unloading. The *Fox* was sitting high in the water, at least a foot above where she normally sat. Her copper was showing.

"That's enough, we can pass over everything in the river now."

The *Fox* was warped away from the dock and flat-bottomed barges were brought in and loaded. They were covered in tarpaulins to keep everything dry and could be either powered by a single gaff-rigged sail or rowed by the six-man crew. When that was done, the *Cub* was brought in. She drew less water than the *Fox* so had to have less removed. Two days later they were ready to sail up the river.

Rodrigo's calculations really did not cover this part of the journey. He knew nothing about sailing, apart from the basic physics of how sails worked. The first phase was easy, as they entered the Chagres estuary and passed through into Gatun Lake. The sailing was actually quite pleasant — with a gentle northerly wind of around ten knots — although the *Fox* tended to heel a bit more than usual.

In an hour they had reached Barro Colorado island and skirted its northern shore to enter the river proper. Past the island they swung south then east — which was fine, but then the river turned north directly into the wind. It was five hundred yards wide and flowed sluggishly, which meant they had to short tack to make progress; they slowed to a veritable crawl, then stopped completely when the river narrowed.

"How far do we have to go before we get to the place where you will take them out of the water?" Richard asked Rodrigo.

"Not far: it's only about five miles from here. Less than an hour."

Richard glared at him then gritted his teeth. He spoke slowly, biting each word off as it formed. "With the prevailing wind we will have to tow the ships up the river using the boats. My men will only be able to make about a knot of headway against the wind and current, which means it will be at least five if not six hours before we get there."

Rodrigo looked surprised and his lips formed an "oh".

Richard stomped off and yelled orders. Sebastian walked over to Rodrigo and put his hand on his shoulder.

"There is enough daylight left today that we might get there by this evening. But Beth tells me that the men will have to be changed every thirty minutes or so, as this is extremely hard work."

And so it was. The men strained to get the ship moving, heaving on the oars so hard they bent. In the *Cub* they ran out the sweeps and pulled them with three men to an oar.

"This is where a steam ship would be so much more convenient. Why, if we had one, we could tow the ships and barges up the river in no time," Beth said.

"And if wishes were ponies, we would all ride," Sebastian replied.

Even the marines took a turn at the oars and they crawled up the river at an average of one mile an hour. Six and three-quarter hours later they arrived at the place where the next group of engineers waited on the shore. Rodrigo asked to be taken across immediately they anchored, after muttering something about modifications. He then disappeared, leaving another engineer in his place.

Enormous sheerlegs had been erected on a barge that was securely anchored to the bank with pylons. The *Fox* was hauled alongside, and the crew started to take down the rigging. Her masts were unstepped and laid on her deck, a tricky and dangerous operation for the crew and the ship. It took two days, by which time Rodrigo had returned with his wheeled contraptions. Four huge, four-wheeled, cart-like wooden vehicles with shaped frames were brought up to a ramp carved into the riverbank. Their wheels were a foot wide and around eight feet in diameter, which matched the frames that were made of heavy timbers curved to fit the hull of the *Fox*. These carts were linked by cables and ballasted, so that when they were rolled into the river they stayed on the bottom. Cables, buoyed to the surface, showed where they were. The *Fox* was floated over them and the buoyed cables pulled up and secured to ringbolts on the deck.

"We will dive down and release the ballast weights. Keep the cables even and tight," Rodrigo said, and promptly stripped to his underwear and waded into the river. "Secure the cables!" he called up to the deck.

The sailors hauling on the cables made them fast. Twenty pairs of draft horses were brought up and attached by more cables to the *Fox*'s stern and the aft cart. On a command from Rodrigo, who was still in his underwear and dripping, the horses started to pull. Men joined in hauling on lines that ran beside the horses and Beth and Sebastian watched in amazement as the *Fox* was slowly pulled out of the river.

The guns and stores were loaded onto a fleet of carts by the crews and then the *Cub* was brought out in the same way.

"Bolívar must have requisitioned every horse in Panama!" Sebastian exclaimed as the mile-long convoy progressed down the road to Panama City.

Richard, who refused to leave his ship, stood at the rail and waved to Beth and Sebastian, who rode in a carriage. The crew members either walked or cadged a ride on the wagons. The road had been prepared by the engineers and was free of ruts and large rocks, and they progressed at a steady walking pace.

Beth suddenly had a thought. "How long do you think Bolívar has been planning this?" she asked Sebastian.

Sebastian held up a finger in a gesture that could have meant *give me a minute*, then jumped from the carriage and trotted over to Rodrigo, who followed them on horseback. He walked beside him for several minutes talking to him before returning with a frown on his face.

"He was first given orders a year ago to clear the river and prepare the road. He understood that was to enable troops to be shipped across the isthmus quickly. Then Bolívar asked him if the same route could be used to transport ships. That was three months ago."

"Do you think he had us in mind?"

"I don't know, but I'm going to ask Bolívar when we see him."

They covered the twenty miles from the river to the docks in Panama City in two days. The road was mainly flat, with level terrain, but with the weight of the *Fox* any incline saw the men heaving on ropes to help the horses and on declines they unhitched the horses from the front and attached them to the back to act as a brake. The horses had to be rested every hour for an hour, which made for very slow progress. Richard insisted on the ships' bottoms being cleaned during the stops until their copper glowed in the early-morning sun.

It took another day to be ready to refloat the ships, a process that was basically a reversal of the procedure used to get them out of the water. After that, a week was needed to step the masts, refit everything and ensure that the hulls had not been damaged.

Eventually, with the stores, water and powder loaded they were ready to sail. Rodrigo came to say goodbye.

"I am staying here for the next year or so. If you need anything, please find me at the garrison and I will help all I can."

Beth kissed him on both cheeks and then had a thought. "Did Bolívar say anything about getting us back to the Atlantic?"

Rodrigo paused in recollection. "All he said was that you would be here until the war ended. Oddly, he never mentioned how you would get back."

"I think we have been tricked," Beth said, as she paced up and down their cabin. "He has manipulated us all the way along. He must have known about Rosa Collins and my activities in Mexico."

Sebastian was sitting on the transom bench and watching Beth. He never got tired of looking at her — and particularly her hips — in her fighting leathers.

"It seems to me that he wanted an extra couple of fast ships in the area and that we presented him with a solution to his problem," he said. "A pair of independent raiders. We have the letter of marque."

Beth went to the desk and took out the envelope containing the letter. She opened it and extracted the single sheet of paper with the seal of Gran Colombia. It was in Spanish and very stylised. This was the first time she had actually read it, as she had only glanced at it before, to make sure it was indeed a letter of marque.

"He knew. This is made out in the name of Rosa Collins."

"What?"

She handed the paper to Sebastian.

"The cunning ..."

"Indeed."

Beth took the letter back and folded it into its envelope. She went to the head and removed a cunningly hidden panel, behind which was a cavity containing a strong box. She brought the box out and placed it on the desk, unclasped a key — which looked like an ornament — from her bracelet and opened it.

"Here are all the papers for the *Fox*, making her an American ship owned by Rosa, and the American letter of marque."

"Two letters; that's handy. Mind you, I do not think the Americans would like us to use theirs in this instance."

Beth put the letter back in the box and relocked it, keeping the ship's papers out. The box disappeared back into the hidden space in the head.

"I didn't know that was there," Sebastian commented as he re-read the Colombian letter.

"What?" Beth said.

"That secret panel — and I have sat on that head countless times."

"It was made by a very skilled craftsman."

"Who?"

"Mr Clough."

"The carpenter? I never would have thought he had such a delicate touch."

"He was a cabinet maker in his youth." Beth smiled, enjoying getting one up on her husband.

"Here is another thing: according to this letter we will give him fifty per cent of anything we make in prizes."

Beth shrugged. "That's standard, the king takes that on an English letter."

"Aah, but Bolívar has to be paid in gold," Sebastian said.

"Do you think he is lining his own pockets?" Beth asked in surprise.

"Wouldn't shock me. I have yet to meet an honest dictator."

Beth laughed. She couldn't have been more wrong: Bolívar was personally poor, as he gave away most of the riches accruing to him as dictator.

"Well, we are here, and our brief is to aid him in whatever way we can."

Just then the sound of the anchor being raised came from above, the stamp of the men's feet as they turned the capstan and the patter of the boys' feet as they nipped the messenger to the anchor cable. The ship heeled slightly as she caught the wind and the helmsmen called, "I have her," as the rudder bit.

Guayaquil

January 1829

The *Fox* and *Cub* flew the Colombian flag as they sailed south from Panama at the end of January 1829, heading along the Colombian coast towards Ecuador. They were initially heading for Buenaventura, which would be their base. None of them knew what to expect, as not a single officer or crewman had sailed the Pacific before. What they found surprised them.

As they sailed into the Bay of Buenaventura, a lookout on the mast kept up a running commentary on what he could see, and a pair of leadsmen called the depth. Both the master and his mates were busy taking sightings of landmarks and drawing sketches of what they saw so they could update the charts. Every Royal Navy ship had an obligation to survey any areas it entered, to improve the quality of the navy's charts. The master's logbook and notes would be sent to the Charting Office on their return to England.

The bay was ten miles long. "It's an island," Richard said. "The chart has it as a peninsula."

"Well, you learn something every day," Beth replied, more interested in an indigenous canoe that was pacing them. Richard put his telescope to his eye and examined the people in the boat. The man wore a simple loincloth and the woman a sarong-like skirt. Other than that, they were naked. The man rowed while the woman held a baby. There was no sign of weapons. Beth smiled and waved to them; the woman waved back, the man ignored them.

The dock had a pier made of stone, which boded well, and there were ship repair and building businesses along the shoreline. They were the only armed craft in port — every other ship was a trader and either unarmed or only carrying a couple of old cannons. Consequently, they attracted attention, and an army officer came to the dock to greet them.

"Hello, may I come aboard?" he called up politely as they tied up alongside the pier.

"Please, come on up," Richard called back.

The man, dressed smartly in the uniform of a captain of infantry, walked up the gangplank and saluted Richard, who wore a coat reminiscent of a captain of the Colombian navy.

Richard saluted back and introduced himself. "Captain Richard Brazier of the *Fox*, a privateer of the Colombian navy."

"Captain Enrico Santiago de Palma. I will need to see your papers, Captain."

Richard took him down to Beth and Sebastian's cabin and introduced him to Beth. Sebastian was nowhere to be seen. Fede raised his head from his bed, decided the new human was no threat, and went back to sleep.

"Captain Santiago de Palma, may I introduce Miss Rosa Collins, the owner of the *Fox* and our sister ship the *Cub*. Miss Collins, the captain wishes to see our papers."

The captain bowed gracefully to Beth, who wore a dress and looked every inch the lady. "You may call me Enrico," he said.

"Then you should call me Rosa," Beth replied in a Southern drawl, and bade him take a seat. She handed him their letter of marque and registration papers. His eyebrows raised as he saw Bolívar's signature, but he made no comment, only handed them back.

"We will be using Buenaventura as our base while we annoy the Peruvians by taking their ships," Beth said, and smiled. Titherton served glasses of Madeira.

"Then we shall see more of each other, as I am in command of the garrison here and am acting governor."

"Do you have a big one?"

Enrico nearly choked on his wine. "I'm sorry, a big what?"

"Garrison," Beth purred. A faint thump came from the sleeping quarters.

"What was that?" Enrico asked.

"My other dog. He likes to sleep in there," Beth said.

A snort was heard. Enrico looked at Fede. If she chose to sleep in the same room as these monsters, who was he to intrude?

"Your garrison?" Beth prompted him.

"Oh yes, I have one hundred men."

"A company all of your own! How delightful."

Enrico smiled, indulging her. *How did she end up a privateer?* "You must come and dine with me before you leave."

Beth smiled brightly. "I would be delighted. When?"

"Shall we say tomorrow night, at seven at the company headquarters?"

Sebastian had a hard time not sniggering or laughing aloud as Beth worked the unsuspecting captain. By the time she finished with him he would be giving her powder and shot for free, and they would have protected berths for both ships. Sebastian's main concern was how he was going to get messages and reports back to London. British ships were not plentiful in this part of the world and he couldn't trust them to other countries' ships.

The sound of the captain leaving was his prompt to go out into the cabin — which was empty, as Beth had escorted the captain to the side. Soon after, she returned and immediately started taking off her dress.

"That went well," he said.

"It did," her muffled reply came as she pulled the garment over her head, giving him a wonderful view.

He put his feet up as he watched her dress in trousers and a shirt. *It is a wonder that women don't wear some kind of underwear,* he thought.

"Have you considered how we are going to get messages home?" she asked.

"I have, and I haven't come up with a single idea."

"That's not good." She plonked herself down in a chair and twirled a lock of hair. "What if—" she wrinkled her nose in thought — "we sent them across the isthmus at Panama?"

"Who with?"

"Good question … we could set up our own courier service." Then she sat upright. "Hold on, we are missing something. Doesn't the service have an office in Panama?"

"They closed it."

"Oh."

They were silent for a minute, then Sebastian sighed and said, "So it looks like we will have to set up that courier service."

* * *

They reprovisioned the ship and Beth went to the garrison for dinner with the captain. She was escorted by Fede and the sisters as it was a fairly uncivilised town even by the standards of South America. The captain, confronted by an array of weapons, was on his best behaviour, especially after Alie pulled her punch dagger to spear an apple from the centrepiece of the table. Fede did what he always did and lay down at Beth's feet keeping a baleful eye on the men in the room.

"We will be leaving tomorrow morning," Beth informed him.

"So soon?"

"We have ships to capture and Peru to annoy," Beth quipped. "By the way, if we have prisoners, should we bring them here?"

The captain looked at his adjutant, his expression one of surprise. "Aah … well, we have never considered that. Do you take many?"

"Well, that depends; if they play nicely we will let the civilians go, but any military prisoners have to be kept, I'm afraid."

"If they *don't* play nicely?"

Beth took a bite of the rare steak on her plate.

"Oh, then we kill them all."

She said it so coldly and matter-of-factly it sent a shudder through the officer's bodies.

"I think we can take a few military prisoners," the adjutant said.

"Can you? Oh, that would be splendid!"

They sailed south, the *Cub* out to windward, the wind from the south-east. Progress was made in a series of long tacks. After a day they entered Ecuadorian waters, where the coast was green and lush. They were heading to the Gulf of Guayaquil, having been told before they left that the Peruvian navy was blockading the city as a prelude to taking it. They had little hope of removing the frigates doing the blockading, but could possibly disrupt their supplies.

Apart from fishing boats, they saw little in the way of traffic for the first few days, and what there was flew a friendly flag. They continued south, stopping any ships heading north for news.

"How could a single corvette repulse two ships of the Colombian navy and cause so much damage?" Beth asked Richard after they had heard an account of the initial battle of Guayaquil.

"Poor sailing and gun handling on the part of the Colombians. Their navy is weak and poorly trained. They rely on British or French officers, who take their money but do little to improve things."

It was becoming clear why Bolívar wanted them in the Pacific. For Gran Colombia to have any influence at all at sea, they needed help.

"What do you think about our chances of relieving the siege of Guayaquil?" Beth asked.

"Little to none unless we can pull off some kind of sneak attack. They do not have carronades, so we would have run the gauntlet of their long guns before we could get close enough to do any damage."

If this is going to be anything more than a pleasure cruise, we are going to have to do something, Beth thought.

They continued south and came up on the Gulf. They could see no warships.

"What do you want to do, boss?" Richard asked.

"Signal the *Cub* to scout the Gulf and see what's in there," Beth said, then had second thoughts. "Belay that." The midshipman responsible for raising signals froze. "Take us in, they won't be expecting us. Fly the Mexican flag."

Richard gave the order to change course and to put two men in the chains to monitor the depth. They had no pilot so would have to feel their way in. The *Cub* dropped in a cable astern. The Mexican flag replaced the Colombian flag in imitation of the *Cub*'s big sister.

"Take us to quarters, Christopher," Richard said quietly to his first mate.

Double lookouts set, the master and his mates commenced furiously plotting and mapping; their charts were sparse to say the least and showed nothing apart from the fact there was a city at the head of the delta. They slowly entered the Gulf. The wind was on their beam and the current from the river sluggishly against them. It was slack water on the ebb and about to start coming in, according to the master's almanac. They could expect a tidal range of ten feet or thereabouts, with high tide around noon.

Their progress increased as the tide started in. Richard kept the *Fox* running just fast enough to maintain steerage. They rounded the island of Puná and were faced with a choice of two channels. They took the western channel that headed a point west of north. The river was wide and deep, the banks lined with mangrove forests that were full of life. Farms dotted the shore in clearings. They soon realised that what they were passing on their port side was an island, and a helpful fisherman told them it was called Isla Mondragón. He also told them that the river continued north for about three hours' sailing before reaching Isla Santay with the city tucked in behind it.

Richard stood the men down; it was pointless keeping them at stations for that long. Suddenly a deck lookout called, "There be pink dolphins!"

Richard first thought the man had gone mad, but he went to the side and there, swimming sedately alongside them, *was* a pair of pink dolphins of between seven and eight feet long. Beth had heard the call and she and Sebastian followed him to the side.

"Well, I'm blowed! I never thought to see such a thing!" Sebastian exclaimed.

"Look, there's a crocodile too!" Beth said and pointed to the shore where an eighteen-foot specimen basked in the sun.

"No swimming in this river, then," Sebastian joked.

Richard walked amongst his lookouts, cautioning them to keep alert and on watch for the Peruvian ships rather than the local fauna. Colourful birds abounded and Beth spotted a large primate in the treetops.

Two and a half hours of nature-spotting came to an end when Richard sent the crew back to quarters in anticipation of coming up on the blockading ships. If the fisherman was right, they should see their masts any time now. They plodded onwards, making no more than four knots, when suddenly the masthead lookout called, "I can see the island and there are masts to the west of it."

Richard came to Beth. "Should we anchor and send the longboat forward?"

Beth thought for a moment or two. "No, we will sail up as if we are neutral. I want to see how the city fares."

Richard shrugged and kept his tongue still. If the boss wanted to be bold then he could do bold, even if he thought she was being rash.

Sebastian didn't have the same restraint. "Is that wise, love?"

Beth was unrepentant. "If we can get past them into the city, we can work out a way to sabotage the Peruvians in some way."

Sebastian shrugged. On this ship he definitely played second fiddle to his wife.

They bore about thirty degrees west to follow the channel around the island and there in front of them, anchored mid-channel, was a pair of Peruvian frigates. The lookout called, "More masts to starboard at the tip of the island in the other channel."

As they closed, they saw the ships were the *Presidente* and *Libertad*, both forty-gun, twelve-pound frigates. The *Libertad* had swung on her springs to bring her broadside to bear.

"Heave to," Beth said. "Bring a boat around."

Richard called the orders, and they backed the foresail to bring them to a halt. The *Cub* slid up beside them before she did the same.

Sebastian took Beth to the side and asked, "Why aren't we shooting?"

Beth nodded to the *Libertad* and then at the *Presidente*, which had also now swung her beam to face them. "We are facing forty guns and an enemy we know has reasonably trained men, as one of their corvettes showed off two Colombian ships. We would take a lot of damage in a fight and still be left to face a third ship even if we won."

Sebastian hugged her. "This is why I leave the ship business to you."

Capitan Alfonso Huamani of the *Libertad* watched curiously as a boat set out from the intruding ship. The schooner and its associated cutter had appeared unexpectedly and only the sharp eyes of a lookout, who had spotted the Mexican flag, had prevented them from being summarily blown out of the water. Now he waited to see what would happen next.

His first mate was looking through a telescope and audibly gasped then gave a low whistle.

"*Dios mío, aye, aye, aye.*"

"What is it, Pedro?"

"We are about to be visited by a *maravilla* with red hair."

The captain took the telescope from him and trained it on the boat. He adjusted the focus and let out a little gasp himself.

A beautiful red-haired woman sat in the stern, dressed elegantly in European attire and holding a parasol above her head. She looked directly at him. Beside her sat what must presumably be an Englishman in a smart suit, wearing a French-style top hat. The boat was being smartly rowed by a professional-looking crew.

"Get a chair ready, she will need to be hoisted aboard."

Beth saw the chair swing out before they hooked onto the chains, and kissed Sebastian on the cheek. "Go up the side, I will meet you on the deck. Introduce me as Felicia Armitage; you are my husband."

"I know ... we went over this on board," Sebastian grumped.

"Just making sure you don't forget." She kissed him again.

Sebastian climbed the battens to the deck then waited for Beth to be lowered, her ankles showing daintily. The captain stepped forward and bowed.

"Capitan Alfonso Huamani of the Peruvian frigate *Libertad*. Good afternoon," he said in Spanish.

Sebastian bowed in return, sweeping his hat off in the process, and said, also in Spanish, "Sir Sebastian Armitage and my wife, Lady Felicia."

"So pleased to make your acquaintance, Captain," Beth said and fluttered her eyelashes at him.

Damn but she is beautiful, Captain Huamani thought, then introduced his officers, who were, to a man, equally smitten as Beth turned on her charms.

Sebastian gave a wry smile as he ended up taking a back seat. When Beth was in this kind of mood, no one was safe.

"To what do we owe the pleasure of your company?" the captain asked once they were below in his state room and had been served drinks.

"We were hoping to water here before sailing south," Sebastian said. "We were unaware there was any kind of conflict going on."

"Why are you sailing the Pacific coast?" the captain asked.

"Why, we are on honeymoon from Alta California. We wish to explore the continent from top to bottom," said Beth.

"You are Europeans?"

"We are naturalised citizens of Mexico and own several ranches," Sebastian explained.

"You are rancheros? My family are also rancheros!"

They all laughed at the coincidence and chatted about their travels until Beth brought the subject back to their needs.

"We really need to rewater and get some fresh food. Can we go to the town and replenish, please?"

The captain smiled benevolently. She was such a pretty little thing.

"Yes, I will permit it, for one day and one night only. Then you must leave."

They moored up at a dock that had seen better days. In fact, the whole town was looking rather the worse for wear. Some batteries were still partially intact and able to respond to the frigates, which Sebastian thought should hold things up for a while.

They made a show of watering, as they knew they were being watched, and held a meeting with the town's mayor, who came to greet them. When he found out they were from Bolívar, he was overjoyed.

"How are you for weapons?" Sebastian asked.

"We have our cannon, but we only have a few muskets. We are lucky they sent ships, not soldiers."

Sebastian had to disappoint him. "They have soldiers on board as well. They are manned in the Spanish fashion."

The mayor wrung his hat in his hands. Beth smiled at him and said, "But we can help with that. Send twenty men to the ships at midnight and we will supply you with one hundred rifles."

That was not all she had in mind. It would be a dark night with no moon and Sebastian spotted her talking to the gunner after they returned to the *Fox* an hour later. He heard her say, "A sealed cask should do it, one of the small ones of pistol powder."

"Should do what?" Sebastian asked as he approached them.

"Cut an anchor cable."

"Oh, of course! I should have known."

Beth put her arms around him and kissed his nose. "I'm planning a little sojourn tonight. Want to come?"

He looked down at her and shook his head. "No, I'm sure you can manage quite well on your own. Who is going with you?"

"A boat crew and the boys."

"Well, Mike should be able to keep you out of trouble."

She blew a raspberry at him.

Meanwhile, the gunner had fetched four quarter-kegs of pistol powder and carefully removed the bungs. Beth opened a wooden box. Inside were a selection of brass timers of different sizes. "What time is it now?" she asked.

Sebastian looked at his pocket watch, a fine French-made specimen that Beth had bought him. "It's ten minutes to seven."

Little frown lines appeared on Beth's brow as she pondered. "Sun comes up at six?"

"About then, yes," Sebastian said, knowing what she was thinking.

She spoke out loud, working it through. "We will sail at first light on the last of the ebb and should be past the frigates by seven. Twelve and a quarter hours should be enough."

She selected four medium-sized timers and, after testing the igniters, set them before placing them inside each of the casks. The gunner sealed them with the bungs and then applied a liberal coating of tar to each before wrapping them in oiled canvas, which was also sealed with tar.

While Sebastian oversaw the offloading of the guns, Beth, Mike, Harry and four oarsmen — all dressed in black with blacked-up faces and hands — climbed down into the gig that sat in the shadow of the *Fox*'s port side. Four neatly bound packages sat innocently in the bottom. Mike had already bound them in messenger rope and left enough to lash them to the anchor cables of the frigates.

The boat pushed off and the men pulled on the muffled oars, being very careful not to make a splash. Mike lay in the bow. He had excellent night vision and directed Harry, who had the rudder. Beth sat in the middle and enjoyed the night air. They drifted downstream towards the *Presidente*, which was their first target.

The frigates were anchored out of line of sight of the shore batteries in the lee of Isla Santay. This was to make them hard targets and they were largely invisible until the boat rounded the corner. Mike signalled that Harry should steer to port and the oarsmen should make headway. Then he held his hand up and they stopped rowing. He knelt and took up a line with a shackle on the end. The ship loomed up on them, and with a flick of the wrist he flipped the weighted line out so that it wrapped the anchor cable, and the weight came back to him. It was nicely done, and the boat swung to a stop.

Beth picked up a cask and moved to the side at the bow while Mike pulled the gig tight up against the cable. Beth held the cask against the cable while Mike secured it, his knots as good as any sailor's.

Job done, they cast off and allowed the gig to drift down past the hull of the ship. The men walked them down the side. That is, the two oarsmen on that side shipped their oars and used their hands to fend the gig off the hull. At one point they did scrape it, but no one on deck reacted; Beth assumed they thought it was one of the many floating logs that drifted down the river.

They found the stern anchor cable and lashed a cask to it. They were halfway done, so now they had to row across to the *Libertad*. The men applied themselves to the oars as they moved across and slightly against the sluggish current. As before, Mike guided them — but even his keen vision did not spot the log coming downstream. It hit the gig aft of the bow with enough force to spring a plank at the waterline and spin the boat around.

They kept going once they recovered their equilibrium, and Mike found the outline of the *Libertad* against the stars. Beth stuffed the small sail the gig carried into the gap to slow the inflow. She started bailing, and the sound of the water being poured over the side seemed preternaturally loud.

They found the forward anchor cable and attached the charge, but the water got ahead of her, and on the way down the side she dared not bail for fear of discovery. By the time they had attached the second charge the water was halfway up their shins.

"Plan B," Beth said as the men struggled to row the heavy boat.

"What's that?" Mike asked as he set to bailing along with Beth.

"Find a sand bar and beach the boat. The *Fox* or *Cub* will pick us up in the morning."

They let the gig drift on the current downriver and bailed like madmen to keep her afloat. Frank grabbed an oar and sculled from the stern to give them a little steerage. The starlight outlined the shore, and he pushed them eastwards until they grounded on a muddy bank.

"At least we won't sink," Mike said as the men hauled the boat a little further up. The smell of the mud at low tide was, however, pretty awful and there was the new risk of crocodiles.

They bailed her out and the crew tied a patch over the sprung plank on the outside. That would hold better than stuffing it from the inside. It was a cold and insect-ridden night. Their only recourse was to smear the stinking mud on their skin to get some protection.

Beth sat dozing until a thump woke her. She was instantly alert and pulled out a pistol, then realised that a shot would give the game away. She reversed the weapon and held it by the barrel.

There was scrabbling and the boat rocked as something climbed the side. Mike had a small signal lantern which had louvres that opened with a lever. It was intended to signal the *Fox* they were returning, but now he used it to shine a beam on their intruder — and Beth found herself face to face with the enormous head of a fifteen-foot-long crocodile that was trying to lift itself over the side of the boat. She swung the pistol like a hammer and hit it right on the middle of its snout. She put all her weight behind it and the gun broke in half, leaving her with the broken barrel in her hand. The monster pulled back in surprise at being assaulted, its claws leaving gashes in the woodwork.

Beth threw away the useless barrel and grabbed her main gauche, ready to stab the beast if it came back. But it had had enough for the moment and went off to seek an easier meal.

Dawn came with a cacophony of birdsong and the roar of howler monkeys. The tracks of the crocodile were still visible in the mud. Forty minutes later the *Fox* appeared around the corner, and they pushed the boat off the bank and rowed to midriver.

Richard looked over the side as they hooked on and noted the damage. "Haul her aboard for repairs," he instructed.

Men climbed down as Beth and the rest climbed up. Sebastian stood waiting for her. Beth was just about to hug him when the first charge detonated. It was followed rapidly by the others.

Sebastian held her at arm's length. "You know you stink?"

"Do I?"

"Yup." He turned her around to face a deck pump that was rinsing down the gig. He slapped her on the backside. "Go wash."

The crews of the frigates found themself adrift as their anchor cables were cut just as the two Mexican ships went out of sight. Orders were shouted and men ran to raise sail, but on the *Libertad* they were closer to the west bank, and before they could get her under control she ran aground in full view of the shore batteries. It would be three long days before they managed to refloat her.

Prey

They sailed out of the river and back into the Pacific, following the coast down into Peruvian waters. The lush greenery of the rainforest slowly gave way to more barren land and then desert, all in less than a day. Beth looked at it and blew out her cheeks. "If the rest of Peru is like that, it is no wonder they want a piece of Ecuador and Bolivia," she said to no one in particular.

She jumped when Christopher Wiggins spoke from behind her. "The interior is more like Ecuador, according to the writings of Pizarro."

"Who is, or was, Pizarro?"

Wiggins put on a scholarly air. "Francisco Pizarro was the original conquistador who discovered and conquered Peru for the Spanish in the 1500s. He was illiterate but one of his companions was a priest, Hernando de Luque, who wrote down his commentary."

"Really? That is so studious of you." Beth flattered the man ingenuously, making Wiggins laugh.

"Not much else to do, other than read, when one is off duty."

Beth looked back at the coast. It was decidedly rocky, arid and barren. "Tell me there are some ports along this blasted waste."

"According to the charts there is a fishing village at Bayóvar, which we should see before the day is out. Then there is Chimbote and Lima."

"That's it?"

Wiggins sighed dramatically. "My dear lady, I am afraid it is."

She was about to curse Bolívar when a lookout called that he could see a sail. Her mood brightened.

"Any idea what it is?" Beth asked Richard as he looked at the ship, which was around four miles away.

"A Peruvian merchantman. A rather old one at that; looks like it used to be a whaler."

"Signal the *Cub* to board her."

Stephen Donaldson, the *Cub*'s skipper, read the signal. "Bring us around to parallel her and put a shot across her bows," he said to George Byker, his midshipman.

"Aye, aye, sir," George warbled. At fourteen years he was going through the final stages of puberty. "Ready to wear ship! Load the forward starboard gun."

Stephen called the boy to him. "Which way will you wear?"

"To starboard, sir," George replied.

"Do you think to turn inside or go around our target?"

"I thought to go around her, sir."

"Then who would have the wind gauge?"

"Oh, *they* would."

Stephen looked at him sternly. "You need to change your orders."

"Aye, aye, sir," George replied a little sullenly.

"Get on with it."

George picked up his speaking trumpet. "Prepare ..." His voice came out in a squeak. He coughed. "Prepare to wear to starboard. Port forward gun make ready!" This time it came out in a manly roar.

The gunners grinned at each other. They had spotted the error immediately and waited for the correction. Stephen watched their target and at the correct moment ordered, "Wear ship, bring us alongside that scow."

The ship didn't wait for the order to stop and shed the wind from her sails as soon as the *Cub* swung around, the Peruvian flag fell to the old ship's deck. A boat took George and three marines across, and she was boarded.

The *Fox* hove to and watched. The manoeuvre was smartly done, and the boarding was unopposed. A signal flew from the *Cub*.

"What does that say?" Sebastian asked as Beth had a fit of the giggles.

"It spells out what the cargo is."

"And?" Sebastian said, a little exasperated.

"G.U.A.N.O." Beth spelled the word out, still giggling.

Sebastian took a second to take that in. "Guano? Bird shit? We captured a load of bird shit?"

Beth calmed down and replied, "Actually, my dear husband, guano is a rich source of phosphate and is worth good money as a fertiliser."

It turned out the ship was heading to Mexico, where they would sell the cargo at a premium. "Do we keep it or sink it?" Richard asked.

Beth thought about it.

"We keep it. Put a prize crew on board and take it to Buenaventura. We will sell the cargo to the highest bidder there."

* * *

They continued south and were soon amongst the Peruvian coastal traffic. The waves were high and rolling and Beth understood why ports were few and far between. They took several coasters, putting the crews ashore before taking the cargo and burning the ships. Beth was, she had to admit, getting bored. Then they spotted a Peruvian navy brig with a corvette escorting it. Beth examined the two ships through her telescope.

"Now that is more interesting."

"How do you want to play it?" Richard asked.

"What do you think?"

"Sail past them, wear and take the corvette with the wind gauge. Then take the brig at our leisure."

"That sounds like an excellent plan," Sebastian said.

Beth gave a wicked smile. "It is, but we will add one small thing."

They contrived to tack so that they would pass within two hundred yards or so from the corvette. Beth and the girls put dresses on over their leathers and went to the fore deck, where they made a show of waving at the approaching ship. Neither the *Fox* nor the *Cub* showed any colours. The girls blew kisses at the corvette's quarterdeck.

The corvette captain waved back, then — as the ships were about to pass — he saw the Colombian flag unfurl on the mainmast. A row of stubby guns ran out and smoke and flame erupted down the schooner's side. He dove to the deck as a hail of chain shot ripped through his rigging. Her mainsail burst apart, splitting top to bottom; the mizzen was struck about halfway up and had a decided list to port in its upper half.

"Wear ship," Richard ordered and the *Fox* swung with the wind in a graceful arc that ended with her directly behind the stricken corvette.

"Let's see if that fore chaser was worth the money," Beth said.

"Prepare the fore chaser! Load with chain!" Richard yelled.

The corvette's crew were frantically making repairs, taking down the torn main and heaving a new sail up to take its place. The fore chaser fired and a double load of chain flew directly down the centre line of the corvette about six feet above her deck. The howl of the chain as it ripped through the air was eerie, with the sound of rendering wood and snapping rigging followed by more than a few screams of terror and pain.

The corvette slowed and the *Fox* came up alongside, her carronades run out. The corvette responded. She had been mauled but was not beaten. Her crew was well trained and chose the right time to fire, which was precisely the same time as the *Fox* did. The main smashers of the *Fox* were loaded with thirty-two-pound balls, the smaller with twenty-four pounds of grape. The corvette, the *Santa Maria*, fired nine-pound balls. Weight for weight it was no contest, but the *Fox* still suffered.

The carronades were faster to load, and as they ran out for a second broadside, the corvette struck.

"Cease fire!" Richard roared. "Back the foresails and prepare a boarding party."

The *Cub*, seeing that the *Santa Maria* had been taken care of, sped off after the brig. She had no fore chasers but was faster than the heavily laden vessel. The brig had a few six-pounder cannons, which the eight twenty-four-pound carronades could easily outmatch. However, Stephen had the prize in mind and went for her rigging. She slowed, but didn't strike.

"Prepare to board! Take us alongside, helmsman."

The two ships ground together, and a volley of swivel guns sent canister shot howling across the deck. Stephen led the charge. The brig had a crew of sixty, being navy rather than a merchant ship, and was determined to resist. Stephen found himself facing men who knew how to fight and was in danger of being overwhelmed before his men arrived and rescued him. The fight was, as all such boardings were, brutal and short.

"What have we got?" Beth asked as she stepped aboard the brig.

Stephen, his right arm in a sling, stepped up with a paper pinned to a board. "Supplies for the blockading ships in Guayaquil. Food, powder, spares, extra men."

"Oh, a good haul, then … that will save us having to return to base." Beth looked at his arm, which had a bloody bandage around the bicep. "Let me see that."

"This? It's nothing."

Beth tutted and told him, "I'll decide that."

She unwrapped the blood-soaked bandage and revealed the cut. It was deep and obviously made by something very sharp. "Hmm, that's nasty and needs stitching. Go onto the *Fox* and see the surgeon."

"He'll take my arm off," Stephen complained.

"No, he won't, he will stitch it — or would you prefer I did it?"

The latter was intended as a threat. However, it backfired.

"Would you?"

Beth rolled her eyes. Men! Fearless in battle but babies when it came to getting repaired afterwards. She took him back to the *Fox* and had Paola and Alie attend. Then she sat him on a wooden stool while she prepared.

A bottle of neat spirit and curved needles designed for suturing wounds were laid out on the table along with a reel of silk thread, two pairs of forceps and a pair of scissors. Clean boiled rags lay in a bowl. A bottle of rum stood open within reach of his left hand.

Beth poured spirit on a rag and cleaned the wound of congealed blood, making Stephen wince.

"Hold him."

The girls held his arm and upper body. Beth poured alcohol into the cut. "Jesus Christ!" Stephen gasped through gritted teeth.

"You think *that* hurt?" Beth said with no sympathy at all. She took a small needle and threaded it with silk. Then she held it in the tip of one pair of forceps and reached down into the bottom of the cut. Stephen braced himself. She inserted the needle into the muscle as low down as she could, but his muscles tensed, trapping the needle.

"Relax; every time you tense, your muscles grab the needle," she told him, then put in a row of stitches that sealed the muscle over the bone. Stephen took a long pull on the bottle. She repeated the exercise further up, ensuring the sides of the cut were closed. A long end of the thread was left to act as a drain, then she put in a layer in the fascia that lay below the fatty layer and finally a row in his skin.

"There, all done," she said and gave it a final wipe with alcohol.

By this time Stephen was rigid and he very slowly relaxed. Alie bandaged the wound and told him, "I will change this every day."

The significance of that simple statement did not sink in until he realised that she was joining him on the *Cub* and would be sleeping in his day room. Now Beth knew that Alie was attracted to Stephen, as she had talked about him in a way that girls do when they like a boy. She knew that Alie had plans for him that Stephen may or may not like.

She shrugged; they would sort it out between them, just as Paola and Harry would.

Now that they had three ships with prize crews, they decided to head back north to Buenaventura. The Peruvians were prisoners of war and numbered about eighty in all, and they needed to get rid of them as they took up a lot of resources to guard. Beth wondered what Bolívar was up to.

As the ships entered port, they saw that the army had reinforced the defences, and a reception committee awaited them on the dock. Captain Enrico Santiago de Palma stood at the fore. "You seem to have been successful in your ventures," he said as he stepped aboard after they tied up.

"Fairly," Beth responded. "These two were going to resupply the blockade at Guayaquil. The aggressors will have to go onto short rations for a while."

De Palma grinned, his teeth white against his dark skin. The grin faded when he saw the prisoners being marched off.

"Don't worry! There are only eighty or so."

"Can't you just sink them, rather than capture them?"

Beth laughed. "Where is the profit in that?"

Sebastian stepped up and asked, "What news of the war?"

"There is word that Sucre and Flores are marching on Peru."

It was now March 1829, and if that was true, then their privateering days were numbered.

Beth sat with Sebastian and her captains.

"I believe our task here is done," she said. "If Gran Colombia forces Peru to the table — or rather, *when* they force them to the table — our letter of marque will be worth nothing."

"Worse, we could be seen as pirates and conveniently abandoned by our sponsor," Sebastian added.

"Time to go home?" Stephen said. His arm was still in a sling.

Beth smiled; she knew the men were getting homesick and she felt the same way. "I believe so, we will head up to Panama and see if we can get taken back across the isthmus. It will be the fastest way home."

The trip north ended in disappointment. There was no sign of Rodrigues or the cradles to carry the ships to the river. They heard that the council had resigned after Bolívar discovered they had voted to invite a member of the House of Bourbon to take his place upon his death.

They only had one option: to round Cape Horn and go home the long way.

The Long Way Round

June 1829

They provisioned the ships for a long voyage and headed south. The journey to Jamaica was over 17,500 miles and the best they could hope for was to do it in around three months.

Sebastian looked at the course that Beth and Richard had plotted on a large chart. "I know there must be a very good nautical reason why we won't follow the coast north on the east side of the Americas but sail all the way across to Africa. But can you explain it?"

Beth pointed to the chart with one hand and held his with the other. "We first follow the west coast south against the wind and current because there is really no alternative in the Pacific. However, once we round Cape Horn and the tip of South America we have the Roaring Forties on our stern that will push us across the Atlantic to the tip of Africa, where we can pick up the south-westerly trade to take us up to Venezuela and from there to Jamaica. It is longer, but believe me it's quicker."

"I've heard about the Horn. Is it as bad as they say?"

Beth smiled. "Going west is far worse than going east. We should have a relatively smooth passage as we will be going with the wind, waves and current."

The voyage south was a series of six long tacks, the first of which took them out to the Galapagos Islands. They didn't go ashore; none of them were naturalists and they had full storerooms. The second tack took them to a point off Lima, where they encountered a ship which they hailed for news. Beth had been right, the Peruvians had been forced into an armistice and the war was over. They changed flags to show the red ensign of Britain's merchant fleet.

Chile offered little in the way of ports so they took advantage of whatever haven they could to restock fresh fruit and lime juice. The crew became tired from the pounding they took during this part of the journey and by the time they reached Cape Horn, all were looking forward to a simpler sail to Africa.

Beth was sitting with Sebastian in their cabin when the rudder was put over to steer them due east. The motion of the ship changed, and they felt her speed up as she took the long Pacific rollers on her stern. Sails cracked above as Richard set all sail.

"Come on, this should be fun," Beth said and grabbed Sebastian's hand to drag him up on deck.

It was almost as if they were on a different ship. The *Fox* flew along, almost surfing the big waves that came up behind her. The sun was shining, and they could see the coast to the north. Beth led Sebastian to the prow and whooped as they flew over the water, her hair streaming out ahead of her. A large grey shape appeared off the starboard bow. "Look, a whale!" she cried.

It was a wicked old humpback, a lone male which casually rolled so his eye looked straight at her. Beth was amazed at the intelligence in that glance and blew him a kiss. The whale blew a fountain of steamy air from his nostrils then slid below the waves, waving goodbye with a flick of his enormous tail.

"My God! That thing was huge!" Sebastian gasped.

"Aye, that were a big 'un," a grizzled ship hand answered him.

Beth laughed. "Old Will there has been everywhere and seen everything!"

"Not everything, miss … not yet, anyway."

Nine days of sailing saw them approach the southern tip of Africa and Cape Town, where they tied up at a dock on the foreshore. The men needed a break, and the plan was to stay there for a week.

Slaves were working the docks under the command of overseers, unloading cargo from a pair of Dutch ships. One particular overseer was an Afrikaner who wielded an eight-foot bullwhip and shouted at them in the local bastardised version of Dutch. Beth and Sebastian were passing when the whip snaked out and hit a slave on the shoulder, leaving an oozing cut.

The man grinned at Beth. "Lazy bastards need a taste of the whip to teach them respect and to work."

Sebastian tightened his grip on her arm before she could respond and clamped his hand on her purse before she could take out her pistol.

"Not now, princess, that's perfectly legal here," he muttered in her ear.

Beth treated the man to a smile that, if he had known her, would have terrified him. As it was he congratulated himself on his cleverness, convinced he had impressed the lady.

* * *

The couple took rooms in a hotel that had a panoramic view of the town and of Table Mountain. They had no sooner entered the rooms and started to unpack when the Wolves arrived. Beth sat with Delfina and Alie and chatted. Sebastian sat with them for a while, then went off to find the commandant of the local garrison. As soon as he left the room, Beth turned to the girls.

"You saw the slaves being used to unload those Dutch ships?"

The girls had. "I thought you were going to shoot that arsehole," Alie said.

"Seb wouldn't let me. I want you to find out where he lives."

The girls grinned. They knew where this would end and were keen to make it happen.

That evening they dined at the hotel and socialised with other travellers who were either on their way to India to take up positions in the East India Company, or on their way home. They got to their rooms after eleven o'clock, but Beth exhibited no signs of weariness.

Sebastian looked at her as she slipped out of her dress and pulled her leathers from her trunk. He sighed; there was nothing he could do to stop her and if he could, she would find some way to work around him.

"I will be on the balcony smoking a cigar and drinking a brandy," he said and walked out through the balcony doors. Ten minutes later, he heard the door to their rooms close.

Beth, Alie and Delfina were dressed in long, hooded cloaks that concealed what they were wearing underneath. They left the hotel by the front door and made their way down into the town, to one

132

of the less-salubrious quarters. Once they had left the hotel district and entered the less well-lit areas, they allowed the cloaks to billow out, revealing their fighting leathers and weaponry. Anyone who saw them gave them a wide berth.

They arrived at a tavern; it was called the Goue Trompet and frequented by Afrikaners. The sound of a half-dozen men laughing came from inside. Beth pulled on a leather mask that concealed her face and the girls followed suit. Beth stepped through the door with a pistol in her hand, the girls on her heels.

The laughter faded as the men saw the gun. Then one said, "*Hulle is vroue, is dit 'n grap?*"

Beth had no idea what he had just said, but she knew what spoke louder than words ... The sound of the shot, and the yelp of the man as the bullet tore up the bar just inches from his fingers, got their undivided attention. Now the men faced six pistols held in rocksteady hands.

Beth pointed at the man she had seen at the docks and beckoned him forward. He stood his ground. She raised her left gun and fired. The bullet nicked his ear.

"*Wat de fok! Is jy mal, vrou?*" (What the fuck! Are you crazy, woman?)

Beth beckoned him forward again. This time he complied. However, he thought she had emptied her guns and made a lunge at her as he did so. Beth was ready for that and stepped neatly aside then clubbed him under the ear as he passed.

Delfina steered him out of the door as he staggered and Beth and Alie followed. Beth stopped the other men from following by slamming the door and jamming it shut with a wedge. By the time they got it open, the girls and their victim had disappeared.

* * *

The next day, Sebastian and Beth were walking around the town when they passed a print shop. Outside, on a pinboard, were copies of the day's news and one headline caught Sebastian's eye. He stepped over to the board and checked the sheet, which had a story printed in both Afrikaans and English.

"What is it, dear one?" Beth asked.

"Something very strange. An overseer was taken from a local pub last night by three women carrying guns. The authorities are bemused as this has never before happened in Cape Town. Apparently, he has completely disappeared and the only thing that has been found is his bullwhip, which was hanging from the entrance to the slave pens."

"How strange."

"The Boers are upset; he was one of the leaders."

Beth managed to keep an air of innocence about her. "Do you think it was the man we saw with a bullwhip?"

Sebastian looked at her, then at Alie, who stood at her shoulder. Delfina was maintaining their weapons back at the hotel.

Sebastian grinned, ending the play-acting. "Where did you dump the body?" he asked softly, his head next to Beth's.

"In the pig yard at the slaughterhouse."

"It will be gone by now, then."

Beth looked around. "They should stop slavery now," she asserted.

"Unfortunately, those already enslaved stay as they are. There is no provision in the act to free slaves, only to stop the trade, but that will come."

In due course, rested and refreshed, they set sail for the Caribbean, picking up the south-easterly trades after sailing north up the west coast to Walvis Bay, Namibia. They steered a course that would make land at or around the equator and from there follow the South American coast up to Venezuela, where they would stop off at Caracas to get news.

The trip was punctuated by weather fronts that rolled off the coast of Africa to cross the Atlantic, propelled by the trade winds. Some moved faster than the *Fox* and *Cub* could sail and came up behind them, forcing a reduction in sail and sometimes a change of direction as well. Fortunately, everyone had their sea legs well and truly under them by then.

They made land on the northern Brazilian coast near to São Luis and followed the current northwest past Suriname and Guyana to pass between Trinidad and Tobago.

"We will need water before we make Caracas. We should stop at Cumana," Richard stated. Beth agreed, and they made their way around the Punta de Araya to what was one of the oldest Spanish towns in Venezuela. The town was situated on the southern shore of the Gulf of Cariaco and provided a sheltered mooring even during the hurricane season. As soon as they docked Beth went ashore to find out the state of things. She returned after just an hour.

"Word has it that the council of ministers and Bolívar have fallen out again. It's also rumoured that Bolívar is not well," Beth reported. "The feeling in the town is that Venezuelan independence is imminent."

"How imminent?" Sebastian asked.

"In the next year. If he resigns or dies, then the federalists will take over and the process of decentralisation will begin."

Sebastian looked at the town and the happy faces of the people. "We will leave well alone. I think our job here is done."

Beth agreed. "Yes, let's go to Jamaica, rest up and refit the ships. We can message London for new orders."

They entered Kingston Bay and tied up at Port Royal. They flew the white ensign and Richard reported to the port admiral. He returned with a grin on his face.

"What are you looking so happy about?" Beth asked.

"The port admiral, Sir Graham Sennett, was not keen to provide our ships with maintenance or supplies."

"Then you showed him your authority from the first sea lord?"

"Yes. After that he was begrudgingly helpful. The ships' bottoms will be cleaned and the rigging overhauled."

"And stores … ?"

"I had a look in the warehouse. The average age of the salt beef was at least twelve years."

Beth pulled a face; that beef would have the texture of mahogany by now.

"We will source our own, once the ships are ready," she told Richard. "In the meantime, give the men leave to go ashore. Sebastian and I will go to the Den. We won't be going anywhere until the hurricane season is over"

Beth and Sebastian wrote a comprehensive report, which they put on the fast packet to London for the attention of Admiral Turner. Then they hired a carriage and went to stay at the Den. They were surprised when they received a letter from Beth's father, twelve weeks later.

"Turner has passed away from cholera. Your father is in charge now," Sebastian told her as he read the letter.

Beth sighed; a tear ran down her cheek. "Oh no, not Uncle James! What about poor Julia?"

"He says they have gathered around her in support."

Beth resisted the urge to go home on the first available ship and waited for Sebastian to tell her the rest.

"Our orders are to take a break in Jamaica and return once our ships are ready. There is a small task he wants fulfilling. But I think the Wolves can take care of it."

"Oh … and what would that be?"

"There is a British slaver in Savannah, Georgia, who has consistently avoided interception by British ships. He is very outspoken about the navy's inability to catch him and has become something of a folk hero to the Southern plantation farmers."

"They want him killed?"

"Publicly and messily."

Beth pursed her lips and raised her eyebrows in surprise at that. They were normally told to "disappear" people.

"What about attribution?"

"Nothing provable, but enough to raise suspicion."

"He has to be killed publicly and messily with a suspicion that the British government or Royal Navy was involved," Beth summarised.

"That's it!" Sebastian grinned.

Beth gathered the Wolves together to brief them.

"We have a mission. There is a man in Savannah, Georgia, by the name of Captain Tristan Montague. He imports slaves from Africa and is adept at avoiding all attempts by the navy to catch him. The government wants him killed in a way that sends a message to other like-minded individuals that this will not be tolerated. Now, that is all well and good, but I have an idea to combine this with finding out how he avoids the navy and to ensure that whatever sources of information he has are closed off forever."

Mike nodded. "Do we know when he is in town?"

Beth checked the decoded version of the instructions she had in her hand.

"He makes regular runs and has a very fast ship. He only trades in slaves and tobacco and never at British ports. For the westward leg of his trade, he calls in at Lisbon. We think he picks up his slaves in Angola, which is a Portuguese colony, thus avoiding any British colonies."

"Will you lead this?" Mike asked.

"No, you will, with the Wolves. I will only help with the planning."

138

Georgia

August 1829

The *Petrel* sailed into the Savannah River.

"That side of the river is the Carolinas," the first mate, Gregory Clarkson, told Delfina as he nodded to the north. "It forms the border with Georgia."

He had taken a shine to her during the voyage up from Jamaica and was very attentive. However, Mike and Harry's presence pretty much guaranteed that his behaviour stayed gentlemanly. They had made it very clear that the girls were under their protection — not that they needed it.

The river was bisected by a string of islands and the *Petrel* took the south channel after taking aboard a pilot.

"That's Shark Tooth Island; Savannah is around the bend up ahead," Gregory continued. The ship had been chartered by Sebastian and would wait in port for the team to complete their mission.

A fort came into view on the south shore. It was obviously manned and the American flag, with its twenty-four stars and seven red stripes, flew above it. Mike asked the pilot, "What's that?"

The pilot pointed at it with the stem of his pipe. "That is Fort Jackson. Built in 1808."

Mike nodded at it in appreciation as the pilot continued, "It will be replaced by the new fort that's being built on Cockspur Island."

"What's wrong with this one?"

"Oh, President Madison decided we needed more forts along the coast to protect against foreign invasion after the war of 1812."

"By that, I suppose he meant the British!" Mike laughed.

Savannah was a green city. Tree-lined avenues draped in Spanish moss interspersed with rhododendrons fronted colonial-style houses. It was warm and humid even though it was early in the morning when they arrived, and a fine mist seeped along the ground, making it very picturesque.

Mike looked for and found a hotel and booked them in as two married couples with their relatives. The owner sniffed at the sight of the obviously Spanish origins of the "wives", but a look from Mike stilled any comment.

House slaves took their bags up to their rooms. They were well-dressed and showed no signs of abuse; however, they didn't speak but silently obeyed instructions. Netta asked Alie, in sign language, why they were so reticent.

"Why do you not speak?" Alie asked one of the young bellboys.

He quickly looked around to make sure none of the others could hear him. "The massa say we must not offend his guests with our talkin'."

Alie passed that on to Netta, whose reply was short and to the point. "Their 'massa' is the one that offends."

The boy grinned when Alie told him that, but had to refrain from replying as other slaves were present.

* * *

Once they were settled, they set about finding their way around the city. It wasn't so big; cobbled streets linked shady squares surrounded by mansion-size houses. There was wealth here. Carriages criss-crossed the streets carrying well-dressed and obviously wealthy passengers. They were driven by Africans in livery, some with footmen riding at the back on a footplate.

"Conspicuous wealth created on the backs of slaves," Mike noted.

He was right: the plantation class formed the upper echelon of Georgian society and ruled by dint of its wealth.

Eventually they found the slave market, which was empty of slaves. They found the man who ran it, a rat-faced man with skin that was pockmarked.

"We only run auctions when the ships come in or when someone is selling off stock," he told Harry.

"When's the next ship due in?" Harry asked.

"You interested in buying?"

"I am, I have just acquired a new plantation which is short of manpower."

"Well, there should be a ship coming in next week. The skipper has a reputation for bringing high-quality stock — mostly to order, mind, but he always has a hundred or so for auction."

"Who is he? I will check his credentials with my contacts."

"Captain Montague. He's a British trader."

That fitted with the information they had been given by the Intelligence Service. Montague had left Lisbon three months ago and, considering the time it would take to gather slaves to match his order book, he should be due around then. They mounted a watch on the dock used by the slavers, and were rewarded when his ship appeared three days later.

Paola was on watch when the ship came in. It docked and soon lines of shackled slaves were being marched down the gang planks. They were naked and filthy and as they stepped ashore were hosed down by a team of slaves operating a fire pump. Paola was thankful the wind was at her back, as the stench must have been horrendous.

Once relatively clean they were sorted, their shackles were struck off and they were placed in pens. A ring of guards armed with whips and clubs kept order. Paola waited until the man who was obviously the captain came ashore and was greeted by the auctioneer. She moved to a spot where she could overhear them.

"Any trouble?" the auctioneer asked.

Montague grinned. "None; the pens are full over there, and I could take my pick. Now my fellow British have banned the trade, the traders are moving up into Angola, though there are still some good pickings in West Africa."

A young slave bolted as soon as his shackles were removed. A whip snaked out and wrapped around his ankle, tripping him. He was dragged to his feet and marched to where Montague stood. He was thrown at the captain's feet.

Montague looked the slave over, assessing his worth. He cocked his head to one side. "Put him to the pole — by his feet."

The terrified boy was dragged to a mast-sized pole with shackles hanging from a hook. The shackles were clamped to his ankles, and he was hoisted up so that he hung upside down facing the pole.

Montague took a whip from an overseer and stood next to the pole. The boy was crying and begging for mercy.

"Listen to me!" Montague bellowed. The slaves all turned to watch him. "There will be no more of this! Escape is futile and any attempt will be punished like this!"

He stepped back and shook the whip out then proceeded to shred the boy's body with stroke after stroke. He didn't spare a square inch of flesh and, even when the boy stopped screaming, continued until he had sated his anger.

They left what remained of the corpse hanging. The boy had bled out and chunks of flesh lay on the ground where the whip had cut them off. Paola felt sick but fixed the image in her mind to fuel a burning desire to avenge the murder.

She followed Montague to a house on Whitaker Street and saw him greeted by a house slave before the door was shut. Through the window she saw him hug a woman and lift a pair of young children into his arms.

"He is married, and lives in one of the bigger mansions on Whitaker Street. He doesn't value black people except as slaves." Paola went on to describe the whipping to death of the would-be escapee to the other Wolves.

"Our brief is to make his death public and messy with a suspicion that the British are behind it," Mike said. "Any ideas?"

There were several suggestions, all likely to result in a gory death, but the conclusion was that they needed to keep Montague under surveillance for a while to ascertain his habits and likely movements. They did this in pairs: Mike and Delfina, Harry and Paola, Alie and Netta. It was their host the hotel owner who presented them with the opportunity. He told them, "There is a regular perambulation around Oglethorpe Square. You should participate; it is good for your health and you will meet many influential people."

That led to a reconnaissance of the square, which was divided into nine sections by a pair of parallel paths running north–south and another pair running east–west. The central area was ideal for what they wanted.

The perambulation started at dusk, when the park was lit by lanterns suspended from the trees. It was quite gothic in its atmosphere, and reminded Paola of Mary Shelley's *Frankenstein*, which she had read on the voyage up to Savannah. As such opportunities go, it was perfect. The team were dressed in black when they snuck out of the hotel and melted into the shadows.

Montague left his house with his wife, and they made their way to the park. They were out to be seen and to show off some of their wealth. Mrs Montague wore a voluminous dress of the latest Southern fashion, with multiple petticoats and layers of lace with blue bows. She carried a parasol and had a wide-brimmed fancy hat on her head. A slave boy of about seven years old followed her to carry her purse.

Their perambulation was disturbed on their second round, just as they entered the central section of the square. An object landed on the path near them and burst into a fountain of brilliant light. Another exploded behind them and a third to the side, forcing them into the middle of the central square. The observant would have noted that the fireworks were coloured red, white and blue. An even more observant person would have noticed the dark shapes dropping from the trees to surround the couple. The other couples moved out towards the perimeter … Whatever was happening was strange and frightening.

Sensing danger, Montague drew his sword and moved in front of his wife. She yelped as a pair of strong arms enveloped her and dragged her into the shadows. A hand clamped over her mouth prevented her screaming.

Now all Montague could see was dark shapes outlined against the glare of the fireworks. He waved his sword to keep them away.

A whip snaked out, stinging the back of his hand. The sword fell to the ground.

"What do you want?" he shouted.

"Justice!" A very British voice shouted back, and a whiplash stung his back. He spun towards it, but another came in from the dark, slashing across his face. He screamed. More blows struck him, and the night air was torn with the sound of whips cracking.

It was over as quickly as it started. The bloody corpse of Montague lay in the centre of the square, beneath a Spanish moss–festooned oak. Of his assassins, there was no trace.

"Did you go out last night?" the hotel owner asked over breakfast.

"No, we stayed in," Mike answered. "Why?"

"Oh, it was terrible, someone was murdered, whipped to death right in Oglethorpe Square, in front of everyone!"

"Whipped?"

"Yes! Cut to pieces, he was!"

Montague's wife was dressed in black at his funeral; she did not, however, look all that upset by the death of her husband. The local sheriff was searching for a bunch of former slaves who had exacted their revenge on the slaver. The assumption was that, as the figures were described as having been black, they must be former slaves. Rumours were rife and were encouraged by the whispering of theories. One in particular was prevalent — that the British were behind Montague's death.

The Wolves stayed in town for another week and heard that Mrs Montague had put her late husband's ship up for sale. A few enquiries to the gossipmongers revealed that hers was an arranged marriage. Montague was rumoured to have bought her from her impoverished family, and though he treated her well, she was still his property.

The last batch of slaves was sold off and Delfina insisted on buying a half-dozen young girls who, she said, would be set free as soon as they left America. Mike decided to leave before the Wolf girls could do any more than that. They were pretty fired up by the whole slave-trading revenge and weren't completely satisfied with the message left by the killing of Montague.

As it turned out he was too slow, for as the *Petrel* left port, smoke could be seen coming up from the slave market. By the time they were level with the centre of Snake Island, the smoke had flames leaping up through it.

"That looks bigger than the slave market," Mike said as he leaned on the stern rail next to Harry.

"The wind has shifted," Harry responded.

Mike sucked his teeth. "Probably spread into the town, then."

"Shame, some nice houses there," Harry said.

The girls whom Delfina had bought were lined up along the side of the deck forward of the mainmast. They were dressed nicely and had been told they were free.

"Does Delfina know what Beth is going to say when we get back?" Harry asked.

"I think she is in for a shock; Beth won't let her get away with merely freeing those girls. She will tell her she owes them a duty of care."

Mike was right, Beth told her protégée in no uncertain terms that she was responsible. The girls, all aged between sixteen and seventeen, were badly prepared for freedom, having been enslaved in Africa only a year before. They spoke no English and had no idea how to survive in American society.

"I hate to say this, but you would have done better to have bought girls who had been on plantations for a year or two," Mike said.

Delfina was having none of that and asked Bertram Berkley if they could be employed at the Den.

He replied, "They can be coffee pickers and go to school here. You know there is always a shortage of girls as there are always more men than women on the plantations?"

Delfina looked shocked, then angry.

"Hold your horses, young lady, I am not suggesting we *force* them into relationships. I am just saying they will attract the attention of the single men. You chose six pretty ones, so you wouldn't expect anything else."

He was right and she knew it. The girls were subtly different from the other girls at the Den, who originated from West Africa. Skin that was a lighter shade of brown, almond-shaped eyes and longer, prominent noses. This made them slightly exotic and was already gaining them admiring glances from the young men on the plantation.

The girls had picked up some English on the voyage from Georgia to Jamaica. One day Delfina took them to the teacher who ran the plantation school. He sat them down and asked their names.

"Ooli."

"Yuia."

"Ailine."

"Beomia."

"Nelma."

"Imani."

He wrote them in the school register, then turned to Delfina.

"Are you going to pay for their education?"

Delfina looked surprised; she had assumed the plantation paid for the school.

"Um, yes … I suppose so."

A short distance away Beth sat on the porch of the plantation house, lip-reading what was being said. She grinned.

"Something funny?" Sebastian asked her.

"Mr Charles has just asked Delfina if she will be paying for the girls' education."

"Did you put him up to that?"

"Of course!"

Meanwhile, Delfina swallowed. "How much will that be?"

"Six pence per girl per month."

"Oh."

She squared her shoulders. "That will be no problem, I can pay you for a year in advance."

She had about five pounds left in the stash which she had saved from her pay. The purchase of the girls' education would put a significant dent in that.

"As long as they are working, they will make enough to live on," the teacher replied. "I will teach them English and basic reading, writing and mathematics. If they wish to go further than that they will have to go to the school in Kingston."

"We will cross that bridge when we get to it," Delfina said, and smiled.

To aid their integration, Bert had the girls lodge with families, and as their language skills improved — surprisingly rapidly — their stories began to emerge. Ooli, Yuia and Nelma were from the Ovimbundu tribe; Ailine, Beomia and Imani from the Mbundu. They had all been put into slavery by their chiefs, who sold them to Arabic traders. Yuia, who was actually a daughter of her chief, told her foster family it was a common practice. Her chief had twenty wives and more children than he needed. Satisfied they were well taken care of, Delfina felt happy to leave the girls at the Den.

That was just as well, as all too soon Richard Brazier appeared and announced that the ships were ready to sail and moored in the Wag Water River. It was time to go home, but first Beth wanted an update on the situation in Gran Colombia. They would stop off at Barranquilla on the way.

Their arrival found Barranquilla subdued, to say the least. It was late April 1830 and the news was that Bolívar had resigned as dictator and was going into exile. The newspapers were full of this and attributed his resignation to poor health. Some speculated that he had contracted tuberculosis, others said he was just worn out. The federalists were taking over and greater autonomy would follow for the individual countries involved.

England

June 1830

They arrived in the Port of London in early June 1830. It was cold and wet, which made the capital's notorious smog lie low, close to the ground.

"God, this is horrible," Beth said, and grimaced as the ships were unloaded. The air was so badly polluted they could hardly see the carriages on the dock beside the ship. The air stank of sulphur and had a yellowish tinge to it.

"We should have debarked in Southampton," Sebastian said. "It would have been a longer road trip but at least we could have breathed."

The baggage loaded, they set out for the Stockley house in Grosvenor Square where they planned to overnight at least, depending on orders from above. The carriage drivers proceeded slowly, picking their way along the streets.

Beth looked out of the window. "These are perfect conditions for a hold-up."

Sebastian agreed and took his pistols from the carpet bag at his feet. Beth reached through the hidden "pocket" in her dress and drew the pistol holstered on her thigh. Sebastian reached out and touched it.

"It's still warm."

"You know all the nice things to say to a girl," Beth said, and kissed him.

There was a jolt as the carriage came to a stop. Beth sighed; London, if nothing else, was predictable. Someone banged on the door and a gruff voice shouted, "Get outta the carriage!" A dirty face appeared at the window and the man waved an old single-shot pistol.

Beth pulled the webbing that dropped the window and shot him in the face. He exhibited a modicum of surprise just as he keeled over backwards. More shots sounded from the girls' carriage behind them and then there was the sound of running feet.

Sebastian stepped out of the carriage and made his way around behind it to Beth's side, while she covered the approach. He found the would-be thief, or rather his body, with a neat hole in the bridge of his nose which had made his eyes cross in death.

"That's something you don't see every day."

Whistles sounded and a constable appeared out of the gloom. He saw Seb and skidded to a stop. More footsteps could be heard approaching.

"Morning, Constable," Sebastian said.

"Is everything alright, sir?"

Sebastian nudged the corpse with his foot. "This fellow and his friends tried to hold us up. I am Major Ashley-Cooper of the 95th Rifles. This is my wife. She shot him."

Beth smiled at the constable and held up her pistol.

Another constable arrived, then a sergeant.

"That's Billy Clements," one of the police officers said after bending over the body. "He didn't have crossed eyes last time I saw him, though."

"They did that after I shot him," Beth said.

"Can you come to the station and make a statement?" the sergeant asked.

"We are on our way to my father-in-law's house in Grosvenor Square, can we do it there?" Sebastian replied.

"Of course, sir."

"Excellent, hop up beside the driver and we will be on our way."

Their arrival at the house was busy. The sergeant waited patiently for the couple to be greeted by the lord and lady who owned it. The lord turned out to be Admiral Stockley, the Earl of Purbeck, and the sergeant was a little in awe of him. He also found out that the second carriage was full of armed people, just as the first had been. His day had become complicated.

The sergeant was asked to wait in an anteroom, where a maid served him with a mug of tea and some biscuits. Eventually a valet came and collected him, and he was brought into what he assumed was one of many reception rooms, where the couple and their people were gathered.

Now they were inside, he had a chance to look at the group. He realised they all had tanned skin. The woman, Bethany, was beautiful by any standards and had a soft honey glow to her complexion. The gentleman was darker and his hair sun-bleached. The four girls who had a Spanish look were dark-skinned anyway and the two other men that were part of the group were swarthy.

The sergeant began to question them. "Can I assume you were on your way from the docks when the incident occurred?" he said.

"Why, yes. We had just landed from Jamaica," Sebastian replied.

He made a note of this. "And at which dock did you land?"

"The Stockley berths in India Dock."

"Had you seen the individual identified as Billy Clements before the incident?"

"No, we could hardly find our own carriages, the smog was so thick. Who would expect London to be like this in the summer?" Lady Bethany said.

The sergeant tried again. "Can you describe the moments up to and during the encounter?"

Beth settled herself, ready to answer in detail. "We were chatting in the coach when it suddenly stopped. Then someone banged on the door next to me and shouted for us to come out. A face appeared at the window and the man brandished a gun. I dropped the window and shot him."

"Milady, do you habitually carry a gun?"

"Oh yes, all the time. We all do."

"May I see them?" the sergeant asked in a way that suggested disbelief. But fifteen pistols suddenly appeared. Lady Bethany had one, Lord Sebastian had two — and the other six had two each!

"What on earth ... ?" he exclaimed, just as Lord Stockley entered the room.

"Sergeant, may I have a word with you?" he said, and indicated he should join him in the hallway.

Once they were alone, he explained, "I can speed this up. Both Bethany and Sebastian work for me, in British Intelligence. They are returning from a mission in South America, where they have been for the last couple of years. They and their team are expected to be armed at all times. Your felons chose the wrong carriages to hold up and are lucky that only one of them got killed. No report is to be made, and the incident never happened."

"But the body, sir ..."

"Will be disposed of by my people, as will any others that turn up, as I am absolutely sure that more than one was shot."

The sergeant looked troubled; this was highly irregular. Marty took a purse from his pocket.

"This is to compensate you for your trouble. The government is grateful to you and the constables that keep our streets safe, but this is a matter of state security."

The next day, Marty asked Beth and Sebastian to meet him in his study.

"Your reports have been taken and noted. There is no more to do in South America and your next mission will not start for some time yet. So, I suggest you go down to Surrey and keep house for a while. The Wolves need to spend some time at the academy so you can have the house to yourselves."

"What about the Rifles, sir?" Sebastian asked.

"You are still on detachment and will remain so until we release you. Now run along and have some fun."

Surrey was a blessed relief after the polluted air of London. As they left the bowl-like dip in the ground that London was built in and emerged into fresh, if not damp, air, they could see the miasma behind them like some glowering, brooding organism that was choking London to death. At this time of year, it should be warm enough that the coal fires at the root of the problem were out. But this year was much colder than usual and exceptionally wet. Businesses in particular kept their furnaces running. Add to that the increase in steam engines that continuously pumped out smoke from the cheapest available coal, and the source of the problem was obvious.

They travelled down the Portsmouth Road, with the roof down on their landau so they could enjoy the weak sunshine that was beginning to peek through the clouds. The girls followed in a second coach and behind them the luggage in a wagon and four. Mike sat next to the couple's driver and Harry rode on the luggage wagon.

They were uninterrupted as they passed Chessington and Claygate, and stopped for lunch and to rest the horses at the Bear coaching inn in Cobham. They had made good time as the road had been recently paved as far as Chessington and was only now unpaved and muddy. Work to pave the whole road was in progress, but it was uncoordinated and patchy, being concentrated mainly around the towns.

Lunch was slabs of cold, good meat pie, fresh-baked crusty bread, freshly churned butter, chutney and cheese, all washed down with beer brewed in the small brewery attached to the inn. It was a rich ale, nutty and dark.

The last leg of their journey was slower as they crossed Wisley Common; the road was drying out, but being unpaved it was full of ruts which slowed them considerably. They arrived in Ripley mid-afternoon to a warm welcome from the full staff of the house.

Being on leave chafed at Sebastian, who was happiest when he was doing something. He waited patiently for the shooting season to start, and on 1 September he took a trip down to the New Forest to shoot black grouse. He broke out his newest acquisitions, a pair of James Purdey fifteen-bore percussion shotguns. These Damascus thirty-inch-barrelled masterpieces of the gun maker's art were muzzle loaded and the best that money could buy.

He took their farm manager, Bradley, as his loader, and a flat-coated retriever to fetch the kills. They drew lots for stands after being introduced to the rest of the guns and many of the beaters. As soon as they reached their stand, Sebastian and Bradley waited for the signal that the shoot could commence.

Sebastian missed his first bird. "Damn, but I am out of practice!"

"It will come, sir. They are new pieces as well for you to get used to," Bradley said kindly as he handed him his second gun.

"It's a good job my wife isn't here. She would be laughing like a drain!" Sebastian grimaced.

"Aye, I have seen her shoot."

"Exactly."

Another rose and flew over them. Sebastian raised his gun and fired in one movement. The retriever shot off to collect the bird, which was a fine cock. Bradley did a great job as loader, keeping him supplied with loaded pieces throughout the shoot so that he tallied fourteen brace of grouse for the day.

While he was in the New Forest, Sebastian took the opportunity to do a bit of stalking as well as shooting, since red deer stags were in season. For this he used a Purdey double-barrelled sixteen-bore rifle with ten-groove rifling that took a lead patched ball. Having two barrels made it unnecessary to carry two guns. He bagged a handsome four-point stag at two hundred yards which, when dressed, would go home with him.

When Sebastian returned home with his prizes for the kitchen, he found that his wife had been busy as well. She had joined the Surrey Union hunt based in Fetcham and was busy getting her horses fit for when the season started in November. Beth was the proud owner of a number of horses, some of which were retired as she had owned them since she was a teenager. For hunting she had bought, at auction, a three-quarter-bred mare cross with Irish draft; it had plenty of bone, lots of heart room, a short back and legs but strong hind quarters and shoulders. She was a prodigious jumper and could run all day. Beth named her Duchess.

Sebastian found his wife at the stables giving Duchess a rub down after a hack. She looked over the horse's back as he approached.

"Hello darling, did you hit anything?"

"I did, it's all down in the meat room. Grouse and a stag."

"Good, I like grouse."

"She is new, isn't she?" Sebastian asked, nodding at the horse, which he cast an expert eye over.

"She is," Beth said, and tossed him an apple. "Meet Duchess. Duchess, this is Seb."

Sebastian offered Duchess the apple on the flat of his hand. She took it, her soft lips nuzzling his palm.

"I bought her for hunting, she can clear five feet easily and can gallop all day."

Sebastian stuck his head into the stables.

"Looking for something?" Beth asked innocently.

"Where's mine?" he asked.

"Your what?" Beth rested her arms on Duchess's back.

"My hunter."

"You want to join the hunt?"

Sebastian approached her as if to give her a hug then reached out and started to tickle her. She squirmed and giggled in his grip.

"Stop!" she gasped.

"Where's my hunter?"

She wriggled free and took his hand, then led him around the stables to the paddock behind them. There stood a gleaming, very solid-looking stallion with a broad chest and very strong hindquarters. Sebastian whistled in appreciation. "He looks powerful."

The horse, which Beth had named Ulysses, perked up his ears at the whistle and trotted over to the fence. Beth gave Sebastian another apple.

"Where are you hiding them?" he said and offered it to his horse.

Bradley saw Ulysses later and was heard to comment he was made like a brick-built barn with a leg at each corner.

Their fun was interrupted at that point by the news that Sebastian had been made a Knight Commander of the Bath — a KCB — for service in the military and had to go to London for the investiture.

When the hunting season began, the riders of the Surrey Union gathered at the Running Horse pub, which was a forty-five-minute ride from Ripley. The hunt offered the couple the opportunity to socialise with the other landowners in the area, and their first outing was preceded by a round of introductions.

"May I introduce Sir Sebastian Ashley-Cooper and his wife Lady Bethany," the hunt master announced as they had their stirrup cup.

Some knew them by reputation, especially the women of Bethany's age group who had seen her on the London social scene.

"You have been away?" Lady Sophia Greenwood asked her.

"Yes, we have been on a diplomatic mission to South America for the last couple of years," Bethany replied.

This was heard by the fairly large group of riders gathered around them and one asked, "Is it as chaotic as the newspapers would have us believe?"

"It is. There are constant revolutions and bids to snatch power.

Bolívar was the only one who managed to tame it, but he has now retired because he is ill," Beth said.

The hunt master blew his horn, and the riders sorted themselves into order. Then one of the whippers-in blew his horn and the hounds bayed as they set off.

The rest of the day was spent galloping around the Surrey countryside. The couple's horses performed well, and they both chose to jump their fences rather than queue at the gates. Several foxes were chased but only one was run to ground and killed.

When the hunt was over and the horses had been cared for, the riders gathered for a drink at the Running Horse. Major Iain Fitzwilliams of the 7th Royal Fusiliers took up conversation with Sebastian.

"You still with the Rifles?"

"I am, but on detachment."

"Doing Wellington's dirty washing, eh?"

Sebastian smiled. "Diplomatic service. I was an envoy at the embassy in Bogotá. What has the Seventh been up to?"

"Two years in Malta, no hunting there worth a damn. It's good to be back."

"I joined a shoot down in the Forest; pretty good sport once I got my eye in. Got a buck as well."

At this point, Beth joined them.

"My wife, Lady Bethany," Sebastian explained.

"Good afternoon, sir," Beth said sweetly.

Fitzwilliam bowed. "I saw you jump that fence by the river. Impressive piece of riding."

"Why, thank you." Beth smiled. "I have a very good horse."

"You both have, where did you find them?"

"At an auction in Guildford," said Beth.

159

The conversation continued in this vein for a while and then they circulated. At around five o'clock the gathering broke up and they started the hack home. The horses were rested and wanted to run, so they let them.

It was Beth who spotted the body lying beside the road on Ockham Common. She pulled up Duchess abruptly, surprising Sebastian, who had to turn around and come back — by which time Beth had dismounted and was kneeling beside it.

It was a girl of around seventeen years old, and she was covered in mud and blood.

"Is she dead? Sebastian asked.

"Almost — she is breathing, but very shallowly. Can you go to a farm and get a cart?"

"We passed one a mile back. I'll go there."

Sebastian left at a gallop. Beth took off her cloak and gently rolled the girl onto it before starting a top-to-toe examination of her. She had clearly been beaten and when she checked, she found she had been raped as well. Someone had left her for dead and that made Beth very angry. She moved the young woman into a position where she was safe from choking if she vomited, and wrapped the cloak around her to warm her up.

Beth checked the ground around the site and the track. She noticed several footprints in the mud and when she stood back, she saw that there were three distinct sets in a circle with the girl's bare footprints in the middle. Then there was a mess of prints leading from there to the spot she had found her. In her mind's eye she imagined the scene. Three men had trapped the girl in the middle of them and pushed her from one to another, probably hitting her as they did. Then tiring of that sport, they dragged her to the spot where they raped her and gave her a final beating. On the track were an assortment of hoof prints and wheel ruts.

The sound of a cart coming down the road at a canter distracted her.

Sebastian arrived with the farmer and his wife. The wife practically leapt from the cart and rushed to Beth's side.

"Oh my Lord! The poor dear!" she cried as she looked down at the girl.

"Do you know her?" Beth asked as the men gently lifted her into the cart, which had a layer of hay on the bed.

"She's not from around here. I've never seen her before."

"Is there a doctor nearby?" Sebastian asked.

"Effingham be the closest, but he's old and won't come out this far," the farmer said.

Beth mounted her horse. "Get her to our house and I will fetch Rutherford from Guildford. He will come if I ask."

Assault and Battery

Ripley Court was only a mile or so away and they took it slowly, so as not to jar the poor girl too much. As soon as they got there, she was taken to a room, washed and dressed by a pair of maids and put into a bed.

The clatter of hooves announced the arrival of Beth and the doctor.

"Where are the farmer and his wife?" Beth asked as she showed Rutherford to the girl's room.

"Gone home. They wanted to get back before dark," Sebastian told her.

Beth sat and watched as the doctor repeated the examination she had made. The girl stirred as he did it and her eyes flickered, then opened. She looked terrified.

"It's all right," Beth said, and mopped her brow with a moist towel. "You are safe now. He is a doctor."

The girl looked into Beth's eyes, then relaxed and her eyes closed again.

Rutherford finished his examination. "Broken ribs, concussion, maybe a cracked skull as blood has come from her ears, bruises coming up everywhere. She is lucky you found her, or she would be dead."

"Not many people use that road. It's more of a track."

Rutherford asked if he could stay the night to continue treating the girl. Beth had a cot made up in the room. She checked on them both in the morning. The girl was sleeping and Rutherford looked tired.

"Go and have some breakfast. I will watch her," Beth said.

Rutherford left and Beth looked at the bruised face. Under the purple bruises she saw a pretty girl with blonde hair which had been shaved in a patch where Rutherford had stitched up a gash in her scalp.

Beth hummed a tune as she sat making notes of what she had seen on a pad with a pencil.

In time, the girl stirred and groaned. Her eyes flicked open again and she glanced around the room in a panic.

"Shh now, you are safe," Beth said.

The girl's eyes were of an icy blue and now they flicked to Beth. "Who are you?" she said. Beth noted her local accent.

"I am Beth, I found you beside the road. What is your name?"

The girl looked confused, "I don't remember, I can't remember anything. What happened?"

"You were attacked and badly hurt. You must stay in bed until you recover."

"My head hurts."

"I am not surprised, you were hit on the head and kicked in the ribs as well as punched." Beth didn't mention that she had been raped.

The girl started to cry, and Beth held her until she stopped.

"They raped me, didn't they? I am sore down there."

"Yes, I am afraid they did. When I find them, they will pay for that."

"She doesn't remember anything. Complete amnesia," Beth told Rutherford and Sebastian.

"Not uncommon in cases like this," Rutherford replied. "She will probably get her memory back in time, but whether she will remember the incident or block it off, I can't say."

Beth sat back and gazed up into the corner of the room. Sebastian braced himself.

"Well, if she can't tell us who attacked her then we will have to approach the problem from the other end," said Beth. "Do we have a map of the area?"

"Yes, I bought a full set of the new Ordnance Survey maps while we were in London."

Sebastian found the map that covered the relevant area and laid it out on the dining room table. Beth examined it and pointed to the spot where they had found her.

"We found her here. So, she was either coming from Ripley or from East Horsley. My guess is she was travelling from East Horsley to visit someone in Ripley or Send." She looked thoughtful. "I wish the Wolves were here. We could do with the manpower."

"Why don't you leave it to the constables?" Rutherford asked.

"Pfft, they won't do more than note it as an incident," Beth snorted. "No, we will find the perpetrators and put them before the magistrate."

Beth asked some of the staff to go around the villages knocking on doors and asking if they were expecting a visit from a relative or friend from outside the village. One by one they returned with nothing — until a maid-of-all-work, Emily, came with more positive news.

"The Arnolds in Send Marsh have family in East Horsley. They say they have a daughter who is seventeen and sometimes comes to visit."

"Go and bring them here, please."

Mrs Arnold and her daughter came and were taken up into the girl's room.

"Sarah, what have they done to you?" Mrs Arnold cried as soon as she laid eyes on her.

Sarah looked at her blankly. "Is that who I am?"

"She cannot remember anything," Beth said. "It's due to the head injury."

The daughter sat on the bed. "Sarah, it's me, Anna. You are my cousin, and you were coming to see me."

Sarah shook her head. "I don't know any of you."

Beth saw that Sarah was becoming distressed, so she asked the Arnolds to come and talk with her downstairs.

"So, her name is Sarah Arnold?" Beth asked.

"No, she is my sister's girl, she married a Shepherd."

"Sarah Shepherd, from East Horsley?"

"That's right, they live on Bluebell Lane."

"What does her father do for work?"

"Like his name, he is a shepherd on the Horsley Estate."

"Did Sarah work?"

"She helped out at the Wheatsheaf sometimes but stayed at home to look after her mother, who has dropsy in her legs."

Beth thanked them and told them that Sarah could stay at the house until she had recovered.

A new face appeared in the Wheatsheaf — a tall redhead. Dressed plainly and barefoot, she asked for work. The landlord saw her potential immediately, as his go-to girl had stopped coming around. The new girl worked for a shilling a week and room. She said her name was Beth and she came from Leatherhead. She looked to be in her late twenties, was very pretty and had no man as far as he could tell.

She was popular with the regulars as she was cheerful and flirted with all the men. However, she deftly avoided any lasting contact. Many a man made a grab for her, only to be left clutching air. She played no favourites and moved with the grace of a dancer — which gave old Ben the landlord an idea.

"If I get a couple of players together, would you dance?"

"What, for the customers?"

"Yes," he said, and grinned. "You will pull them in."

He was right: entertainment was scarce in the villages in the countryside. Men and women came from all around to see the show.

She stayed a month, then told him that she was moving on to Ripley where she had family. She noted that a couple of locals paid particular attention to that, and she was careful to keep an eye on the road behind her as well as ahead.

Beth was approaching Ockham Common when a cart overtook her. She recognised a couple of the men from the pub and waved. She checked the pistol in its thigh holster and the knuckle dusters tucked in her belt.

The fresh ruts in the track told her the cart had pulled off the main track onto a side track. She noted that the horse had a loose shoe that left a distinctive print. She cast her mind back to finding Sarah; had there been a similar track? She shook her head, it was too long ago to remember so fine a detail. A movement in the gorse bushes caught her eye and she made sure she didn't react — other than to slip her fingers through the knuckle dusters.

A squelch as someone trod in the mud behind her was all the warning she needed. She dropped to a knee at the same time as spinning around. The club that was aimed at her back flew over her head just as her right fist came forward and up, striking her would-be assailant in the groin.

His eyes crossed and the club fell from his fingers as he sank to his knees. No more than a squeak came from his mouth. Curses emanated from her right as a second man appeared out of the gorse; in his hurry he got tangled up in a bush. Beth waited until the man broke free and then swung a haymaker of a right cross, which contacted his cheek with an audible crack. He howled and clutched his face, which now had a tear from below his eye to his chin. She kicked him in the balls and followed that up with a left hook that put him on his back.

A third man erupted from the gorse and ran in the direction of East Horsley. She shook the brass knuckles from her right hand and drew her pistol, pulled back the hammer to full cock and took careful aim. The shot rang out and the man stumbled, hit in the right buttock. He looked back at her and limped away. She let him go, he would be easy to find.

The sound of hooves approached from the direction of Ockham and Sebastian and a constable galloped up. Sebastian looked at the man still lying prone in the mud and the other by the roadside whose face was bleeding profusely.

"You've been busy."

Beth smiled and put her gun away, causing the constable to raise his eyebrows as he caught sight of her legs as she pulled up her skirt.

"That one tried to club me, the other was coming to his aid. There is a third hobbling back to East Horsley with a bullet in his bum. They have a horse and cart up that side track somewhere."

The constable set off to pick up the runner while Sebastian found the cart. He returned leading the horse. "It's got a loose shoe."

"I know, they rode past me to set up their ambush," Beth said. She prodded the first thug with her toe. "Get in the cart. Help your friend."

Sebastian pulled a rifle from a saddle holster and covered them as they climbed in. Beth climbed up and took up the reins. She looked up the track.

"Constable's coming back," she said. "He has the third one."

The men were delivered to the magistrate at Guildford. All three were hurt in one way or another. A broken cheekbone, a split scrotum and badly bruised penis, and a hole in the arse. The doctor patched them up and Beth brought Sarah to the jail. She had been gradually getting her memory back, but the events of the day of her attack were still missing.

The men were held together in a cell and Beth brought Sarah to the door, accompanied by a constable.

"Look through the grille, see if you recognise any of them," Beth told her.

Sarah stepped forward and looked. Suddenly she went rigid, her hands at her face, then she fainted.

She came to lying on a chaise longue. Beth sat beside her. "It's alright, you are quite safe," she told her.

"Where am I?" Sarah asked.

"The magistrate's house. You fainted when you saw those men."

The magistrate sat across the room. He stood and walked over to stand beside her. "Young lady, you had quite a strong reaction. Did you recognise the men?"

Sarah looked at Beth, her eyes wide. Beth nodded.

"I did. They are Bert Selby, Trevor Rash and Jimmy Smith."

"Why did you faint?" Beth asked.

"I suppose it was the shock, ma'am, everything came back in a rush."

The magistrate leaned forward. "Are they the men that attacked you?"

"Yes, sir, they are," Sarah said, and started to cry. Beth held her and made comforting noises. "Oh, I wish I didn't remember it," Sarah wailed.

The men were brought before the magistrate. With Sarah's sworn testimony and Beth as a witness, their guilt was not in question, especially as Smith pleaded guilty and testified against the other two. Ultimately, the men were sentenced by the magistrate.

"Bertram Selby and Trevor Rash you have been found guilty of assault, causing grievous bodily harm and rape. On the count of assault, you are sentenced to the maximum that the law will allow, which is five years; for causing grievous bodily harm, ten years; and on the count of rape, five years. These sentences to be served consecutively."

The magistrate paused.

"However, as the Crown has requested that we reduce the numbers in our jails, you will serve your sentences in exile in Australia. There will be no parole, and you may not return to England for twenty years."

The two men were taken down by the bailiff with their heads hung low, leaving Smith on his own.

"Now to you, James Smith. As you gave testimony as to the actions of the other two offenders, and by their admission you only played a minor role and did not take part in the rape, you will serve five years in Andover jail with the possibility of parole after three years."

Beth was satisfied and Sarah much relieved that the men would be no threat again. Beth offered to take Sarah to Southampton so she could watch them be put aboard the convict ship.

"Thank you, ma'am, that would be good," the young woman replied.

They followed the prison wagon to the port. The men inside were shackled to ring bolts in the floor. When they got to the port, the converted frigate that would transport them was moored offshore, and a boat was sent across to take the convicts. Beth and Sarah sat in the landau and watched.

The guard was only armed with a truncheon and when he released Rash's shackle, the man struck him in the head with the chains and bolted. Beth was surprised at how fast he could move wearing leg irons, but kept calm and simply lifted the forward seat cushion in the landau. She lifted out a Durs Egg carbine that had been converted to percussion cap. It took her eight seconds to load it, then she brought it to her shoulder.

She took aim and fired. The rifled sixty-calibre bullet flew straight and true and hit Rash in the back of the neck. The impact sent him tumbling forward in a sort of forward roll — only he ended up flat on his back in a pool of blood.

Beth reloaded and gave the rest of the prisoners a pointed look. None of them moved, giving the guard time to regain his senses. The boat pulled up at the dock and a bosun's mate from the ship ran up the steps with a pair of marines at his back. They ran to where Rash lay. One had obviously never before seen a dead body that had been hit with a large calibre bullet in the back of the neck, because as the other marine rolled the body over, he took one look and threw up.

"You near on blew his head off, ma'am; the bullet took his spine out as good as a hangman," the older marine said when he returned to the coach.

Sarah stood up. "I want to see."

"Are you sure, miss? It's not a pretty sight."

But Sarah stepped out of the coach and walked to the corpse. She looked down at the face of the man who had raped her then drew back her foot and kicked him solidly in the ribs. She then spat in his face.

"Better?" Beth asked as Sarah rejoined her.

"Yes."

Captured

Sarah accepted Beth's offer for her to join her staff at the house and soon settled in. The permanent removal of Rash, and Selby being on his way to Australia, had settled the girl more than any treatment could.

Six months had passed and 1831 was just around the corner when the Wolves returned home for Christmas.

Beth was watching when Sarah first saw Harry, and she grinned as the girl flushed and went all shy. Harry, being typically male, didn't notice and neither did Mike, but Delfina and Paola did, and they nudged Netta and Alie. Paola took the initiative and went up to Sarah to introduce herself.

"Hello, I'm Paola. You're new, who are you?"

"I'm Sarah, I started three months ago."

Paola took Sarah by the hand and dragged her over to the other Wolves. "Everybody! This is Sarah. She is new here. Sarah, these are my sisters, Alie, Delfina and Netta." Netta signed, *Hello, nice to meet you*, which Paola translated. "Netta is deaf; we talk using sign language. This is Mike, he is the leader of the Wolves, and this is Harry."

As she got to Harry she pulled Sarah to stand in front of him, and as he looked at her she blushed. Harry did a double-take and when she looked at him with those ice blue eyes …

The relationship started slowly, which was understandable under the circumstances and Beth made sure to warn Harry about Sarah's history. She need not have worried; Harry was empathic and gentle in his courtship.

However, all good things come to an end, and at the end of January a courier arrived from London with a summons for the couple to attend her father at his office. It was signed *M*, so they knew this was official business.

London still stank and the air was full of smoke as they pulled up in front of the Foreign Office. Sebastian held out his arm to help Beth down and then she took it as they entered the building. The clerk at the entrance lobby nodded them through to the inner sanctum.

M's office was on the third floor, and they were greeted by Adam as they approached along the corridor. "Good afternoon, Lancelot, my lady Chaton." He bowed and then held out his arm to direct them into M's office.

Marty sat behind his desk and immediately came around to hug his daughter and shake hands with her husband. "You two look in fine health, even if your tans have faded," he said with a smile.

"Hard to keep a tan when it doesn't stop raining," Beth quipped. Then she asked, "What's the problem?"

Marty sighed, obviously troubled. "Belvedere has got himself locked up in a Bulgarian prison. It's a trumped-up charge, of course."

"That's not good, he knows who everybody is."

"That's exactly the problem. Bulgaria is an Ottoman state, and if they get it into their heads to torture him, well … he might break."

Beth looked at her father, he almost seemed not to age, but this was causing a wrinkle or two to show.

"How can we help?"

"Glad you asked," Marty said. "Get him back."

The *Fox* was waiting for Beth and Sebastian at Portsmouth. The Wolves accompanied them, of course, and Sarah came along as her lady's maid. Sarah was there for two reasons. The first was that she felt safe with Beth around and the second was that she had actually taken a real interest when the other girls trained. She had learned how to shoot a pistol and some unarmed combat. Harry had taken her under his wing and the two were generally accepted as being at the walking-out stage.

Richard greeted them at the entry port. "Welcome back. Where are we going? I was just told to provision for three months."

"Greece," Sebastian said. "The Port of Kavala."

Richard looked quizzical and walked over to the chart room, where he asked the master for a chart. He used a magnifier to examine the coast of Greece.

"There it is, right up in the north of the Aegean near Thessalonica. Why there?"

"It's the closest place to Bulgaria that isn't in Ottoman hands."

Richard looked at the couple and then at the Wolves.

"Tell me once we are at sea."

They set sail on the tide and as soon as they were out at sea headed west to gain sea room to pass the Bay of Biscay. Richard, Beth and Sebastian gathered in Richard's cabin.

"The Bulgarians arrested our man using trumped-up charges that he was responsible for the assassination of the Ottoman sultan," Sebastian explained.

"He wasn't?" Richard said sceptically.

Sebastian shook his head. "Actually no, he wasn't. He was on a watching brief only. We think the Bulgarians killed the sultan and are looking to shift the blame on to the British. Belvedere is being held in the Turkish Barracks, which is a sixteenth-century fort with dungeons."

Beth held up a docket with their briefing in. "Unfortunately, that is about all we know. We have the name and possible location of a contact and that is about it."

The voyage gave Beth time to study a pamphlet of Bulgarian phrases. After an hour she put it down.

"This is impossible. It's not a language, it's a bloody tongue-twister. Hello is *zdravejte*. There is no way we will be able to say anything apart from hello and goodbye."

Sebastian looked up from his book. "Well, we had better hope we find our contact, then."

Twenty days later, they came into Kayala Bay. They anchored off the town and a boat took the team ashore.

"I will wait here for as long as it takes," Richard told them.

"We will try and get a message to you," Sebastian said.

There was supposed to be a contact in the town who could guide them to the border, and Beth led them to the church of Saint Nicholas. When they got there, she covered her hair with a scarf and wrapped her cloak around her before entering. The church was empty apart from an old woman, who sat in the nave. Beth went to the altar and lit a candle; she placed it in the far right of the sand tray that the candles were pushed into and leaned it to the right. Then she took a seat in the front pew.

A priest came out and looked at the candle, then at Beth. He walked back to the door he had come in through. Beth stood and followed him through the door. The old lady snored.

"I am Father Marcus," he said quietly. "The spring is the best time for flowers."

"But the autumn is the best for fruit," Beth replied, and held out her hand.

He gave her his hand and she kissed his ring. "We need to get to Sofia," Beth said.

"You are here to get Belvedere?"

"Yes, do you have any information?"

The priest went to a desk, opened a drawer and took out a thin packet of papers. "This is all we have."

Beth scanned them; there was a drawing of the barracks and a map showing where it was in relation to the town. Notes told of the number of troops stationed there.

"You will need horses for your pilgrimage to the Cathedral of St Alexander Nevsky," Father Marcus said.

"Will you lead us?" Beth asked.

"Of course, my child." Marcus grinned.

The port town was a centre for trade and regular convoys of pack horses and wagons made their way to destinations across northern Greece and into western Bulgaria. They needed to get all eight of them to Sofia, which was 170 miles away. Father Marcus took them to a breeder who had riding and pack animals for sale, and they found themselves at a farm with horses in the fields. A large Greek stepped out of the house to greet them.

"What do you want?"

Father Marcus stepped forward. "My friends here want to buy ten horses."

The breeder kissed the Father's ring then looked the team over, noting the girls and their weapons. He finished his appraisal by giving Beth the once-over.

"Ponies will do for them."

"They will have to carry us all to Sofia," Sebastian said.

The breeder gave him a long, slow look. "What do you want to go there for?"

Sebastian stared at the man. "A friend."

"My horses are bred to work, not ride."

"But they are broken to the saddle," Beth said, and stepped forward. Her cloak opened, revealing the fighting leathers underneath.

The breeder looked at her, then pointed to a horse in a corral. "That one isn't. If you can stay on him, I will sell you the horses."

Father Marcus went to object, but Beth touched his arm. She shed her cloak and walked to the corral. The big black stallion snorted and trotted towards her, stopping six feet away. *He's got a lot of Arab in him*, she noted, looking at his head.

Beth climbed through the pole fence and held out her hand. In it was an apple. She cooed soft words to the animal as she approached and he stretched his neck forward for the apple, which she let him take. Then she turned and slowly walked away at an angle to him. The horse snorted, tossed his head and then followed her. She stopped, and he stopped too, keeping his distance. She looked at him over her shoulder.

"What is she doing?" Father Marcus said, fascinated by her actions.

"Making friends," Sebastian answered.

Beth looked forward again and took several more steps. The stallion followed. She stopped again and this time he took the extra few steps to come up beside her.

She gave him another apple.

Where does she hide them? Sebastian thought.

The stallion stood and let her stroke his head. He nuzzled her shoulder. Beth reached out and took a handful of mane. The stallion didn't react. Running her hands down his neck she worked her way to his flank. He looked back at her, eyes bright and intelligent. Her hands made their way up onto his back; her left moved forward and grabbed the mane again. She jumped and laid her body across his back, talking to him all the time. As her weight came onto him he skipped sideways, then forwards. Beth stayed in place, talking softly to him all the time.

He settled, and Beth just stayed where she was for a couple of minutes before sliding down to stand beside him. Another apple was offered and accepted.

Beth took a deep breath and, holding his mane in her left hand, swung herself up so she straddled his back. Her long legs gripped the barrel of his chest. The stallion stood rigid for a second then neighed in outrage and bucked. Beth kept her seat, moving with him. He jumped forward, so she kicked him on and in surprise at the command he walked forward then remembered someone was on his back. He reared; she handled that masterfully.

"Open the gate!" she called as his front feet touched the floor. Mike ran forward and unhitched the gate to swing it open. The stallion, seeing a route out, shot forward. Beth gave him his head.

"She's crazy!" the breeder said, seeing his prize stallion disappearing into the distance.

Sebastian grinned. "Just wait."

The stallion ran like the wind and Beth let him, guiding him with her knees. Eventually he slowed to a canter, then a trot, and she steered him back to the corral.

The breeder stood open-mouthed as Beth rode the stallion up to them and stopped him directly in front of the breeder.

"Now," Beth said. "About those ten horses …"

The line of horses made its way up into the mountains with Father Marcus in the lead.

"Presumably that distance of one hundred and seventy miles was measured on the map?" Beth asked Sebastian, who rode beside her.

"Yes, I fear it may work out to be closer to two hundred with these mountains," Sebastian replied. He dropped back behind Beth as the track narrowed. There was a sheer drop of four hundred feet to their right.

Beth was riding a bay mare; the stallion wasn't for sale, and anyway, he needed a lot of schooling before she could ride him in these conditions. The track widened again as it sloped down into a broad valley with a village at the bottom.

"We will stay there overnight," Father Marcus called out.

Beth looked up at the sun that was behind a thin layer of cloud. It would get dark early in the mountains. As it was, the valley was already in twilight when they got to the village. They dismounted in the courtyard of a tavern.

Father Marcus slipped from his saddle and rubbed his backside. "This is a regular stop for the traders who travel to and from Bulgaria, though I have to admit they take a longer route that avoids the mountains. The boys will look after the horses."

Stable boys came and took their horses as they dismounted. Beth gave them a small coin each and told them to rub the horses down and give them some oats. The Wolves grabbed their baggage from the pack horses.

Inside they found a clean, well-kept establishment that was around half full of men drinking ouzo and smoking pipes. The landlord met them and bowed to the priest.

"My son, we need rooms for the night."

The landlord scratched his ear and looked the party over. "I have four rooms, that's all."

"That will suffice," Beth murmured from behind the priest's back.

"Perfect." Father Marcus beamed.

The rooms worked out well. The girls had two beds in theirs, which they shared. Mike and Harry had the same, and Beth and Sebastian shared a largish bed. Father Marcus had a room to himself. They ate in the bar — a rich, slow-cooked lamb dish, prepared with vegetables and herbs. They washed it down with locally made red wine that was fruity and strong.

They slept well; the beds were comfortable, if a little soft. They rose before dawn, breakfasted on fresh bread, yoghurt, ham and cheese and were ready to leave as the sun rose over the mountains.

"We will stop once more before the border," Father Marcus told them as they mounted.

The border, when they reached it, was a non-event. There was no checkpoint, and they simply rode across. Apparently, Bulgaria and

Greece had been on peaceful terms since Greek independence. The terrain didn't improve — if anything, the Bulgarian mountains were higher and steeper. They made their way through snow-capped mountains to a monastery.

"This is the Rila Monastery," Father Marcus told them as they approached a series of buildings with richly decorated, arched colonnades and a red-and-yellow-brick church. "We will stay here tonight. Ladies, keep your heads covered at all times, and all of you stay silent. I will do all of the talking with the monks."

Scarves were tied to cover their hair and everyone made sure their weapons were out of sight. The monks were fairly friendly and one or two even smiled as they showed the visitors to their rooms.

It's a cell! Beth thought as she was taken to a room with a narrow cot that took up one side of it. Apart from the cot there was a jug and bowl on a stand. She would not be sleeping with Sebastian tonight!

Food was served in a refectory to the sound of monks singing somewhere in the depths of the building. It was solid fare, but well-cooked and tasty. Breakfast was early, and when they took to their horses they found that loaves of fresh bread and cheeses hung from their saddles.

They continued their journey through a forest that smelled of pine and wild garlic before emerging into a wide valley that was covered in fields.

"We will enter Sofia once we get through those hills ahead," Father Marcus said.

Sebastian looked at them.

"I hope there is a pass."

"Do not worry, there is. From here on, we are back in civilisation."

Jailbreak

They went to the cathedral and Father Marcus introduced them to Bishop Petar Kostoff, who spoke Greek.

"Welcome my children, you have travelled far. The church has a hostel where pilgrims can stay. It is secluded and the authorities leave it alone."

Beth recognised an ally when she saw one, even if public appearances suggested otherwise. She understood why the bishop wanted to have deniability when it came to helping his Greek friends. As he talked to them, she came to understand — from little hints he gave — that he was a Bulgarian nationalist and took the view that "an enemy of my enemy is my friend".

They slept in the hostel in the now-familiar cells: they had expected this, as Father Marcus told them before they got there that it was run by monks from the same order as those they had met in the mountains.

The barracks where Belvedere was being held was right behind the cathedral. It housed a regiment of janissaries, as well as many political prisoners in the dungeon.

On the day of their arrival, Beth and Sebastian, Mike and Paola, and Harry and Netta took a walk. Sebastian's stride was almost military as he paced out the dimensions of the walls.

"You look like you are up to something, walking like that," Beth said.

"We need the dimensions."

Beth sighed. "You are thinking like a soldier, not a spy. We need the layout and the location of the entrance to the dungeons. Dimensions are secondary."

Sebastian nodded towards a pair of guards patrolling along the wall that ran beside the road. "We need to get past them first."

Beth smiled. "Yes, they take thirty-two seconds to walk the length of the wall. From the point they cross the gate to the time they turn around is fifteen seconds."

Sebastian rolled his eyes. Beth didn't let him off. "Netta is memorising every aspect of the barracks, and we will get her higher so she can look down into it. Then she will produce pictures and plans."

Sebastian gave up: Beth was the expert here. She frowned as a thought came to her. "What we could do is to find someone who has been a prisoner here."

"How are you going to do *that*?" Sebastian asked.

Beth smiled. "I will ask a priest."

Netta was busy sketching what she had seen. They had found an empty house with a roof that overlooked the barracks, and she had all the images in her head. Beth went to find the bishop.

Bishop Kostoff was in his study when Beth knocked on his door. He was not surprised to see her. She was dressed like a Bulgarian woman, and he nodded in approval.

"What can I do for you, my child?"

Beth treated him to her smile. "I want to talk to someone who has been a prisoner in the barracks."

The bishop nodded and stroked his long grey beard. "Come back this afternoon, after prayers."

Beth returned with Netta at the appointed time. The bishop had a man with him who was missing a hand and had scars on his face.

"This is Dimitar. He was confined and tortured in the barracks for three years."

Beth looked into Dimitar's eyes. They were defiant, even though she could see his pain in them.

"Did they take your hand?"

"Not directly; they broke all the bones in it trying to get me to give the names of all my comrades. It had to be taken off after I was released."

Beth nodded sympathetically. "If we show you some drawings of the barracks, can you tell us where the entrance to the dungeon is?"

Dimitar nodded and Netta laid out her drawing of the barracks from above.

"These two buildings are the living quarters. These are store rooms. This is the commandant's office, and this little building beside it is the entrance to the dungeon."

"Is it locked?" Beth asked.

"Yes, with an iron bar and padlock. The key is in the commandant's office."

Beth had Netta make notes on the drawing. "How many guards are down in the dungeon?" she asked when Netta had finished.

"Is she deaf?" the bishop asked.

"Yes. How many guards?"

"None, they can't get out."

"When and how are they fed?"

"Everything is lowered through a trap door once a day."

Netta signed back, "Where is it?" and Beth translated. Dimitar pointed to a dome in the centre of the barracks between the two living-quarter buildings.

"In the centre of that dome. That is the roof of the dungeon."

The team gathered. Beth briefed them. She had Netta's pictures pinned up on the wall.

"This is the barracks. Tonight is a full moon and at two in the morning the sisters and I will infiltrate it and extract Belvedere. Mike, Harry and Sebastian will provide cover from these three rooftops using the airguns. I've chosen this time as it's two hours into the guards' shift."

The air rifles were Austrian, made by Girandoni, and had an air reservoir in the butt. They carried twenty 0.46-inch balls in a tube magazine and fired them at six hundred feet per second. They each had two spare air flasks and a pump. They were quiet and didn't make smoke. However, they were deadly in the right hands.

The briefing continued with timings and questions until everybody was happy.

That night at midnight Beth and the girls prepared. Knives and clubs were the weapons of choice. Each had their preference. A strong thin rope of woven silk was extended and inspected before being rewound in a skein that could be slung over a shoulder. They were dressed in black linen coveralls with hoods and mesh veils, soft-soled shoes and black calfskin gloves that were so fine, Beth could feel the eyes on a fly through them.

The boys stripped and serviced the airguns. The main point of attention was the leather gaskets of the reservoir, which were kept moist to ensure a good seal. The flasks were filled and they too dressed in black coveralls.

They moved out at one thirty and slipped between shadows cast by the moon. They split as the boys went to their vantage points that overlooked the barracks. From there they could cover the girls if they had to.

At two, the girls were in position in the alley opposite the barracks. Beth watched as the sentries crossed by the gate. She moved fast and was across the road in seconds with the girls right behind her. She put her back to the wall and cupped her hands. At the count of sixteen, Paola was flipped up onto the wall, and she was followed by Alie then Delfina. Beth reached up and the girls grabbed her hands, allowing her to fold upwards to gain the top as well.

All of this was timed to perfection. The guard turned at the end of his patrol and was none the wiser.

The four dropped to the ground in the shadow of the wall. Delfina and Paola slipped across the open square to the doors of the living quarters. There they jammed the locks with spikes to stop anyone getting out.

Beth and Alie made their way to the domed roof and the hatch. Beth picked the padlock that held the locking bar in place and slid it free. She took the rope from her shoulder and tied it around her so she could be lowered through the hatch. Delfina and Paola arrived, and the three girls took up the rope. Beth slipped over the edge and was lowered into the dungeon. Once she was below the roof she opened the shutter on a lamp. Below her was a mass of bodies. The air stank. She was close to the bottom and looking for a space to put her foot when the whites of the eyes of the man below her suddenly shone in the lamplight.

"Give me some space!" she hissed in Greek.

The man looked shocked and stood up, making a gap. He nudged someone else and like a ripple, the whole place came awake. She untied the rope and tugged it. The girls pulled it up.

"SSHHHHUUSSH!" Beth whisper-bellowed, and the place went quiet. She realised she must look menacing with the hood and veil in place so pulled it back, revealing her face.

"I am looking for the Englishman," she hissed. A muttering spread around the room, then a hand touched her, and she looked around. It was a young boy and he beckoned her. She followed him to a niche in the wall. Within it lay Belvedere.

"Oh my, what have they done to you?" she said.

He opened his eyes. "Beth?"

"Yes, it's me. I've come to get you."

"Too late. They broke my hands, and more. I'm dying. I didn't tell them anything."

Anger raged through her; somebody would pay for this. She took in a deep breath and nearly choked on the stink. She checked his hands; they were useless. Systematically, every bone had been broken. She ran her hands over his ribs. Several were broken, and at least one had punctured a lung as she could hear it suck as he breathed. She couldn't get him out in this state.

"Help me die," he said. "A good clean death is better than this."

"Peter," she said, using his real name, "I will tell them about this at home. Who did this to you?"

"Pasha Mohamed ben Yusaf. He is the head of the Ottoman secret police in Sofia. He was the one who killed the sultan. It's a typical Ottoman power grab."

He broke down coughing and blood ran from his mouth.

"Tell my mother I love her."

"I will," Beth said, then she slipped the stiletto between his ribs and into his heart. She felt it stop beating as he sighed and lay back.

"You," she said to the boy. "You are Greek?"

"I am."

"Come with me."

She returned to the hatch, ignoring the many hands that reached out to her. She shone the light up and the rope snaked down.

"I cannot take you all," she said in Greek, "but I can take one. This boy will live and tell of what is going on here. The revolution and independence will come."

The men cheered as the word was passed around by those who spoke both Greek and Bulgarian. Beth hoped the dungeon was soundproof.

She tied the boy to the rope and gave it a tug. The girls pulled him up. When the rope returned, she wrapped it around one of her wrists and gave it a tug as she scanned the faces below in the light of the lamp. She would not forget.

Revenge

They made a clean exit from the barracks, as Sebastian had the clever idea of setting up a diversion. He and Mike stood at the corner of the wall and threw stones at the sentries, both of whom ran to that end of their patrol line and threatened to shoot them. While the sentries were distracted, the girls slipped over the wall with the boy and got away.

The next morning, Mike and Sebastian stood over a tub of cold water and handed the boy a bar of soap. "Keep scrubbing, you still stink," Sebastian said in Greek.

The boy, whose name was Niko, picked up the soap and sniffed it. It smelt of roses. He shrugged and applied it to his untidy mop of hair. At this point the bishop, who had heard that there was a new addition to the team, wandered over.

"So, this is your rescued orphan?"

"Yes, your eminence, we are trying to get the stink of the jail out of his skin," Sebastian answered.

"Cleanliness is next to godliness."

Niko snorted as if to deny that.

"What happened to your parents?" the bishop asked.

"They were killed when I was a baby. My aunt cared for me and then she was killed when a Turkish soldier raped her."

"How old were you then?"

"I don't know how old I am; it was two years ago."

"I am sorry for that. Why were you in the prison?" the bishop asked sympathetically.

"I was working for the Englishman; he treated me well. He was my friend."

The bishop sighed. "So young for so much loss. God bless you, my child." He walked away, muttering.

"Do you know why Peter was arrested?" Beth asked Niko.

"He knew that Pasha Yusaf had killed the sultan, and somehow the pasha found out. They were looking for someone to blame for the killing and they chose him. They tortured him for the names of other British agents and to confess to the killing. He never did."

"You were working with Peter ... What did you do?"

Niko's head rose proudly. "I watched the offices of the secret police. Nobody notices a boy in the streets."

Sebastian interjected, "How come they picked you up at the same time as Peter?"

"I lived in his house. We were asleep when they came."

"Together?"

Niko looked confused by that question. "No, I had a room of my own."

"Is there something I should know about Peter?" Beth asked Sebastian as they sat by a fountain in the cathedral grounds later that day.

Sebastian sighed and looked her in the eyes. "He was a good agent, but he was also a homosexual."

Beth looked surprised. "I never knew."

"It was kept quiet as long as he was discreet. Your father knew."

"Do you think ... ?"

Sebastian smiled sadly. "That he and Niko ... ? No, boys were not his style or interest."

"How old do you think Niko is?"

"I would guess sixteen or thereabouts."

The subject was abruptly changed when Niko came into the courtyard. He was squeaky clean, had received a haircut and was dressed in newish clothes. "Well, look at you!" Beth exclaimed.

Niko did a twirl, then bowed. "It will be no good for watching though, I would stand out like a shiny nail."

"Oh, we can dirty you up again if need be. I want you to sit with Netta and describe the secret police headquarters to her."

"How can I do that? She cannot hear or talk."

"One of the others will sign for you."

Niko looked puzzled. "Sign?"

Beth signed *hello* then continued to sign as she talked. "Like this. It's how we talk to her."

Niko looked at her hands, his eyebrows raised in surprise. "That said what you just said?"

Beth laughed. "Yes, all of it."

Niko, Mike and Netta sat together under a tree. Niko described what he had seen, Mike translated it to sign language and Netta drew it.

Niko stopped her and shook his head. "Not like that. May I?" He took her charcoal and made an adjustment that was artistically as good as Netta's work.

She looked at him in surprise. "You can draw?"

"I can make pictures. Can you teach me to sign?"

Netta agreed eagerly. She had never met a boy who could draw like her before. Between the two of them, they produced an almost lifelike representation of the building from three sides. She was more precise than Niko, whereas he tended more to give the impression of what he had seen.

Beth was impressed and sat with the Wolves around the pictures. Sebastian translated for Niko.

"How high is this window?" Delfina asked.

"A bit higher than I am tall," Niko replied.

"We could use that as our entry point. Beth can reach the catch from the ground," Delfina suggested.

She was right: Beth was a good six inches taller than Niko, who, like most Bulgarian boys of his age, was around five feet three.

Niko had also told them that the pasha lived in the headquarters in an apartment on the top floor. He was paranoid and the building was constantly guarded inside and out by men he trusted.

"There will be no way to do this without a lot of bloodshed," Sebastian said.

"That's alright," Beth replied, and looked at him defiantly.

Sebastian gave her a hard look, which she returned. He shook his head. "Alright, we will do it your way. Who goes into the building?"

"You, Mike and Harry will be on sniper duty. The area is well lit, so you should have no trouble picking off the outer guards."

"All of them?" Mike asked.

"Yes, all of them — when they get to the far ends of their patrols. We will deal with the two on our side of the building."

The pasha had four sets of guards patrolling each face of the building in pairs. "Would it be better if you entered through two points?"

192

Sebastian asked. "That way you divide the inside guards, so they won't gather to oppose you."

Beth considered this. "As we don't know the interior layout beyond a best guess based on similar buildings, I would rather we stuck together and moved in waves."

Sebastian knew what she meant. With four of them they could work in pairs, and while one pair dealt with a guard, the second pair would move ahead, and so on.

"We clear the building one floor at a time, moving up after each level is secured. We keep it quiet, using knives and our new air pistols."

The "new air pistols" were, like their rifle counterparts, built on the Girandoni principle with changeable air flasks and tube magazines that held six .42 balls. They were effective at short range — that is, up to about twenty feet — against a human. They had been around since the beginning of the century and the Toolshed, the Secret Service's workshop of useful tools and gadgets, had refined them, making them usable in situations like this.

That night, at just after midnight when the streets were empty, shadowy figures moved across the rooftops. They leapt from one roof to another across the narrow streets and made no noise that could be heard at ground level. The three moved to individual houses that gave them a clear line of sight to the headquarters of the Ottoman secret police.

Simultaneously, another group of four dark figures made its way through the streets to the courtyard of a house next to the same building.

When everyone was in position, the song of a nightjar rang out.

Sebastian watched his quarry approach the end of their patrol along the front of the building. He took careful aim at one of the men — the range was around twenty yards and he targeted a point at the base of the skull. He squeezed the trigger gently; the mechanism was smooth. The bullet left the barrel at almost a thousand feet per second and the man crumpled as his spine was cut, dead before he hit the ground. His companion looked at him in shock, then looked up. A hole appeared in his forehead, and he collapsed on top of his comrade.

Sebastian re-cocked the gun and was on the lookout for any more targets when a guard ran from the side of the building that Harry was covering. He took him down with a body shot to the chest and then shot him in the head for good measure.

Harry dropped his first target in a similar fashion to Sebastian's opening attack. However, when he tried to re-cock his gun, it jammed. The second guard bolted to the front and started to shout as he turned the corner, but that shout was cut off abruptly.

Mike had no such trouble. Both of his targets died within seconds of each other. They were walking one in front of the other, so he took the rear one first and the second in identical fashion. *Just like shooting geese.*

Beth and Paola slipped over the wall of the courtyard after the guards had passed. Beth had an eight-inch dagger and Paola one of her favourite punch daggers. Beth moved to the right, so Paola crept up on the man on the left. They moved simultaneously, each girl's left hand covering their target's mouth while their right thrust forward … and there the similarity ended.

Beth's blade slipped downwards between the third and fourth rib, shredding a lung and piercing the heart. Paola was shorter and couldn't get the angle for that thrust, so she went for the kidneys. Four rapid punches to the kidneys had her victim fold and then a final punch to the neck, below the ear, severed his artery and main vein.

"Messy," Beth said, looking at the large pool of blood as Paola cleaned her dagger on the dead man's cloak. Paola shrugged; he was dead, wasn't he?

Beth moved to the window and pulled a slim jim from her belt. The sprung steel strip slipped between the window and the frame and, when slid up, opened the catch. Delfina stepped up and offered her cupped hands to boost Beth through the window. Paola followed, then Alie, before Beth reached down, grabbed Delfina's hands and pulled her up.

The room was empty and there were a series of soft clicks as they cocked their air pistols. Paola moved to the door and tried the knob — it opened. The hall outside was lit by lamps, and a small mirror was used to scan the corridor. She held up two fingers, folded one down and pointed left then raised the second and pointed right.

In the meantime Beth had taken a small flask from her pouch and, using a straw, oiled the door's hinges. Delfina and Alie moved up, pistols at the ready. Beth held the doorknob and when Paola moved back, pulled open the door. The sisters moved through the door together and stood back to back in the corridor. Several soft *phuts* were followed by the sound of bodies hitting the floor. Beth stepped out, followed by Delfina. They moved to the right towards the open end of the corridor.

Delfina and Alie checked their victims then proceeded to the closed end to check the door at the end. It was locked, so they moved back up to join the others.

A mirror was employed again to check around the corner. Beth held up one finger, raised her pistol to the ready and stepped forward. *Phut, click, phut.* She stepped forward and Paola followed.

Delfina and Alie moved ahead. Another man died, shot at point-blank range through the temple.

The ground floor was clear. They replaced the pressure flasks and filled their magazines before moving to the stairs. Delfina and Alie covered Beth and Paola as they moved up to halfway, where they stopped and covered the top of the stairs while the other two passed them to the top.

There were just three guards on that floor. One died in his sleep, his throat cut; the other two were shot. That left just the one guard at the top of the stairs to the pasha's apartment.

Beth took the direct approach; she walked up the stairs and as her head came up above the top stair, she raised her pistol and shot him in the face. She cocked and fired again. It was not a clean kill and his heels drummed on the floor as he died.

The sound of someone moving came from the other side of the door. "Burak?"

The knob turned. Beth waited until the door moved a mere fraction, then kicked it with all her might.

There was a grunt as the door crashed inwards. The room was lit by candles. Beth moved in fast, with the rest of the girls behind her.

The pasha was on his back, blood pouring from his nose — it had taken the full impact of the door. He was dazed and the girls tied his hands behind him before sitting him up.

Beth pulled up a chair and placed it in front of him, with the back towards him. She sat with her arms resting on the back and her legs on either side, a position calculated to offend the pasha.

She pulled off the hood and veil. The pasha's eyes widened as the rest of the girls followed suit.

"*Kadınlar mı? Bu nasıl bir büyücülük?*" (Women? What witchery is this?) he said in Turkish.

Beth poked his nose. "Speak Greek."

"Who are you?"

"Your worst nightmare. You killed a friend of mine. The Englishman." Beth was icily calm as she spoke.

"He killed the sultan!"

Beth poked his nose again. It had been broken and the poke hurt like hell. "Naughty! You know as well as I do that he didn't. You did."

The pasha struggled to his knees. "He was a spy, he paid the price."

Beth spat in his face. "So am I — and now you will."

The door opened and Beth looked around expecting perhaps Sebastian, but she was surprised when she saw that it was Niko.

"What are you doing here?"

"He tortured my friend."

Beth looked at the boy and saw determination, fear and anger. "What do you want?"

The pasha went to interrupt but Paola kicked him in the side to shut him up.

"I want to be the one to kill him."

His lip trembled. Beth stood and put her hands on his shoulders. "Have you killed anyone before?"

"No ... well, not directly. I caused a man to fall off his horse and break his neck."

Beth looked him in the eyes and saw the need. "This will be far more personal. Are you ready for that?"

Niko nodded and she handed him her dagger. She gently led him to stand beside the pasha and pointed to a spot on his neck below his ear. "Stand in front of him to avoid the blood, hold his head up by the hair with your left hand and then push the dagger in there for at least half its length. Pull it forward as you pull it out, it will cut his jugular vein and carotid artery."

The room was silent except for the sound of the pasha begging for mercy. Niko did as Beth instructed. He stood in front and slightly to the side of the pasha, wrapped his left hand in the man's hair and pulled his head up and to the left. He looked him in the eyes and said, "You tortured my friend and your men killed my aunt when they raped her. This is for them."

The knife flashed in — once, then again. Blood spurted. The pasha cried out once, then collapsed. In around ten seconds he was dead.

There was a whimper from the back of the room. Alie moved immediately and returned with a naked young woman.

Niko, who was still looking down at the pasha, looked up and saw her. "That is his mistress," he said.

Beth looked at the woman, who was looking at the pasha's body and crying sadly. She couldn't leave any witnesses. She stepped past her, drew her air pistol, cocked it and shot her in the back of the head.

"Let's get out of here. Burn it."

The girls set fire to the room and every other room in the building on their way down to the ground floor. Sebastian and the boys were waiting in the entrance, a pile of bodies beside them.

"Oh good, you cleaned up," Beth said, and kissed him.

The team, including Niko, was out of the city before dawn. It had been Beth's intention to leave him behind originally, but now he had been blooded she felt a responsibility for him. He was quiet and a little withdrawn as he rode one of the pack horses. Netta rode beside him and her presence gave him comfort.

Father Marcus rode ahead. He had said nothing when Sebastian woke him in the early hours of that morning. He just saddled his horse, tied his small pack to the saddle and mounted. He did see the flames from the burning headquarters, which by that time were spreading through the Turkish quarter, and he made the sign of the cross in that direction.

The bishop watched them leave from the window in his room that overlooked the courtyard, and smiled as he blessed them.

Reassignment

It was March 1831 by the time they got back to England. By then, Netta and Niko were an item, even though she was at least two years older than him. He had learned English, knew how to sign and was a promising agent. Beth wrote in her report that he should be admitted to the academy for training and would be an ideal candidate for deployment to Greece or Bulgaria.

They went to the house after a short stay in London. Surrey was pretty at the end of winter; it was enjoying an early spring and the trees were covered in buds. M sent a letter saying that Niko would join the academy in the summer. Another letter from him, written this time as her father, invited them to Cheshire for Easter. They accepted, of course.

The temperature dropped again in early April and it seemed there may be another snowfall, as had been the case in 1830. That previous year had seen an abnormal amount of snow, and Dickens wrote "Christmas at Dingley Dell", which was published in *The Pickwick Papers*.

Coaching to Cheshire would take too long, and with the risk of late snow they decided to go to Poole, from where the *Fox* and *Cub* would take them and their Dorset relatives up to Liverpool. It was just before they left that Beth started to get morning sickness.

They told no one outside their immediate circle, although the household and the Wolves knew of course, and there was a feeling of happiness throughout the house. The journey down to Poole was comfortable for Beth, as her ever-doting husband went out and bought a new carriage with the latest suspension and made sure that foot heaters were in place, with plenty of blankets and furs to keep them warm.

Beth was happy — a baby would complete their marriage — but taking it easy was not in her make-up. When they arrived in Poole, she took charge of the transfer of the baggage and presents to the ships. The rest of the Stockleys met them there and she organised who got what cabin in which ship. Her uncles, aunts and cousins were well used to Caroline, Beth's mother, and noted how similar the two women were.

However, Beth's happiness was not fated to last. As they rounded the *Lizard*, she had cramps in her abdomen during the night and found blood spots on her sheets in the morning. Her morning sickness had disappeared.

Sebastian woke to find her crying. "What's wrong?" he said as he took her in his arms.

"I've lost the baby," she said and showed him the blood.

He took her in his arms.

"Shh, you can't be sure of that. Annabel will be at the house." Annabel was the wife of the Special Operations Flotilla's physician, Shelby, and a doctor in her own right — although not one of the medical institutions would certify her as such.

* * *

Liverpool was covered in a layer of slushy snow, and Sebastian sent a fast courier to the house to let them know they had arrived. They took rooms in a hotel for the night and, as expected, by midday a line of carriages and a couple of carts were lined up outside of it to take them to the house. It was all rather jolly with the children playing around the carriages as the adults got organised, but Beth was crying inside.

Finally, with everyone and the baggage loaded, they set off. The girls sat in the coach with Beth and Sebastian. Harry, Mike and Niko sat on top. The temperature had risen from around freezing in the morning to a balmy thirty-six degrees and as they left Liverpool, a light snow began to fall. The countryside looked enchanting. Icicles hung from the eaves of houses and the fields were white.

The road was, however, treacherous as there was a layer of ice under the thin layer of snow. The coach carrying Beth and Sebastian lurched and slid towards the ditch at the side of the road. The coachman tried to correct by asking the horses to pull harder, but it was to no avail; the coach slid into the ditch and, with a loud crack, a wheel broke. Beth found herself trapped between Sebastian's body and Paola's as the coach settled at about a thirty-degree angle.

"This is very cosy but …" she said with a giggle.

Paola wriggled free of the entangling blankets and followed her sisters out of the door, which was now above them. Willing hands helped them out. Beth and Sebastian followed. Mike and Harry stood beside the coachman, who was looking very worried.

"Where is Niko?" Beth said.

"Over here!" Niko called from the other side of the hedge.

"What are you doing over there?"

There was a rustle and a small shower of snow and he pushed his way through a gap.

"When the coach tilted, I was thrown off." He grinned.

The men were looking at the coach. "That isn't going anywhere even if we lift it out," Sebastian said.

Mike turned to him, smiling broadly. "With all due respect, you think like an officer, sir."

"Oh? I suppose you have a solution?"

"I might. How much does Lord Martin value those?"

The coach was relatively new and had metal mudguards over the wheels. These were unique, made to Marty's own design, and were there to keep the mud from splashing up on the footmen at the back and the doors at the front.

"What do you intend?"

"We take off the back ones and fix them to the rear wheels, like skis."

"Won't the wheels still try and turn?" Sebastian asked.

"Not if we lock them with the brake."

One of Beth's uncles was a master blacksmith, and he took charge of getting the coach out of the ditch and lashing the mudguards to the wheels. Luckily, Marty always had tools stowed on his coaches in case of times like this.

Two hours after the incident, just as the sun was setting, they pulled up in front of the Stockleys' Cheshire stately home. Marty and Caroline came out to greet them. Marty looked ruefully at the carriage.

"A nice piece of improvisation, but how did the wheel get broken in the first place?"

Sebastian came to the rescue of the coachman, who was looking wretched. "It was a pure accident. The coach slid on the icy road and into the ditch. Your coachman did all he could to stop it but to no avail, I'm afraid. Mike came up with the idea to use the mudguards and Uncle Arthur made it work."

The coachman looked at Sebastian gratefully as Marty clapped Arthur on the shoulder and said, "Well then, you can make new ones and help refit them."

That caused everyone to laugh at Arthur's expense.

Beth said nothing to her mother but sought out Annabel at her first opportunity.

"Let me examine you," Annabel said after Beth had told her what had happened.

The examination was intimate and thorough. "I believe you were pregnant and have indeed lost the foetus," Annabel said.

Beth wept. "I didn't realise I wanted a baby before. Does this mean I can't have one?"

Annabel hugged her and reassured her. "Not at all, it is thought that two in every ten pregnancies end this way. Popular opinion amongst doctors is that the baby was not viable anyway and the body rejected it, but they are all men, so what do they know? You are young and will fall again."

Beth mopped her tears with a handkerchief. "Oh, I do hope so."

Easter was wonderful. The weather improved and the children were able to play outside. Playing with the children helped to heal Beth, who had told all to her mother after seeing Annabel. Caroline also reassured her. On Easter Monday her father asked her to meet him in his study. Beth wondered why Sebastian wasn't invited but knew all would become clear in time.

"Come in," Marty called when Beth knocked on the door. He was standing by the window, looking out at the children playing. Hector, his big shepherd–mastiff cross, was chasing a ball thrown by the children. Fede, Beth's dog, lay under a tree and watched.

"He thinks he's still a pup." Marty smiled when Beth came to stand beside him. "Your mother told me about the miscarriage."

He turned to her and pulled her into his arms. He let her go and led her to a pair of club chairs in front of the fire.

"We have a job for you."

"Just for me?" she said.

"Yes, well … you and your team."

Beth looked at him curiously. Marty continued, "We want you to get close to Prince Leopold. We believe he will be crowned king of Belgium."

"Aren't the Dutch threatening to invade?"

"Yes, King William of the Netherlands is not happy about what is happening in Belgium, and we expect he will try and retake it. It represents a significant chunk of his revenue."

Belgium had achieved partial recognition as an independent state at the 1830 London Conference of Europe's five major powers — Austria, Britain, France, Prussia and Russia — where France had supported them. However, the rest supported the Netherlands on the basis that they would rather have Belgium owned by the Dutch than influenced by the French.

Marty continued, "France will stop them as they are supporting the Belgians."

"Won't that bring them into conflict with the other nations that support the Netherlands?" Beth asked.

"Probably not, as we all have our own problems."

"What am I expected to achieve?"

"He lives at Marlborough House, where he has lived since he married Princess Charlotte of Wales. She died, and now he is a widower. He will probably be asked to marry the eldest daughter of the French king, Princess Louise of Orléans. The French king does not give his support for free. Make sure that you establish yourself as a trusted advisor before he leaves."

"So, I am to become their best friend. Do I use a cover story?"

Marty sat back and grinned. "You are the daughter of an earl whose husband has been deployed to foreign climes with his regiment. The king will introduce you at an intimate supper he is throwing for a number of people at the beginning of February."

Beth gave him a very straight look. "Does Sebastian know that?"

Marty looked out of the window. "He will receive his orders in the next day or so. I'm telling you now so you can prepare. He will be going to India for three years and will be stationed in the north, near the Khyber Pass. We will be rotating the Rifles battalions there for some time to come."

Beth knew the potential threat there was from Russia, but control of the whole region was contested between the British, Sikhs and Afghans. Her husband would probably only see the odd skirmish during his stay.

"When does he leave?" Beth asked.

"When his battalion marches in late January."

"That soon?" Beth exclaimed.

Marty looked at her sympathetically. "The battalion has been preparing since November. This rotation has been planned for a long time, but they didn't expect Major Burrows to fall ill with a wasting disease."

Beth frowned. "You are saying that Sebastian would not have gone otherwise?"

"No, the powers that be had other things planned for him on the diplomatic front, but that has been put back now until he returns. Arthur has his reasons."

Beth was about to ask what they were, but her father's blank expression told her she would find out in good time.

Sebastian's orders arrived two days later. They returned to Surrey via Liverpool and Poole, and left for Winchester as soon as he could collect his uniforms and weapons. They would stay in a rented house until the end of January, so that they could be together.

After a long day of Sebastian organising stores to be sent to Portsmouth, the couple sat together.

"It's a bloody good thing we don't have to worry about horses," he grumped.

Beth laughed. "You will have to get used to walking again."

Sebastian winced and rubbed his feet. "I already am, I must have walked ten miles today."

Beth went to give his feet a rub but wrinkled her nose. "Phew! They stink! Go and have a bath and I will give you a massage and foot rub."

All too soon their time together was over, and Sebastian loaded his campaign chest and furniture onto a baggage cart that called in at the house. Beth accompanied him to the barracks that morning to watch the brigade march off.

The parade ground was full of the 1st Battalion, 95th Regiment of the Rifles. Wellington was there, as their colonel-in-chief. The regimental band played "I'm Ninety-Five" and the battalion set off at the usual quick march pace of the Rifles, which was 140 paces a minute.

Sebastian was at the front and took the salute from Wellington. Once they left the town they would slow to a walk and break step. As he passed Beth, he blew her a kiss. Wellington turned his head, saw her and gave her a haughty look down his long eagle-like nose.

Beth was not fooled. Uncle Arthur's bark was far worse than his bite, especially where she was concerned.

After the men had left, she went and found him standing with some other generals on the edge of the parade ground. "Hello, Uncle Arthur," she said.

"Bethany, my dear. How are you?"

"Considering you just sent my husband away for three years, I am fine, thank you."

"Exigencies of the service."

"Yes, I know."

"You will be kept busy, the time will pass quickly," Arthur said with a knowing smile.

Beth gave him a look. "Hmm, so it seems. I think perhaps you and my father just want me out of the way."

Arthur looked at her. "Didn't he tell you?"

Beth looked up at him. "Tell me what?"

"Belgium would have been an ambassadorial posting if Sebastian was not needed by his regiment. As it is, you will be filling in for him until his return, working with the chargé d'affaires."

Wellington looked over her shoulder; Beth caught the look and turned. Her father stood there, dressed in civilian clothes. Beth opened her mouth to bark something at him when he held up his hand.

"Walk with me, Beth."

She curtsied to Arthur, then reached up and kissed him on the cheek.

"I didn't tell you that because I wanted you two to enjoy your month together. If I had told you, you would both be planning and plotting and, well, you might not have enjoyed yourselves so much," Marty said as they walked across the parade ground.

Beth waved to an officer's wife she knew. "Does he know what he will be doing when he gets back?"

"Not yet. Arthur is going to let him have one last fling with the Rifles before he is put on the reserve list and enters the diplomatic corps. This was too good an opportunity to miss."

Beth sighed. She knew Sebastian loved his regiment and could understand what Arthur was doing, even if her husband would be away for three long years.

The Prince

Her invitation to the dinner at St James's Palace arrived, and Beth immediately replied she would attend. She thought about Leopold. If Charlotte had not died in childbirth at twenty-one years of age, he would have been the crown consort in waiting. Now, with Victoria the heir, he would not get anywhere near the British throne. She had no doubt that if he was offered the throne of Belgium he would accept. Then the French would use their leverage to marry him to Louise. Beth would have to influence him to resist any overtures that the French made to annex Belgium.

She dressed spectacularly, in a pale sapphire-blue dress that was ornamented with silk bows and appliqué flowers along the hem. It was tastefully off the shoulder, and she accessorised it with a stunning sapphire-and-diamond necklace and tiara.

Beth was met at her coach by an equerry and shown into the reception room, where the guests met for drinks and introductions. As soon as she entered, Queen Adelaide took her under her wing and, after Beth had paid her respects to the king, walked her amongst the attendees.

"Georgie was your godfather, wasn't he?"

"He was, Your Majesty. I miss him."

"You must call me Adelaide; we are practically cousins."

Beth thought Adelaide was sweet. How she lived with knowing that her husband had something like nine illegitimate children while she had lost two to early deaths and had suffered two miscarriages, she did not know.

Adelaide introduced her to the French ambassador and his wife; he gazed into her eyes, kissed her hand and said — in French with a sultry tone — "Madam, I am very happy to make your acquaintance."

"Charmed, I am sure," Beth replied, and was happy when Adelaide moved them on quickly. Next were the Russian ambassador and his wife, Princess Dorothea, who Beth already knew very well.

"Hello, Bethany," Dorothea said, and smiled delightedly.

"Dorothea, how are you?"

"I am well. So, you are the one they are putting into Brussels."

"I am?" Beth said disingenuously, knowing that there was very little the Russian didn't know. Dorothea was a socialite and the power behind her husband's embassy. She was very intelligent and quite ruthless in her way.

Dorothea laughed, enjoying the game. "Watch out for the French ambassador — he has wandering hands and thinks he is quite the Lothario."

Beth looked across at him. He saw her look and struck a pose.

"*Bleugh*, I wouldn't get near him even if I was single."

Queen Adelaide had listened to this exchange and giggled. "You two are quite wicked."

"If he tried anything, Sebastian would kill him," Beth told her. "And as he *isn't* around, I would have to do it."

"You could just prick him with one of your knives to dissuade him." Dorothea laughed.

"Knives?" Adelaide gasped.

Beth changed the subject. "Who is that?" she asked and nodded to a balding man with a severe face.

"That is Heinrich von Bülow, the Prussian ambassador. A dreary man — a bureaucrat," Adelaide said.

"*Now* who is being wicked?" said Dorothea, and laughed.

Adelaide blushed. "But I still need to introduce you."

Von Bülow was as dry and dusty as Adelaide had said. They moved on, and Beth greeted the foreign secretary, Lord Palmerston, and his wife, and the prime minister, Earl Grey, and his wife Mary.

Then it was time to meet Prince Leopold. Beth's first impression was of a rather sad man. He was handsome, with dark wavy hair, and was forty-one years old. Apart from Beth, he was the only unaccompanied person in the room.

Adelaide interrupted his conversation with King William and introduced her. "Leopold, I would like you to meet Lady Bethany Ashley-Cooper."

Leopold kissed her hand. "Any relation to Earl Shaftesbury?"

Beth smiled. "My husband is his youngest son."

Leopold looked around. "Aah, I see ... But where is he?"

Beth smiled a little sadly. "He is a major in the 95th Rifles. He has been deployed to India for three years."

"Beth is being assigned to our embassy in Brussels in her husband's absence. You see, he was due to take the position but had to replace a sick officer at short notice." Adelaide's words surprised Beth. The queen had obviously been briefed.

"I am sure you will love it there. It is a beautiful city."

Adelaide quietly slipped away, leaving the two together.

"Oh, I expect I will see you there," Beth said. "Have they asked you yet?"

"To be king? Not directly, but they have, how should I say, 'explored whether I am interested'."

"It is a golden opportunity," Beth said. "Belgium is the buffer between France and the Netherlands and Germany, a country that will be in the centre of Europe in the future."

"Do you think so?" Leopold said, looking at her quizzically.

"With the right leadership and as long as it stays neutral, yes."

The call to dinner rang out and they made their way through to the dining room. As the only two single guests they were seated beside each other to the right of the king.

That is deliberate, Beth thought as she sat down. She could see Leopold pondering what she had said.

"But why do the British support the Netherlands?"

"Probably to put the French noses out of joint and because the government is worried about France annexing Belgium. But if it were guaranteed to stay neutral, Belgium would be our new best friend and ally."

"What does your family do? I mean, one doesn't just drop into the diplomatic corps."

"My father is Earl Purbeck."

"Aah, I have met him. He is an admiral and friend of the Duke of Wellington."

"Yes, he and Uncle Arthur are old friends."

"So, you are very well connected."

"My family is."

"Beth is being modest," King William interjected. "I value her father's advice, and she has his level-headed common sense."

Leopold smiled. "*Very* well connected."

"Her mother is a tutor to Princess Victoria," William added.

Leopold looked disapproving at that. "What the duchess is doing with that St James's system is wrong."

Beth sighed. "Mother is teaching the princess world affairs and politics interlaced with a large dollop of independence. But I wonder if it will be enough; she will be eighteen in six years. Mother says she has developed a strong character in spite of her mother's machinations."

Leopold was quiet for a long moment. Then he said, "I can see that you and your family have ties to my family. I would be honoured to call you friends as well."

When Beth reported back to her father, he was very pleased with her progress.

"This is good. Now you have made the connection, move to the embassy. I am reliably informed that the Belgian congress has exhausted all the candidates and rejected the French ones. Leopold was rejected in the first round but has been reintroduced now."

"Why was he rejected?" Beth asked.

"Because he is a British citizen and our candidate," Marty answered. "The French objected to him. However, the French king is no fool and knows that any member of his family would be even more objectionable to the other powers. Now he is looking like the only one that is universally acceptable."

"I see." Beth smiled. "A compromise for the powers, but in my view a victory for the Belgians."

Marty nodded. "Now get your household together and get yourself over to Brussels. We want you there before he arrives."

* * *

Beth would eventually live above the embassy, on the corner of the Rue de Spa/Spastraat and the Rue de la Loi in Brussels. The apartment was unfurnished, but she had an allowance to furnish it. She decided the shopping could wait until she got to Brussels.

Getting the Wolves and herself packed was enough of a problem. Sarah would be coming as her lady's maid along with her butler, cook, scullery maid and two maids-of-all-work. When Sebastian eventually joined her, he would bring his batman and valet.

Beth was beginning to suspect that there was more to his posting than Arthur or her father were letting on. She had heard that there were at least two other men of sufficient rank who could have gone in his place. But the machinations of senior officers were not her concern; they both had their orders and would do their best to fulfil them.

Having packed, they coached to London and were put on a Royal Navy seventy-six-gun, third-rate vessel, HMS *Imaum*. The captain, Sir Patrick St John-Stevens, was polite and respectful.

"Welcome aboard, Lady Bethany."

"Thank you, Captain. I am afraid we will make your ship a little crowded."

"Not to worry, we will make the crossing to Antwerp quite quickly, as the wind is favourable."

Beth scanned the rigging and looked down the deck. The ship was tidy; clean but not "pretty". The men were likewise clean and smart.

"Your ship is a credit to you," Beth told him.

"Thank you, milady." He didn't mention her father.

Their luggage had been loaded early that morning as it had been sent ahead, so as soon as the tide was right, they warped out and set off down the river.

* * *

Even though it was early in the year, the crossing was relatively smooth. That was helped by the size of the ship, which was around 180 feet along the deck, fifty feet wide and very weatherly. It took a full day to make the port of Antwerp and the captain and his officers gave up their cabins so Beth's party could sleep.

Antwerp was a fortified city that was nominally held by the Belgians. The declaration of independence made the year before stated that it was part of Belgium, but the Belgians' hold was tenuous. Yet the fact that the British and others were establishing embassies gave validation to the declaration.

Even if Britain's embassy would be run day to day by a chargé d'affaires, Beth was there as the wife of the ambassador in his absence. She would entertain and … Well, she wasn't sure what else.

The officer on the dock when they tied up was of the bureaucratic type. He spent an age checking papers through his pince-nez glasses, until Captain St John-Stevens lost patience and took the papers from him.

"Lady Bethany is a registered diplomat. As such, she has diplomatic immunity and can travel where she wants without hindrance. Now, get off my ship or I will throw you in the brig."

"You dare not! She cannot be a diplomat; she is a woman!"

"I do dare! Master-at-arms!" Beth grinned as a burly master-at-arms and two mates stepped up. "Now, it is your choice." The captain's voice was low and threatening.

Just then a line of carriages pulled up at the dock and a tall, well-dressed man of middle years stepped down from the first. "Permission to come aboard?" he called up.

Captain St John-Stevens looked down from the side and gave him permission.

"Welcome aboard Mr ... ?"

"Sir Euan Williams, chargé d'affaires in Brussels."

Sir Euan was in his forties, about five feet ten inches tall with a shock of fair hair that was greying at the sides. He spoke with a noticeable Welsh accent. He was followed up the gangplank by a woman carrying a parasol.

"My wife, Evelyne ... and you must be Lady Bethany." He bowed over her hand.

Sir Euan looked at the officer, who was bridling. "You can go. I have spoken to your senior officer, and he assured me there will be no restrictions placed on the movement of diplomatic staff."

The officer persisted. "But—"

"No buts! Lady Bethany and her staff have diplomatic status. Now, I advise you to leave before the good captain here asks those gentlemen to throw you off his ship. Which, by the way, is British soil as long as Lady Bethany is on board."

The mates stepped forward eagerly. However, deciding that discretion was the better part of valour, the officer gathered his dignity and strutted down the gangplank unaided.

Sir Euan and his wife shared the coach with Beth, who had Sarah in with her and Mike and Harry on top. The rest of the Wolves were in the following carriage and the staff were in the third, with the luggage spread over all three. That meant all the carriages were heavy and moved slowly. Beth stopped them as they passed a wagoners' yard and had Mike pay them to bring the luggage along behind.

The coaches rode much higher and softer after that. "That's much better," Beth said as the horses set off at a fast walk.

"You are one for direct action, Lady Bethany, it seems," Sir Euan said.

"Oh *tush*, call me Beth. All that 'sir' this and 'lady' that is so cumbersome, don't you think?"

Evelyne looked at Beth with a smile. "We were told your husband has been posted to India."

"Yes, Arthur — Wellington, that is — decided to give him one last command and delay his posting to Brussels."

Evelyne looked slightly puzzled. "Don't you think that odd?"

"Frankly, yes I do," Beth responded, showing her frustration.

"I am sure the duke had his reasons," Euan interjected.

"Oh, of that I am absolutely sure ... and it was *not* to give Sebastian a last fling at command."

Euan looked thoughtful. "I have read both of your dossiers. You have had colourful careers to date. Could it be that Sebastian has some other task to perform out there?"

"Probably, but if he has, he didn't know before he left."

The conversation shifted to the situation in Brussels. "We have just taken over the embassy building, so it is a bit sparsely furnished at the moment," Euan said. "Until you have your apartment in a habitable state, we have arranged for you to have rooms in a hotel just down the road."

"I decided to buy furniture locally; I was told that the Belgians make good furniture," Beth said.

"They do," Evelyne replied. Then she commented, "You have a very large retinue. The apartment has servants' quarters, but I do not think that they will all fit in."

"There are only seven servants, including Sarah here. The rest are my ... How should I say? ... staff."

"*Staff?*" Evelyne said, confused.

Euan chuckled. "Aah, they would be the infamous Wolves."

Beth frowned. "How — ?"

Euan raised a hand. "I had a long talk with Wellington and Palmerston before I came out. They commented that I should not be surprised at your entourage. Then Wellington mentioned that you are still a member of the Intelligence Service as well as the diplomatic corps."

"This is all too complicated," Evelyne declared, deciding that she didn't want to know.

Brussels turned out to have a plentiful supply of quality craftsmen making furniture locally, and shops that sold French and German furniture. Beth spent her allowance and then some of her own money furnishing the apartment. She left the hotel and moved in after just two weeks.

Time flew by and before she knew it Leopold was on his way to Belgium to be crowned king. He landed in Calais and entered Belgium at De Panne on 17 July 1831. He travelled through Ostend, Bruges, Ghent and Aalst, and in every town he was greeted by rapturous crowds of celebrating people who drowned out any remaining pro-Dutch sentiment completely. Church bells rang and 101-gun salutes were fired. He arrived at Laeken Castle on 19 July, where forty thousand people waited to greet him.

Beth made a point of going to see him soon after he arrived. "How did they persuade you?" she asked after he had greeted her with a kiss.

"They didn't, you did," he replied as they sat down.

"Me? How was that?"

"You told me that Belgium could be at the centre of Europe. I have every intention of making it so."

"They will want you to marry and beget an heir."

Leopold laughed. "I know, I have already been introduced to Princess Louise."

"You do not seem unhappy about that."

"That is the irony; I took one look at her and my heart sang. I intend to marry her next year. She is very politically astute. I think you two will get on famously."

"I cannot wait to meet her," Beth said.

When 21 July came, an atmosphere of hope for the new nation state prevailed. A committee arrived at Laeken Castle to invite the future king to enter Brussels. Leopold wore the uniform of a general in the Belgian army and mounted his horse. Then, with a royal escort and civic guard, he left Laeken at eleven and rode towards the city.

Beth wasn't about to take any chances with Leopold. There was still enough Orangist sentiment around for some idiot to take a potshot at him. She instructed the Wolves, "Harry and Mike are to shadow the royal party for three hundred yards out on horseback. Girls, you are to take the high ground that is suitable for a shooter along the route and make sure it stays empty." They had scouted the route over the previous few days and knew every hiding place and vantage point along the way. The girls would lead the party like beaters to make sure no one could get within shooting range. Beth would wait at the steps of the royal palace.

Leopold rode, unhindered, along the road, which was lined with celebrating Belgians, until he reached Molenbeek-Saint-Jean, where he was offered a glass of wine and enjoyed the view of the city from outside the entrance gate.

As the soon-to-be king approached Molenbeek-Saint-Jean, Paola moved ahead and worked her way through the crowd gathered there. The only place with a clear line of fire was the city wall and that was lined with soldiers, so she moved into close-protection mode. She had to push her way through and was three rows from the front when her elbow hit something hard.

She turned and looked up into the face of a man who was not cheering. In fact, he looked angry. Paola pressed against him as if she had been pushed, and he looked down at her.

"Sorry," she said.

As bodies crowded in all around, she felt the outline of a pistol under his coat. Her right hand moved up his side then punched inwards and upwards. The blade of her knife entered below the bottom rib, angled up behind it and pierced his heart. He died, but the press of bodies was such that he could not fall down. Paola squirmed free of him and continued on. The easy kill had been pure luck.

Totally unaware of the drama unfolding thirty feet away, Leopold entered Brussels through the Porte d'Anvers, where the longstanding mayor of Brussels, Nicolas Jean Rouppe, presented him with the keys to the city.

The streets were festooned with garlands covered in red, yellow, white and blue flowers. Bells rang and the people cheered. The roads had been covered with fresh sand and triumphal arches had been erected — three on the north side of the canal and two near the entrance.

The escort took him along the Rue Neuve, through the Place de la Monnaie, Place de la Madeleine and on to the Mont des Arts before they arrived at the Place Royale, where the regent and the new Belgian congress awaited. People cried "Long live the king" as he climbed the steps.

The regent, Érasme-Louis, Baron Surlet de Chokier, read the new Belgian constitution with tears of joy in his eyes and then handed it to Leopold. He found Beth with his eyes and gave her a wink. Then he read the document from end to end before rising from his seat.

Slowly and with great dignity, he read the oath.

"I swear to observe the constitution and the laws of the Belgian people, and to maintain the national independence and the integrity of the territory."

A table was brought forward and Leopold signed the constitution into effect. His attempts to address the congress and crowd were drowned out by cries of "Vive le roi". Cannons were fired and trumpets called.

Belgium had been officially born.

Diplomacy

After his coronation, Beth organised a ball at the embassy for the king. He was the British choice, after all. She invited the good and the great from both the Walloon and Flemish sides, who were for once in accord. In fact, the population of the newfound country was so diverse it had six distinct governments. Leopold held them together.

The embassy was officially guarded by marines and the corps had kindly made sure that there were enough musicians amongst them to form a band. The embassy staff plus her own were enough to cover the event — especially as the Wolves would circulate with trays of drinks and canapés. They would, of course, be armed and provide a layer of security inside the ballroom.

Catering was taken care of partly by Beth's cook, along with the embassy and a local restaurant. Between them they provided a sumptuous buffet. Beth was very aware that events such as this performed diplomatic functions such as promoting British interests, as well as facilitating the informal exchange of information and making of contacts.

Having opened the dancing with Leopold, Beth circulated. The new king was a very competent dancer, and she would dance with him again before the night was out. Meanwhile she talked with the French ambassador as she danced with him, and he confirmed that they expected Leopold to marry Princess Louise the following year. He sounded very smug when he said it, but Beth knew that Leopold took his oath very seriously and there was no danger of that marriage resulting in a merger between France and Belgium.

Slightly disturbing was a warning by a prominent politician from the Catholic party: "There is still a significant Orangist Protestant faction in the countryside and in Brussels. They resent the king and the people who put him there. I have heard they are plotting an assassination in support of an invasion."

Beth thought that could be just the politician trying to generate antipathy towards the Orangists; however, it *could* be a genuine threat. But more pressing was the threat of invasion from the Netherlands.

The Netherlands invaded two weeks after Leopold's accession, on 2 August 1831. Prince William of Orange of the United Kingdom of the Netherlands, to give it — and him — their full titles, did not want to lose his southern province to independence as that would put a large hole in his revenue.

Beth was with Leopold when they struck. An army officer rushed in and stomped to attention. "The Dutch have crossed the border at Poppel and are moving on Antwerp."

Leopold was incandescent with anger. "What forces do we have in the area?"

"Not many, sire. Our scouts have blocked the roads to slow the Dutch down but we have only a few hundred troops and they have an army numbering thousands."

Beth touched his arm. "You need better intelligence than this. Let me help." Leopold looked at her, momentarily surprised. "I can send two of my men down there to observe and report back," Beth continued.

"Are they trained?" Leopold asked.

"They are the best," Beth assured him.

Mike and Harry were despatched to the north. They took a crate of homing pigeons with them to send messages back. However, Beth was more worried about the local Orangists taking action against Leopold, now that *their* king was on his way.

Harry and Mike rode through the night, changing horses frequently and using a letter from the king as authority. They arrived on 3 August, just in time to see Turnhout fall. A long line of refugees showed that the population in general was heading for Antwerp.

Some sneaking and observing revealed that this was a multi-pronged attack. The first and the second divisions — from Breda and Rijen, respectively, and both around 11,000 strong — were heading for Turnhout, while the third division, from Eindhoven, had crossed the border. There was a reserve from St Oedenrode stationed to the east of Eindhoven and heading south by south-east towards Oostham.

Pigeons were sent and arrived at the British embassy. Beth went straight to the palace.

"You are facing thirty thousand Dutch troops on two fronts. The Prince of Orange is leading them himself. You have lost Turnhout and Antwerp will fall without a fight."

On 4 August, Antwerp fell. The Dutch forces tore down the Belgian flag and raised the Dutch. However, King William of the Netherlands had the flag taken down because it symbolised occupation rather than the restoration of Dutch ownership.

More messages arrived and Beth went once more to the palace.

"The Dutch have split their forces; my people think that is because they have faced little opposition so far and are moving further south."

On 5 August, the second division took Geel and Diest and the third division took Beringen. The third division continued to advance, and on 6 August, under the command of Prince Bernhard of Saxe-Weimar — an extremely experienced commander who had fought at Waterloo — clashed with the Belgian forces on the border of Limburg province at Houthalen-Helchteren. As before, the Belgians were vastly outnumbered and the Dutch had another decisive victory, after which they moved into Limburg. On 8 August, the third division clashed with the Belgian Army of the Meuse near Hasselt.

The second division made its way south to link up with the third at St Truiden and defeated the Belgian Army of the Scheldt near Boutersem on 11 August. The very next day, they took Leuven.

"We could barely stay ahead of them," Mike said when he and Harry got back to Brussels and reported to Beth and Leopold in the palace. "If you ask me, Belgium is lost."

"Belgium is not lost until Brussels falls," Leopold barked.

Mike bowed his head in apology. Leopold sighed; he had to acknowledge that the situation was desperate. "We need help. I will ask the British and French to intervene," he said and called two of his senior diplomats to attend him.

"Sylvain, please travel to London with all despatches and try and solicit some support from the British. François, please go to Paris and beg the French for help."

Good luck with the British, Beth thought.

Beth was correct in her suspicion that the British would not or could not help. However, the French had no such reservations.

The French immediately despatched their Army of the North under Marshal Étienne Gérard to aid the Belgians. In their haste they "forgot" to inform the other great powers — which immediately raised suspicions that this could create a threat to the European balance of power. The French crossed the border on 12 August.

Beth decided to do something direct. She assembled the Wolves and called for a carriage.

"What will you do?" Leopold asked.

"Well, the last thing the Dutch want is another war with the French, so I am going to talk some sense into William."

The carriage left through the east gate with a Union Jack flying proudly above it and drove straight through both lines of troops to the elaborate tent that had the royal flag of the United Kingdom of the Netherlands flying above it. The coach stopped and Beth waited.

"Aren't we getting out?" Delfina asked.

"We need to give the king time to organise himself," Beth replied.

In this she was correct. One of the king's officers approached the coach and was informed who was in it. However, the king was not dressed for a visitor of her status, nor was his tent in a state to receive her. Frantic efforts were made to rectify both conditions. After a wait of just five minutes, a captain stepped out of the tent and opened the carriage door. Beth, with great dignity, allowed him to aid her in dismounting.

"The king will see you now," he said in English.

Beth did not comment and let herself be led into the tent. She was aware of the sound of her team deploying around the coach, but ignored it.

Inside, the tent was lit by lamps, which made it warmer than outside. A table had been set up, and the king and his generals stood ready to receive her.

"Good afternoon, Your Majesty, gentlemen," she said with a bow of her head.

William stepped forward and bowed over her hand as she curtsied deeply. "What can we do for you, Lady Bethany?"

"Can I be blunt?"

William smiled. He knew her father and his position of influence in Britain. He had also been on the end of some blunt advice from Marty in the past.

"Let us sit, before you tell us why you are here."

The men waited for Beth to sit before taking their own seats. Then she said, "Can I assume that you do not want a war with the French? Because if you do, they are just about to arrive and join the Belgian lines."

The generals looked surprised and the king slightly abashed. "We were not aware they had chosen to intervene."

"Well, they have. The Army of the North is marching as I speak."

Just then, trumpets and drums started to be heard faintly. *Oh! Right on time!* Beth exulted silently. A soldier burst in through the tent flap and gabbled something in Dutch. Beth caught the gist of it from a few key words: "*Het Franse leger komt eraan!*"

Beth looked William in the eye. "May I suggest that your best course of action is to cease your assault, leave Leuven and agree an armistice."

William looked at the tent flap. The sound of the drums and trumpets was getting louder. Beth upped the pressure.

"Be sure, there will be another congress in London after this. You do not want to give the French the excuse to annex Belgium, as North Brabant and Limburg will be their next target."

William sighed; his great gamble had failed. Without the support of any of his allies he stood no chance against the French.

"Gentlemen, we will withdraw our line two hundred metres. Lady Bethany, please inform King Leopold and the French commander that we are willing to enter negotiations."

Beth stood, and the men stood with her. She curtsied and they bowed. The king then escorted her to her carriage, and raised his eyebrows at the sight of her heavily armed escort, which was facing off against William's guard.

"My team," Beth said by way of explanation.

"*Aftreden*," William ordered, and the guards relaxed.

Beth returned directly to the palace and reported to Leopold, who sent a messenger to Marshal Étienne Gérard. The French made camp, and the marshal joined Leopold, who asked Beth to bring King William to the palace. She returned to the Dutch pavilion.

"Your Majesty, would you care to accompany me to Brussels to attend an armistice conference?"

The king was prepared for this and agreed. As he approached the coach, he noted the team was in attendance again, but this time all but Mike rode horses and held rifles. Mike sat in the driver's seat of the coach, holding the reins.

"We will get an honour guard once we enter the city. Until then I will keep you safe."

William looked at her admiringly. "I have complete confidence in you, my lady."

* * *

Beth's work was not finished. The Orangists in Belgium had been celebrating the victories of the Prince of Orange and were angry that the French had intervened. Beth agreed to help prevent any incidents that could give the French an excuse to intervene again.

She asked Leopold for access to his Secret Service. But what she got access to was a disorganised group of policemen. She rolled her eyes when she saw them for the first time but, speaking through an interpreter for the Dutch-speaking contingent, she found they were all keen and dedicated to the cause of Belgian independence.

The Orangists were predominantly Protestant and Flemish. There were some Protestant Walloons, whose lineage dated back to the sixteenth century and the Reformation, and they could not be ignored either. Beth's strategy was to have the Belgian Secret Service agents, such as they were, visit the Protestant churches and meeting houses and listen for any rumours of insurrection.

Beth herself went to a Walloon church — she was, after all, a Protestant. The minister knew all his congregation and spotted a new face immediately.

"My child, I do not know you. Are you new to the city?"

Beth was plainly dressed and had her hair covered. The service had been in French, or rather something close to it. Beth answered with a quiver in her voice. "I am here from Paris with my mistress, I am a servant. I came here because I only speak French and felt the need for God's comfort."

"My child, are you afraid?"

"My mistress says that the Catholics will try and kill us for being of the same faith as the Dutch."

The minister sat beside her. "That is her fear talking; the Belgians are afraid that all Protestants are Orangists and will revolt against the new king. We Walloons will not revolt because we know that if the French gain control we will be persecuted. The Flemish Orangists want the Dutch to be in control, and ignore the fact that the French have intervened. Your mistress would do well to cast her eye over them."

The man was so sincere, she had no doubt that he believed what he was saying. But she was a professional and wanted more than just his word. There was a Protestant meeting house set apart from the church a short walk away and she asked when the next meeting was.

"We meet every Sunday for prayers and discussion after the morning service. You would be welcome to attend."

Beth duly attended the meeting. She kept her head down and listened more than she talked. There were only around twenty people there and she found nothing out of the ordinary; they talked politics but at the party level, with no mention of direct action.

On Monday her agents reported in, and in general all had, like herself, discovered nothing worrying — except for one agent, who had overheard something very interesting.

"There was a group of three who were very intense. I got close enough to hear what they were talking about, and they were discussing how to disrupt the armistice talks. They mentioned a bomb targeted at Leopold when he takes his walk in the grounds tomorrow."

Beth frowned and pulled out a map of Brussels. "Where was this?"

"Here — at the Holy Trinity."

"That is damn close to the palace. Do you have names?"

The agent passed over a sheet of paper. On it were three names and addresses.

Augustus Bertus Bargan, Rue Bosquet 43
Cornelis Faggart, Rue Stassart 94
Thijmen Hemmerling, Rue Jean Stas 20

That evening three houses were raided and three men taken into custody by the army. Beth and the Wolves searched each of them and found bomb-making components in the house of Thijmen Hemmerling. At midnight, she went to the barracks where the men were being held.

"Where did you plant the bomb?" Beth asked Hemmerling.

The man stayed stubbornly silent.

"I don't have time for this. Talk or suffer the consequences."

Hemmerling kept his mouth firmly shut.

Beth took out a tool roll and opened it on the table. In it were a variety of surgical and dental tools. She selected a drill that had a hand crank and fitted a bit.

"Open his mouth."

Mike pinched Hemmerling's nose and covered his mouth so he couldn't breathe. When he started to struggle, Mike uncovered his mouth. Hemmerling's reflexes opened his mouth to gulp in air and as soon as he did that, Beth shoved in a wooden dowel to keep his mouth open. Mike clamped his arms around the man's head, immobilising him.

Beth took the drill and placed the bit on one of his incisors and started to drill. She did not hurry. The drill hit the nerve, he screamed, and she stooped and swapped the drill for a probe. She probed the hole, and at that point the pain he felt was more than he had ever experienced.

"Where did you plant the bomb?"

She looked at him, probe poised. He nodded vigorously and the dowel was removed.

"I made it, but Bargan and Faggart planted it. They have access to the palace gardens."

Beth was astonished ... they were *gardeners*?

"Take him to his cell, bring Faggart." She gave Hemmerling a small bottle of clove oil to ease his pain.

Faggart was brought in and looked terrified. He had heard the screams and now he saw the woman dressed in leathers and the tools. Once he was secured to the chair, Beth leaned down so that her hair brushed his face, her mouth by his ear. "You are going to tell me where you planted the bomb and how it was to be detonated," she breathed into it.

He shook his head.

"That is foolishly brave," Beth said. "You *will* tell me. You know I found a violin at your house, and lots of sheet music. Your wife said it was yours. She also said you were passionate about playing."

She took a pair of pliers from the tool roll and considered them for a long moment. Then she discarded them in favour of a hammer and a sharp chisel.

"Mike, would you be so kind as to lay his hand on the table?" Mike forced Faggart's hand onto the table and spread his fingers. "Where should I start? The index finger?" She placed the chisel on the middle knuckle. "It is hard to play the violin with no fingers." She raised the hammer.

"No! No! It is in a rhododendron beside the path near the kiosque de musique! There is a tripwire to activate it."

"There ... That wasn't hard, was it?" Beth smiled.

At dawn, the Wolves and Beth moved through the gardens towards the pavilion that was the kiosque. They knew the low angle of the sun should make spotting the wire easier.

It was Sarah who spotted it. She had come along as she had very good eyesight and told Beth that she wanted to be a Wolf.

"There, about a yard and a half ahead of me."

Beth moved forward and looked for it. Sarah had to point to it from a foot away for Beth to see it.

"That is quite cunning, they chose a thread that is the same colour as the path," Beth said and chased it back to the shrub at the side of the path.

The bomb was in an iron pot which had been wrapped in half-inch-thick rope and tied to a vertical stem. Beth took a pair of scissors and cut the thread. Harry crawled in beside her and supported the bomb with his hands. Beth gently cut the ties that held it to the stem and Harry squirmed out of the shrub, holding the bomb. He carefully placed it on the path. It rocked as he released it and they all held their breath.

"The detonator is inside. See where the thread enters the saucepan through that small hole?" Beth said.

Mike sat back on his haunches after examining it. "Probably a spring-loaded striker."

"And if that thin a thread can trip it, it will have a hair trigger. Disarming it will be dodgy," Harry added.

Beth stood and looked down at it. "Suggestions?"

"At the academy they talked about directing the blast; could we direct it upwards?" Alie suggested.

Beth thought about it. "It will take a strong, open-topped vessel of some type."

Sarah coughed meaningfully. "You have an idea?" Beth asked.

"Would a large cauldron work?"

Beth looked at Mike, who returned her expression of surprised realisation. "Where can we get one?"

"I know," Paola said, and rushed off with Delfina in tow.

While the others waited, they established a perimeter a hundred feet out from the bomb in all directions. A contingent of royal guards came out on patrol and were conscripted to help. The king was told that his walk had to wait.

The girls returned with a handcart and the biggest cauldron Beth had ever seen. It was made of cast iron and weighed an absolute ton.

"Where did you get that?" Beth asked.

"The glue factory, they boil bones in it."

"Did they agree to you taking it?" Mike asked.

"When Paola pulled a pistol, they did." Delfina laughed.

The cauldron was set on the path and the bomb very gently placed in it. Beth made up a small charge of priming powder in a sealed jar with a timer inside set to one minute. She placed that between the bomb and the wall of the cauldron. "Everybody back to the perimeter," she shouted, and sprinted back herself.

Leopold stood watching, surrounded by guards. He beckoned Beth to him.

"What will happen?"

"It will go bang," Beth said, and grinned.

And bang it went. The ground shook and the blast shot a fountain of shrapnel straight up into the air.

"Looks like they packed the pot with scrap," Beth said, and frowned as the shards fell to earth. She walked forward and examined a piece twenty feet in front of them. "Yes, this is a large bolt."

Astonishingly, the cauldron had survived all of this, and a trail of smoke rose from its mouth.

The armistice was agreed and signed later that day. The Dutch packed up and went home; however, the force in the Antwerp citadel stayed. It would take more than this to shift them. Gérard initially returned with his army to France, but because the Dutch persisted in bombarding Antwerp from the citadel he would return in November 1832, besiege it and succeed in taking it at the end of December — just in time for Christmas Eve.

The Khyber Pass

Sebastian sat in a canvas chair on the deck of HMS *Ptarmigan* — a converted former seventy-four — and watched as Madeira slid by on the port side. A midshipman approached and touched his hat in salute.

"Captain's compliments, sir. Would you care to join him in his cabin?"

Sebastian looked at the boy quizzically, then stood and followed him. The marine at the door announced him and the captain called for him to enter. The mid stayed outside.

"Ah, Major, good morning. We have reached fifteen degrees south, so as instructed, I am giving you this."

He handed over a packet with what looked at first glance to be a plain wax seal. Sebastian took it and asked, "Who gave you this?"

"It was delivered by courier at Portsmouth with this letter."

Sebastian took the offered letter and saw that it was a simple set of instructions, signed by Wellington. "Things are becoming clearer," he muttered.

"Sorry, did you say something?" the captain asked.

"No, nothing. May I use your dining room to read this? I will need privacy."

* * *

The package contained a letter with his orders/instructions and a packet of information including maps and a portrait. The letter from Wellington was typically curt.

> *Lancelot,*
>
> *You are to find Sultan Mohammad Khan and give him the message in the packet. The gold is with the captain of your ship; it will be loaded onto the cart with your baggage. Your contact will guide you to wherever you need to go in Afghanistan to achieve your mission. I recommend you elimi-nate any opposition.*

Hmm, that means the Russians, thought Sebastian.

> *The gold is to buy his co-operation. If you have any doubt that he will fulfil his end of the bargain, eliminate him and do business with his successor.*
>
> *Your second task is to eliminate Mohammad Yama, the current chief of the Tadjiks. He is pro-Russian and opposes Khan in his collaboration with us. His eldest son, Sarbaz, who will replace him, is against all foreign influence but is at least consistent.*
>
> *Once these tasks have been accomplished, you will be replaced and able to come home.*

It was signed with the ornate *W* that Wellington used.

Sebastian spread the documents out on the table. There were portraits of the two men, maps, the name of his contact and recognition phrases. He studied the portraits; the one of Yama showed an older man, grey-haired and bearded with hard eyes, the one of Sarbaz showed a sharp-faced character who, in Sebastian's opinion, looked decidedly shifty.

He folded the documents and remade the packet. He left the dining room quietly after telling the steward he was done.

Back in his chair on deck, Sebastian contemplated what he had learned. The camps of both targets were well inside Afghanistan, that meant he had to travel incognito. He had an idea for a disguise that he would refine when he saw exactly how the locals dressed. Additionally, he would need a guide. The contact should be able to provide that or even be the guide themselves. He would need a team — that was easily provided by the battalion, and he had six men in mind who would do nicely. All were sharpshooters, brawlers and knife-fighters.

It took another two months to reach Karachi, and another ten days' march to get to the garrison. The Rifles marched fast; they would trot for three paces (left foot to left foot, six steps) and walk for three paces. This got them to where they wanted to go faster than regular foot soldiers. Local Indians watched — some amused, others puzzled — as the green-uniformed soldiers passed by. They travelled light, with their kit carried in ox carts that followed along behind.

That first night, tents were not needed, for it was warm even that far north. Camps were set up quickly with a fire, a bed roll and food being all the Rifles needed. However, the further north they went the colder it got, and eventually tents *were* needed as the temperature dropped.

When they were a day away from the garrison in Kohat, Sebastian asked his chosen men to attend him. Sergeant Atwood, Corporal

Jennings and privates first class Stonewall, Barnard, Dyer and Greeves came to his tent.

"At ease, men. You and I will be going on a little expedition. We will be dressed as locals and carry local-style weapons. I want you to observe the people who regularly travel through the Khyber Pass and acquire clothes and weapons accordingly. We will be mounted for this exhibition — am I right to think that you can all ride?"

"Aye, sir," they all said.

"Good, take a look at the Afghan tack. Make sure you are familiar with it. Sergeant, I will need you to accompany me on a little side trip tomorrow night. Wear your civilian clothes."

The following day, the Rifles battalion formed up and march-trotted into the garrison. They were a fine sight, and they were greeted by the outgoing battalion commander.

"Welcome, Major Ashley-Cooper, I didn't expect to see you at the head of the 1st. What has happened to Willy?"

Willy was Major William Gordon, the former commander of the 1st who had succumbed to a wasting disease.

"I'm afraid he has had to retire from the regiment due to illness. I was brought in at the last minute."

As the two men — Sebastian and Major Graham Stanley-Wood — walked together, Sebastian filled his fellow officer in. "Willy has a wasting disease. The doctors say he has had it for some time but has been hiding it. Unfortunately, it progressed faster than he expected."

Stanley-Wood nodded. "Last I heard, you were on detachment. South America, wasn't it?"

"Yes, and this will be my last posting. It's the diplomatic corps for me next."

"Well, I will be staying with the regiment. No cushy job for me."

"Diplomatic posts are hardly cushy. We are the country's eyes and ears inside the foreign power."

Graham laughed cynically. "And knowing you and that wife of yours, manipulating and spying."

Sebastian gave a wolf-like grin. "Possibly, if the situation demands it."

The men having been billeted and fed, Sebastian got ready to find his contact. He was dressed in dirty-white nankeen trousers and a jacket more suited to a farmer than an officer. His head was covered by a rather tatty top hat. He had a sabre on the left side of his belt and a pistol in a holster on the back.

The door to his quarters was open and Sergeant Atwood stepped through it. He was dressed in what looked like a grey pair of sailors' trousers, a collarless shirt and a jacket. He carried a stick with a gnarled knob on one end and had a pistol shoved through his belt.

"Well done, Atwood, you look just the part," Sebastian said.

"Thank you, sir."

"Right, follow me."

Sebastian left the tent and slipped into the night shadows with Atwood hot on his heels. They made their way out of the garrison and headed into the town. Once they were clear of sentries Atwood asked, "Who are we looking for, sir?"

Sebastian didn't slow down as he replied, "A horse trader called Assam; he will be our guide and the interpreter for our mission."

"That will be the six of us lads and you, sir?"

"Absolutely."

Atwood didn't ask any more. If the major wanted to tell him, he would.

* * *

They came upon a number of corrals, some containing goats or sheep but most holding horses. Sebastian skirted around the outside of them until he found a crude lean-to with an odd sigil carved into the lintel of the door. He knocked on the lintel and a rough voice said something. Sebastian responded, "I am looking for a white colt."

A head appeared through the rough blanket that served as a door. "I only have a grey. You are early." He held the banket open and Sebastian stepped inside after signalling that the sergeant should stand guard. Atwood slipped into the shadows and settled himself.

"We made good time from Karachi. Can you guide us now?"

"I can, where are we going?"

Sebastian grinned; his teeth shone white in the light of the moon that came through the badly fitted planks.

"That depends on where Sultan Mohammad Khan is right now."

"This time of year, he will be in Kabul."

"And where will Mohammad Yama of the Tadjiks be?"

Assam grinned. "He will be at Kabul as well, at the annual council of chiefs."

Sebastian knew he wouldn't get a better chance than this to fulfil both of his missions, so he brought his plans forward. He and the men acquired local clothes, and Assam supplied the horses. Their cover was that they were guards of a string of horses for sale in Kabul. Sebastian bought them all rather good locally made rifles and swords. Now he had to tell his number two that he would be gone for a while. He summoned him.

There was a knock on the door. "Enter," Sebastian called.

Captain Mullins stepped inside smartly, came to attention and saluted. "You wanted to see me, sir."

"At ease. I do. I have a mission that the powers that be have sprung on me. It is secret, clandestine. I will be taking six men and leaving you in command."

Mullins was an old hand in the 1st and had done his fair share of "off the books" missions. "Lucky you, sir. This place is shaping up to be rather routine." He smiled.

Sebastian smiled back. "We will leave tomorrow. If anyone asks, I have gone down with a malaria fever that I picked up in the Caribbean. My batman will help create the illusion that I have been shipped back to Karachi for treatment."

"Very good, sir. Do you know how long you will be?"

"I will either return successfully in two months or not at all."

The next morning before dawn a string of thirty horses, guarded by ten men, left the town and headed into the Pass. As the sun rose, they were well into the Khyber, hooves echoing off the mountains. Horses were valuable and an attractive target for brigands, so the men were alert and looking for trouble. Two men rode at the front.

"It is rare for any trouble to occur inside the Pass. It mostly happens once we leave Torkham. We will have four or five days in the hills then," Assam said.

Assam had not been told about the gold — that was in two chests, each on different animals as a precaution against either one bolting. They stopped at Basawul that first night; there were no lodgings and Assam pointed out that he would normally just pitch a tent near his horses.

Sebastian spotted the watcher on a peak halfway through the next day and pointed him out to Assam.

"I saw him. He is probably a scout for the governor of Jalalabad. He likes to know who comes from the Pass."

The man did not move, and Sebastian concluded they were not considered a threat. They overnighted in Jalalabad, which had corrals for horses and lodgings for traders. The latter consisted of one big open common room full of cots. Apparently, the man in charge didn't like tents cluttering up his town.

On day three they rode along the valley of the Kabul river. It was a green and pleasant land with farms. Children ran alongside the horses laughing and shouting while dogs paced them and barked at the children. However, Assam warned that everyone should take extra care at night. "Do not be fooled, they treat theft as a pastime and will take anything."

The baggage, including the gold, was kept under guard the whole night with the marines splitting the night into three watches. Sebastian woke around three in the morning as he felt a hand searching his bed roll. The hand was connected to an arm that came in under the side of the tent. Sebastian watched as it made its way along his bed roll to the corner where his pack stood.

He took a club from the top of the pack and, as the hand continued exploring, waited for an opportune moment. When the hand passed over the butt of his rifle, the club hit it with the satisfying crack of a bone breaking. There was a hearty scream from outside. The hand disappeared and the sound of running feet interspersed with sobs could be heard disappearing into the distance.

The next day they were up at dawn as usual, and packs were checked and loaded. Nothing was missing and the grins on the faces of a couple of his men confirmed they'd had similar experiences. They mounted, and a mile up the road came to a small hamlet of half a dozen ramshackle huts. A man stood outside one of the huts glaring at them, his hand wrapped in a dirty cloth. Sebastian grinned at him and flipped him a coin. His left hand snaked out and snatched it from the air, but the glare didn't change.

Kabul was a bustling town. White stuccoed buildings predominated as they made their way through to the livestock market and their lodgings. Sebastian had Assam deliver a pre-prepared message to the palace. Then they waited.

They waited for a week, watching the palace every day, then they saw the flag dip twice. Sebastian and his men took the gold and approached the gate. Guards stopped them.

"The sun shines on the sultan and the earth shudders at his passing," Sebastian said in well-rehearsed Farsi. This was a line mentioned in the message and Sebastian hoped the guard had been made aware of it. He was disappointed. The guard looked at him blankly and raised his pike. Then a man stepped out from behind the formidable gatepost and said something. The guard immediately snapped to attention and stepped back to his post.

"You are the English bringing a gift for the sultan?" the man said in refined English.

"Major Ashley-Cooper, 95th Rifles, at your service," Sebastian said with a bow.

"I am Gulyar Khan, the sultan's chancellor. You are underdressed, Major. Have you brought your uniform?"

"I have, as have my men."

"Then come with me."

They were led to an anteroom and servants brought water for them to clean themselves with. Gulyar Khan instructed the servants to take the uniforms and make sure there were no creases or stains. They were all returned in pristine condition.

As he dressed, Sebastian hoped that the sultan would keep this a private affair and not try to make some kind of spectacle out of it. He need not have worried — the sultan didn't want the tribal chiefs to know about the gold and they were led into a private meeting room, along a route through the palace that kept them away from prying eyes.

Sebastian marched beside Gulyar Khan.

"Your English is very good," Sebastian said.

"Thank you. I studied at Cambridge — King's College. My father was the chancellor before me and wanted his son to have the advantage of a Western education."

They came to a large pair of doors, which were guarded by four soldiers in a different uniform to the others they had seen. Sebastian mentioned this.

"These are the sultan's personal guard. They are fanatically loyal to him and him alone," Gulyar said.

The guard snapped to attention as they approached, and a pair of halberds was lowered to block the doors. Sebastian realised this was a ritual and waited while Gulyar spoke the phrases necessary to gain entry. The halberds snapped upright, and the doors opened. In perfect step, the men marched in with Sebastian in the lead, the sultan ahead of them on an ornate throne. Other than guards, the room was empty.

"Guard halt," Sebastian said, just loud enough for his men to hear, and they stamped to a parade-ground halt. Sebastian bowed deeply and returned to stand at attention. The sultan spoke and Gulyar translated.

"Please relax, Major, the sultan welcomes you."

"At ease, men." The squad stood at parade-ground ease. Sebastian started the formalities with a deep bow as he said, "I bring greetings from King William the Fourth, by the grace of God, of the United Kingdom of Great Britain and Ireland, Defender of the Faith and King of Hanover. He wishes his brother ruler a long life and prosperity."

Gulyar replied with an extended list of the sultan's titles and holy attributes, ending with a wish for long life and prosperity as well. Then he asked, "You have brought me a gift?" He grinned at Sebastian. "The British never give without wanting something in return. What do you want?"

Sebastian gave a discreet signal, and the men put the chests on the floor and opened the lids. They were full of gold sovereigns.

"My government offers this for an alliance and continued co-operation between our nations."

"This alliance is for what?"

"To keep Afghanistan independent of all foreign interference."

"I see; you want us to be the buffer between your possessions in India and the Russians."

"That is one way to interpret it, Your Majesty, but we prefer to describe our relationship as one of mutual support."

"And will this 'gift' be given every year?"

"It will, Your Majesty."

The sultan grinned then and gestured for the gifts to be brought forward. Sebastian signalled to the men to bring the chests. They placed them at the sultan's feet, then retreated back to their positions.

The sultan picked a coin at random and examined it. It was a newly minted sovereign with King William's face on it. He examined it and weighed it in his hand. He refrained from biting it to test the gold content. He nodded. "Tell your king and government that we have an accord." He gestured for a guard and said something to him. The man left and they stood in silence, waiting.

The guard returned with a small chest, which he gave to the sultan.

"Your king has graced me with many portraits of himself. I wish you to give him this from me as a gesture of our friendship." He opened the box and handed it to Sebastian. Inside was a plaque. In the centre, surrounded by a golden frame encrusted with precious gems, was a portrait of the sultan on what looked like porcelain. It was of exquisite craftsmanship.

"I am sure he will treasure this generous gift. I thank you on his behalf."

They changed back into civvies before they returned to their lodgings. Assam was waiting there.

"There is a Russian delegation in town."

"Where?"

"They are staying in the house of Mohammad Yama."

Sebastian grinned. This way, he could kill two birds with one stone.

Assam led Sebastian and Atwood on a reconnaissance of the area around the house. They stood and looked at the house from an alley across the dirt track that passed for a street. It was large and made of stone and stucco.

"Do these houses burn?" Sebastian asked.

"Not well."

That was true — stucco was naturally fire resistant as it contained no flammable materials.

"How many Russians?"

"Three," Assam replied, wondering what Sebastian was thinking.

"I think the Russians are going to fall out with their hosts and as a result, several people will die."

* * *

All seven riflemen slipped through the streets, ending up at the house of Mohammad Yama. There were guards but they were not a concern as the plan was not to enter by the front door. Instead, they climbed up onto the roof of the house next door and laid a plank across the alley separating it from Yama's. They crossed silently.

The house was built around a central courtyard, and they slipped down the stairs from the roof into it. A guard walked a patrol. Corporal Jennings, a master of the garrotte, dealt with him. They entered the house and split into two teams of three. Sebastian led one and Atwood the other.

Atwood's team moved towards the front of the house and the east side, which Assam had said would contain the guests. They searched the rooms quickly and efficiently. The Russians were all in one room and were sleeping soundly. They quietly gathered all their weapons then Atwood woke the first by laying a knife across his throat. His eyes opened and he was pulled to his feet, the knife biting his skin. The other two had equally rude awakenings. They took them to the courtyard and forced them to kneel. Their hands were tied behind their backs with ribbons that would not cut in or leave marks, and each one was gagged.

Sebastian and his team visited the chief and rapped him on the head after killing both his guards with knife thrusts. Sebastian then went to the courtyard and signalled that they should bring the Russians.

"Who is the leader?" he asked in Russian.

One of the men's eyes flickered. Sebastian took him by the collar and dragged him into the chief's room. He took a Russian knife and thrust it into Yama's chest, straight through the heart. The Russian's eyes were wide with horror as he realised what was happening, and he tried to bolt. Sebastian caught him by the collar and dragged him to the dead chief's body. Then Sebastian took a knife that he had found in the chief's room and slashed the Russian across the inner thigh — cutting the femoral artery — then stabbed him in the shoulder, leaving the knife embedded.

When the man had bled out, Sebastian removed the gag and binding on his wrists and adjusted his position to make it look as though he had stabbed Yama. Then he stood back, taking care not to tread in the large pool of blood.

Outside, the Russians' knives were used to cut the guards' bodies and the guards' swords were used to kill the Russians.

"All done? Let's go," Sebastian said, and they exited the way they had come in.

As they were about to leave, Gulyar paid them a visit. He was accompanied by two guards. Sebastian had already mounted and pulled his horse around to speak to him.

"You are returning home, Major?"

"Why, yes we are. Our business here is concluded," Sebastian said.

"Are you aware that there was a Russian delegation being hosted by the chief of the Tadjiks?"

Sebastian pursed his lips and shook his head. "Any reason why I should?" Then he looked at Gulyar in surprise. "You said *was* — has something happened?"

"Oh, nothing serious. Ride carefully, I'd hate for something to happen to you on your way home."

"I am touched by your concern."

Gulyar gave him a grin and slapped his horse on the rump.

A Wedding and a Siege

Sebastian surprised Beth by turning up a year and a half early. He walked into the embassy unannounced, surprising everyone. Beth was in a meeting with a British merchant who wanted to establish an export business in Belgium. He left and as she walked out of the meeting room she was yawning; she found this kind of humdrum activity extremely boring.

Then she saw Sebastian, and her first thought was that he must be another merchant coming to complain or ask for help. She looked at him then looked away before recognition worked its way to the front of her brain. Then she stopped dead, looked around, screamed and launched herself at him, ending up with her arms around his neck and her legs around his waist — much to the amusement of the embassy staff, who were awed at the length of the kiss.

"They have to come up for air at *some* time," one of the maids said with admiration in her voice.

They did, eventually, and went to the apartment. After they had said hello properly, Beth asked, as they lay in their dishevelled bed, "How come you are back so soon?"

"Ah well, therein lies a tale. On the voyage over I received an envelope with special orders which made the reason for the deployment clear."

"Ooh, what was it?"

"I cannot tell you; in fact, I cannot tell anyone. The only person who knows, apart from me, is the man who wrote them and my team — and the team have never seen the orders."

"Let me guess, you cannot show me either?"

"Nope. Anyway, the mission, at first glance, looked difficult and would take a lot of setting up. But, as it turned out, a stroke of luck put me in the right place at the right time and the mission was accomplished quickly. As soon as I reported that, my replacement was miraculously sent out on a fast packet, and I returned on the same ship."

Beth snuggled into his chest. "I'm glad. I missed you terribly."

"As Leopold is on the throne and is getting married, I assume all went well here."

"We had, and actually still have, an Orangist threat. They tried to blow up Leopold. Those three are in jail now but there are still plenty of others."

Sebastian assumed his position as ambassador the next day and Beth took him to the palace to introduce him to King Leopold.

"I am very pleased to meet you, Sir Ashley-Cooper. Lady Bethany has been doing a sterling job in your absence."

Sebastian smiled lovingly at Beth, who practically glowed.

"I am to marry Princess Louise of Orléans on the ninth of August. You will attend, of course." It was not a question, but Sebastian agreed as if it was.

"Of course," he said. "We wouldn't miss it for the world."

The situation in Antwerp was still a thorn in the Belgians' side. The Dutch still occupied it and refused to recognise the Treaty of the Eighteen Articles; meanwhile, they also placed an embargo on Belgian shipping and goods into the Netherlands, denying the Belgians their largest market. Successive attempts to resolve this diplomatically all failed.

Sebastian returned from one such attempt frustrated and somewhat angry at the stubbornness of the Dutch. "They are greedy and rude," he exploded when Beth asked how the last lot of talks went. "They want everything and to give nothing. Their famous directness has been extended to become downright rude bluntness."

The wedding took place as planned at the Compiègne Palace on 9 August 1832 and they got their first look at Princess Louise. She was pretty, with brown hair styled fashionably in ringlets. She was a Catholic and Leopold was a Calvinist Protestant, so there were two ceremonies. Beth knew that Louise was not happy with the arranged marriage and made sure she got close to her to provide encouragement and support.

Leopold, aware of her feelings, treated her with consideration and respect, which won her heart in the end. Beth found her to be a shy girl, and Leopold's desire for her to live a quiet life suited her.

Beth and Sebastian continued to keep an eye on Orangist groups in and around Brussels, building an extensive network of agents and informants.

"I think we know more of what's going on than the police do," Beth commented.

Sebastian steepled his fingers under his chin and looked thoughtful.

"I know that look; what do you want to do?" Beth asked.

"I was just thinking … we do not know much about what is going on in Antwerp," Sebastian said.

"We have people in the city," Beth replied.

"But not in the citadel."

Fede wandered over from his place by the fire and put his head on Sebastian's lap. He scratched the big dog's ear absently. "We *must* be able to get someone in there. The locals are supplying them with food and there are local servants."

Beth decided a visit was in order. She asked an agent to act as an interpreter and the Wolves set off for Antwerp, leaving Sebastian in the embassy. Once they reached Mechelen, they changed personas. The stately coach was abandoned in favour of a four-wheeled cart, and they became German traders dealing in iron pots. Mike took the lead with Beth acting as his wife. They made themselves look much older and only Sarah stayed with them, playing their daughter. The rest of the team stayed as a separate group. Beth told them, "Harry has learned Dutch, so he will be the husband, Paola is his wife, and the rest of you are his in-laws. If that doesn't get the sympathy of any soldier, then I don't know what will. Girls, you are Spanish from now on. You are travelling to Antwerp because Harry's family are there."

Paola grinned like a cat that had got the canary and winked at Sarah. Harry had a hunted look in his eyes as Sarah gave Paola a look that said, *You dare!*

The sound of cannon fire could be heard as they got to within five miles of Antwerp. Half an hour later they could see that the Dutch in the citadel were bombarding the town.

"What a cowardly act!" Mike exclaimed. "There they sit, snug and warm in the citadel, lobbing cannonballs at defenceless civilians."

Beth agreed; her opinion of the Dutch sank to a new low. What made her angry was a line of carts entering the citadel from the north-east. They flew orange pennants.

"I want to know where those carts are coming from," she said.

They set up base in an abandoned farmhouse outside Antwerp. Beth considered it too dangerous to set up within the town. Harry and the Belgian Secret Service agent, André, scouted the citadel's perimeter and got close to some of the wagons supplying it.

"The citadel is strong," Harry reported. "It is a pentagonal bastion fort with a moat, and probably built three hundred years ago."

"During the time of the Dutch revolt against the Spanish," Beth concluded. "What about the wagons, where do they come from?"

"Mainly the Netherlands — from Hoogerheide and Leemberg, which are just over the border in North Brabant — and some from Orangist supporters locally. The Dutch cavalry are patrolling to the south of the citadel."

"That explains why this farm is abandoned," Beth said and looked out of the window, deep in thought. "Can we get into the citadel?"

"The gate is well guarded and every cart that enters is thoroughly checked," André said.

"But as long as they have the correct papers, they are let in," Mike added.

"I want to know how much food and ammunition they have stockpiled. We need to get inside."

Beth came up with a plan which, as usual, was debated by the team and improved upon. Harry and André would follow one of the

Orangist carts back to its source, which Beth and the rest of the team would take over.

Two carts, which looked to belong to a common merchant, were followed from the citadel to the town of Berchem. They noted that the orange pennants were removed well before they got back there, and that they slipped into a warehouse on the edge of town.

"I bet the locals have no idea that they are supplying the citadel," Mike said.

"Probably not. We will take over the warehouse tonight and when the owners arrive in the morning we will have a chat with them," replied Beth.

Under the cover of darkness, they moved into the warehouse. Inside were sacks of flour and pulses, carrots in sand-filled crates, bags of potatoes and strings of onions and smoked sausages. A stack of wine crates was off to one side along with cooking oil in demijohns. There were two carts of a type similar to British hay wains. To the side was a corral with eight heavy draft horses. Mike searched the carts and found the orange pennants.

Morning approached and Beth woke with an idea. A very wicked idea.

The sound of voices announced the arrival of the merchant and his men. They opened up the doors and entered as the early-morning sun lit up the countryside.

"Get the goods loaded, we are to deliver two cartfuls today," one of the men shouted. This identified him as the owner. The team stayed hidden until the carts were loaded and the horses brought around and hitched on. Then, when they could be sure that all the men were present, they moved.

"Stand still and raise your hands above your heads," André shouted.

One of the men, seeing only Alie in front of him, rushed forward — only to end up on his back when she thrust-kicked him in the face. She stood over him, her gun pointing straight between his eyes. The others stayed right where they were.

André barked instructions and soon all of the men except the merchant were tied up and gagged in the depths of the building.

"You are coming with us," André told the merchant.

Mike drove the first wagon with the merchant beside him. André sat on the goods in the wagon and kept a pistol pressed into his back. Harry drove the second wagon with Beth beside him and Niko in the back. The rest of the girls stayed at the warehouse to guard the prisoners.

The ride to the citadel took a couple of hours and they rolled up to join the short line of delivery carts with the orange pennant flying. André kept the gun barrel firmly against the merchant's spine, covering his arm with an old sack to hide it.

"Back again?" the guard asked as he cast an eye over the bed of the cart.

"Yes, this week's order was too big to bring in one go," the merchant replied after a prod from André.

"Fine, we are glad to get it. In you go."

The cart trundled forward and followed the one ahead of it to a warehouse where everything was being unloaded and sorted. Beth noted that the two carts ahead of them were carrying kegs of powder — the sheer volume meant it was probably for cannon, so it was coarser than rifle or pistol powder. She did a quick count: thirty kegs per cart. That was a grand total of fifteen hundred pounds of powder.

While they were waiting their turn she wandered off. The soldiers whistled at her, and she swung her hips in response. No one stopped her. She came upon the armoury and glanced through the door long enough to get an impression of the number of rifles in there. Men were carrying kegs of powder to what she assumed was the magazine.

A soldier shouted at her in Dutch; she replied in French. He walked over to her and spoke to her in French. "Don't get too close, that's the magazine."

She put on an awed expression. "Is that where they store all that gunpowder that was just delivered?"

The soldier laughed, thinking her naïve. "That's just to top up what we use in a week shelling the town. There's ten tons of the stuff in there."

Beth returned to the carts in time to help them unload. The food was taken to a store near the kitchens, the wine to a small building that was at the entrance to a cellar. André told her later that the cellar was directly under the officers' quarters.

"Don't the ordinary soldiers get wine?" she asked.

"They get beer brought from Leishout," André replied. "It's good stuff."

They returned to Berchem and parked the carts in plain view with the orange pennants flying. The merchant was taken inside and tied up with his men. Beth had André translate for her.

"In one hour, this building is going to catch fire. If you are lucky, someone will find you here and release you. If you are not … well then, I guess you get your just deserts. Do not try to find the device that will start the fire, because we have laid booby traps all around it and you will only get yourselves killed and start the fire earlier."

She turned to leave, then stopped and looked over her shoulder. "Oh, and I do not think you will be welcome at the citadel anymore. You see, I doctored the wine."

When the French Army of the North arrived to finish what Beth and her team had started — namely, retake the citadel and Antwerp — they had valuable information on how long the Dutch could hold out and how much ammunition and stores they had.

The siege lasted from 15 November to 23 December 1832. It was ended by a predominantly French force under the direction of François, Baron Hexo, a siege specialist. Their efforts were helped by recurring bouts of dysentery amongst the Dutch officers. In the end the Dutch retreated into the Netherlands, but for the Belgians that wasn't the end of the struggle for true independence. Skirmishes would continue for another seven years until the Dutch were brought back to the table and pressured into agreeing that Belgium was an independent sovereign state.

Epilogue

Sebastian and Beth spent three more years in Belgium and in that time Beth became firm friends with the queen. She was present at the birth of her first child and at his funeral less than a year later. The future King Leopold II of Belgium was born in April 1835 with Beth in attendance once again. They were recalled to England in June 1835.

In 1834 anti-Orangist sentiment boiled over and riots broke out in Belgium which were only quelled when Leopold himself gave a speech to the masses and promised that pro-Orangist propaganda would be outlawed. However, a further riot — one that attacked the former residences of William of Orange and his family — had to be put down by the army, which had been forewarned by the British embassy.

Back in England, three men met at the Foreign Office. They were George Hamilton-Gordon, the new foreign secretary; William Lamb, the prime minister; and the Earl of Purbeck.

"So, Purbeck, what is your assessment of the Belgian situation?" William Lamb asked.

"It is as we intended. The Dutch will succumb to international pressure and acknowledge that Belgium is a sovereign state in the next few years. Meanwhile, we have excellent relations with the Belgians, who provide us with a substantial buffer between the French, Germans and Dutch. They are growing their industrial base with our help and are licensing patents and designs."

Hamilton-Gordon said, "The embassy is now being staffed by Thomas Waller, the chargé d'affaires, until Charles Ellis goes over next year. Will your daughter and son-in-law be available to brief him?"

"Naturally. We will also send a military attaché to take over the network that they put in place," Marty replied.

"Has Wellington decided who that will be yet?" Lamb asked.

Marty shrugged. "No, but I suspect that it will be another officer from the Rifles."

"What will Sir Sebastian and Lady Bethany be doing now?" Hamilton-Gordon asked.

Marty smiled. "If my wife has a say in it, starting a family."

Bethany and Sebastian were at home. The house was just as they had left it, and they wanted simply to enjoy being together without worrying about networks or foreign relations.

Their respective mothers visited, and both made comments to the effect that Beth was not getting any younger. Beth had to be honest with herself that she wanted children and that her clock was ticking. She told Sebastian, "I want to try for another baby."

He was overjoyed and enthusiastic, threw away his condoms and went to work with manly enthusiasm. Beth was, of course, delighted and dreamt up many ways to keep his enthusiasm going. She even consulted Annabel Shelby, who told her what was known about the woman's cycle and when she was receptive.

However, it was another year until she fell pregnant — and by then, the service had another job for her.

THE END

Author's Notes

References to the real history behind the stories in this book can be found online. Just search for Gran Colombia, Simón Bolívar or Belgian Independence/King Leopold I of Belgium. I try and stick to the timelines of the events but sometimes the story takes priority and, well, these are works of fiction, not textbooks.

The British did, in fact, have a special mission in Belgium from 1831 to 1835 and Robert Adair was the real person who did what Beth did, i.e. prevent a war between Belgium and the Netherlands.

Burglary equipment for spies

Slim jim — a strip of sprung steel that is slipped between a window or door and its frame to spring the catch

Lock picks — a set of specially made tools that are used to open a lock by manipulating the tumblers

Jimmy — A ten-inch long prybar or crowbar with an angled tip

Screwdriver — for undoing screws

Pliers — for cutting

Light mineral oil — for lubricating hinges, usually applied with a hollow straw

Gloves — self-explanatory

Blackjack, sap or slungshot — a small cosh made of leather with a stuffed leather knob on the end full of lead shot

Paper — for copying information

Pencil — useful for copying

Can of ether and a cloth — for rendering people unconscious

Small shuttered lamp with a mirror reflector — predecessor of the torch

Soft-soled shoes — for silent sneaking

Black coveralls with hood

Burnt cork — for camouflaging light skin

English barrel sizes (liquids)
Hogshead = 54 gallons/432 pints
Barrel = 36 gallons/288 pints
Kilderkin = 18 gallons/144 pints
Firkin = 9 gallons/72 pints
Pin = 4.5 gallons/36 pints

English barrel sizes (gunpowder)
Barrel = 100 lbs
Half-barrel = 50 lbs
Keg = 25 lbs
Half-keg = $12^{1/2}$ lbs
Quarter-keg = $6^{1/4}$ lbs

British money
Farthing = 1/4 penny
Halfpenny or ha'penny = 1/2 penny

Penny = 1/12 shilling or 1/240 of a pound
Threepence or thruppence = 3 pennies
Sixpence, or a tanner = 6 pennies
Shilling, or bob = 12 pennies or 1/20 of a pound
Florin = 2 shillings
Half-crown = 2/6 (i.e. two shillings and sixpence)
Half-sovereign = 10 shillings
One-pound note = 20 shillings
Five-pound note

Imperial weight

One ounce (oz) = 28.34 g
One pound (lb) = 16 oz = 0.45 kg
One stone = 14 lbs
One hundredweight = 8 stone or 112 lbs = 50.8 kg
Large sack = 16 stone

Imperial volume

One fluid ounce = 28.4 ml
One pint = 24 fluid ounces = 0.56 l
One gallon = 8 pints = 4.54 l

Fahrenheit to Celsius

30 °F = 0 °C
Celsius = (Fahrenheit −32)/1.8

The Lume & Joffe Books Story

Lume Books was founded by Matthew Lynn, one of the true pioneers of independent publishing. In 2023 Lume Books was acquired by Joffe Books and now its story continues as part of the Joffe Books family of companies.

Joffe Books began in 2014 when Jasper agreed to publish his mum's much-rejected romance novel and it became a bestseller.

Since then we've grown into the largest independent publisher in the UK. We're extremely proud to publish some of the very best writers in the world, including Joy Ellis, Faith Martin, Caro Ramsay, Helen Forrester, Simon Brett and Robert Goddard. Everyone at Joffe Books loves reading and we never forget that it all begins with the magic of an author telling a story.

We are proud to publish talented first-time authors, as well as established writers whose books we love introducing to a new generation of readers.

We won Trade Publisher of the Year at the Independent Publishing Awards in 2023 and Best Publisher Award in 2024 at the People's Book Prize. We have been shortlisted for Independent Publisher of the Year at the British Book Awards for the last five years, and were shortlisted for the Diversity and Inclusivity Award at the 2022 Independent Publishing Awards. In 2023 we were shortlisted for Publisher of the Year at the RNA Industry Awards, and in 2024 we were shortlisted at the CWA Daggers for the Best Crime and Mystery Publisher.

We built this company with your help, and we love to hear from you, so please email us about absolutely anything bookish at feedback@joffebooks.com.

If you want to receive free books every Friday and hear about all our new releases, join our mailing list here: www.joffebooks.com/freebooks.

And when you tell your friends about us, just remember: it's pronounced Joffe as in coffee or toffee!

www.ingramcontent.com/pod-product-compliance
Lightning Source LLC
Chambersburg PA
CBHW010818250626
47156CB00011B/3120